MW00711441

The
Inconvenient Corpse

The
Inconvenient Corpse
A Grace Cassidy Mystery

Jackie King

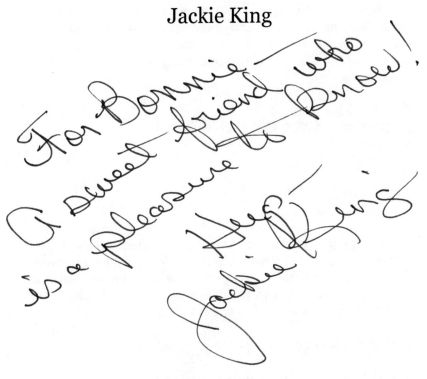

For Bonnie —
A sweet friend who
is a pleasure to Bnow!

Her —
Jackie King

Deadly Niche Press
Denton Texas

This is a work of fiction. Names, characters, places, and incidents are products of the author's imagination or are used fictitiously and are not to be construed as real. Any resemblance to actual events, locales, organizations, or persons, living or dead, is entirely coincidental.

Deadly Niche Press
An imprint of AWOC.COM Publishing
P.O. Box 2819
Denton, TX 76202

© 2009 by Jacqueline King
All Rights Reserved.

No part of this publication may be reproduced, stored in a retrieval system, or transmitted in any form or by any means, electronic, mechanical, recording or otherwise, without written permission, except in the case of brief quotations embodied in critical articles and reviews.

Manufactured in the United States of America

ISBN: 978-0-937660-53-9

Visit the author's website: www.jacqking.com

For My Children

Susan King Keithley, Jennifer King Sohl

and John David King

Chapter 1

Grace Cassidy stared at the stranger's body. He was about sixty, pot-bellied, naked, and very dead. She knew he was dead because his skin was the color of concrete. Worst of all, he was lying smack dab in the middle of her bed.

Icy fingers gripped her heart then rose to close her throat. Her sweat-soaked silk shirt clung to her skin, and a chill permeated her soul. She shivered. Why in the world did I wear silk to walk on the beach, she wondered, and then gave herself a mental shake. A ruined outfit was the least of her problems.

How did a native Okie end up alone in a Northern California town with some stranger's corpse on her bed and a dead cell phone in her Louis-Vuitton purse? This couldn't be happening. Not to her. She was Miss Goody Two-Shoes from Southwest Suburbia, USA.

She couldn't just stand there, looking at the body, doing nothing. Grace searched her mind for the names of the two women she had met earlier. The zany ones, who had asked endless questions that she found herself answering for reasons she couldn't understand.

"Help me! There's a man in my bed!" She backed out of the room, flew down the creaking stairs of the Victorian inn and into the second-floor sitting room. Empty. Where was a busybody when you needed one?

Her gaze swept across the hall and her dazed brain noted that the brass plaque on the door read "The Elizabeth Barrett Browning Suite." She lifted a hand to pound solid, antique wood.

"Let me in. Help me. There's a dead man in my bed. A *naked* dead man!"

Footsteps sounded, a deadbolt scraped, and a mature woman stepped into the hallway. She was short, dark, and moved with dramatic, decisive movements. Theodora. That was her name, Grace remembered.

"Did I hear you say that a naked man is in your bed?" Theodora threw a fringed, gauzy wrap around her shoulders to cover a fuchsia silk caftan that clung to her rounded, still-sexy body. "I'm assuming from your hysterical tone that he's not your husband."

"Of course not! I don't know who he is, but he's dead and naked." Grace blushed, and then bit her lip in self-annoyance.

"Better let me call Pansy," Theodora said and knocked on the door to her right. "Pansy!" she called loudly. "A woman here says she's found a naked body."

The door opened and an obviously amused blonde stuck her head into the hallway. Both women were a young sixty-something.

"You're kidding, right?" Pansy ran tapered fingers through her blond hair, and then shook her head so every strand settled into silky perfection. She looked at Grace. "Surely you didn't find a *naked* body," she said. "I'll bet you fell asleep reading a mystery. Just a bad dream, I expect."

Grace wanted to shout that her whole life was suddenly a bad dream, only it didn't include unknown corpses in her bed. She took a deep breath, exhaled.

"I wasn't sleeping. I had just returned from a long walk. You gave me directions for the scenic route to the beach, re-member?" She had wanted to walk forever, and almost had. The crisp air, the sun on her back, walking past the rows of Victorian houses to the rocky beach had been the purest of therapies. She had shelved her anger with Charlie and con-centrated on long strides and deep breathing.

"You're sure he's not your husband?" Theodora stepped forward, reached up and patted Grace on the shoulder. "Didn't you tell us the two of you had a little spat in San Francisco? You said—"

"I'm sure." Grace cut the woman off mid-sentence, vexed at the quantity of information the two women had pried from her in the short casual conversation before her walk.

"Believe me. I'd know my own husband, dead or alive." He may be dead after I get through with him, Grace thought.

The women exchanged a look and Grace read their thoughts.

"I'm not making this up. Where's a phone? My cell needs recharging and I've got to call the police!"

"Of course dear," Theodora exchanged another look with Pansy then stepped forward and took Grace's elbow. "But first let's step into the guests' parlor and make ourselves a nice cup of tea. There will be time enough afterwards to bother the police. After all, if the man is dead, he's dead. Another ten minutes won't alter that fact." She waved airily toward the small sitting room at the top of the stairs.

"I can't believe he was naked. Perhaps I should run upstairs and take a quick peek." Pansy's eyes sparkled, mischievous as a small child. "I might know him."

"In that case he'd have been in your bed." Theodora said.

"I've got to call the police." Grace tugged against Theodora's firm grip, but the woman was strong for her age.

"Now, now, dear, let's just stay calm." Theodora kept a firm hand on Grace's arm and led her into the cozy room, and then pulled her down onto the Victorian sofa. "First we'll drink some tea." She waved ringed fingers in a graceful movement and looked at Pansy with an expression that suggested they should be tolerant of the madwoman before them. "I don't think we've ever had a body at Wimberly Place before," she said in what seemed to be a forced conversational voice.

"Dear me, no." Pansy assumed the same tone and stepped to the small sink and took floral teacups from an open shelf. She paused a minute as if she were seriously considering the question. "Not a naked one anyway. There was that sweet old lady who passed away quietly in her sleep last March while we were here on spring break, but she wasn't naked. I saw her, she wore a really sweet gown. Yellow sprigged batiste, I think it was." Pansy studied an assortment of tea bags.

"You were here last spring?" Shock numbed Grace. I'm Alice in Wonderland in a deep hole, she thought, with outrageous characters acting a fantasy. "Do you live here?" What kind of kinky inn had she stumbled into in her eagerness to distance herself from Charlie?

"Only during vacations and holidays, Pansy and I love Port Ortega and spend a great deal of time visiting here at Wimberly Place," Theodora said. "It's rather like our home-away-from-home, both reasonable and charming. We come often and sometimes stay for extended periods of time." She smiled and lowered her voice to a conspiratorial tone.

"Small-town teachers must escape from time to time, you know."

Grace took a deep breath. None of this was happening. She was dreaming. Soon she would wake up and her only problem would be Charlie and how to tell their nineteen-year-old son Brand about the divorce.

"I think we'd better have chamomile," Theodora said. Her gaze fastened on Grace, a curious, studying look that alarmed Grace. "To steady our nerves."

"Excellent." Pansy chose three bags, stripped the paper covers with a neat movement and put them in the cups. "We'll need to be calm. If someone really is dead I expect Mr. Wimberly won't like it at all." She pulled a tap and boiling water poured from an automatic jet. Pansy handed the first cup to Grace. "Was the man big?"

Grace's hand shook, rattling the teacup in its saucer. Neither woman believed her. This Pansy person must be stretching for conversation to ask such a question. Grace set the cup on the table. It was going to take more than chamomile to settle her nerves in this stage center scene from the Mad Hatter's tea party.

"Medium height, I'd say," Grace said to humor the woman, glancing around to spot a telephone.

"Oh, height." Pansy raised an eyebrow at Theodora who smiled.

Grace rolled her eyes.

"I'm calling the police." She stood and headed toward the stairs.

Theodora rose with unexpected speed and grabbed Grace's arm.

"I suggest that the three of us go upstairs together and look at whatever it is you've seen."

"I told you, I saw a dead man." Grace forced herself to speak calmly. "If you don't believe me, come on up and see for yourselves."

"I believe we'll do just that." Theodora's authoritative tone verified that she had taught public school for what Grace suspected was most of her adult life.

It took a few minutes for the three of them to reach the top of the stairs. Pansy, who was athletic, paused considerately to wait on Theodora who seemed to favor her right foot. They walked to the open door and peered in.

"Good grief, he really is naked." Theodora panted, breathless from the climb.

Pansy moved to the edge of the bed, her hand fluttering around her throat. Grace kept her gaze on Pansy. She didn't want to look at the body.

"This man isn't a guest here." Pansy leaned forward, studying the corpse. "And not really medium sized either." She sounded disappointed. "Of course being dead might be a factor."

Grace blinked. The scene was surrealistic. Like a clip from a weird movie. Get a grip, she told herself. But she couldn't move. All she could do was stand there and think about how the heavy floral scent reminded her of a funeral home. Potpourri, she supposed. The stuff seemed to be scattered everywhere throughout the inn.

"He's lying in an odd position," Theodora said.

Grace forced herself to glance at the body. Everything about the guy looked odd to her. A bit pathetic, too, stretched out straight in a helpless manner for all the world to view. She looked away.

"His eyes look like a raccoon's," Pansy said. "The poor man must have never slept." She shot a look at Grace. "You're sure you've never seen him before?"

"I'm sure. We've got to call the police, and also tell the owner, Mrs. Wimberly." Grace could barely speak. She wanted to walk away, but her legs wouldn't cooperate.

"I hope this won't ruin the trip Mrs. Wimberly is planning." Pansy turned away from the body seeming to dismiss it entirely. "She's supposed to fly out of San Francisco for Hawaii, tomorrow."

Were these women crazy? Grace took a deep breath and tried to pull herself together. She had to call the police.

"Why should it?" Theodora said. "The inn sitter, that nice Mrs. Smith is due in tonight. Why make a big fuss over the dead body of a person we don't even know? He probably just wandered into the wrong bedroom and fell asleep—had a heart attack or stroke or something."

Relief washed through Grace and she took a deep breath. Of course, that had to be what happened. A body in her bed

could only be some sort of bizarre mishap. The shock lifted
and her indecision evaporated. "I'm calling the police," she
said and raced downstairs toward a phone.

"You say you don't know this man? Never saw him before?" Sam Harper's tone was flat, his eyes bored, as if dip-
lomacy were a dishonest quality to him. Grace figured that
was why he was still a sergeant at his age, which she guessed
to be about fifty. His tone indicated that Grace was lying.

"I've said it three times." Grace hoped her tone told him
she didn't care what he thought. "I've never seen him in my
life. He evidently wandered into my room thinking it was his,
undressed, and had a stroke or something. Ask the other
guests, I'm sure someone knows him."

"Hmmm," Harper lifted an eyebrow and looked annoyed.

Grace figured he hadn't learned anything from the other
guests, but he wasn't going to admit that, at least not to her.
He had ordered the others to stay in the upstairs sitting
room, and then led Grace down to Wimberly's office. Grace
had glanced backwards to see everyone clustered about in a
gaggle of excitement, with their tongues wagging at a non-
stop pace. And even with the horror of murder, Grace could
hardly keep from smiling when she thought of Theodora's
and Pansy's attempts to take another peek at the body. The
Sergeant had been furious.

She watched as Harper scribbled something on a pad.
What was he writing? Was he just killing time to make her
more nervous than she already was? She fought to keep her
face expressionless as he lifted his gaze and gave her a drill-
to-the-soul look.

Grace met his stare. The man was making her nuts. Desperation caused her to long for support, any support. Where
was Charlie? Much as it had galled her she had called his
convention hotel room three times but received no answer.
Maybe it served her right for storming out in a rage after the
nasty confrontation with Clover McBride. But how did a
woman make polite conversation with her husband's
girlfriend? Certainly not a situation she could handle gracefully. Instead she threw around a few nasty threats and then
packed a bag and headed north. She needed some time alone.

But now this wanna-be Columbo seemed to think that she was lying.

"I don't know anyone in this town. I drove to Port Ortega on a whim and landed at Wimberly Place by accident. Why can't you accept the truth?"

"Two things bother me." Harper stretched his long legs in front of him and shifted his weight without breaking eye contact. "One," He held up his index finger. "According to the owner, you walked in unannounced and insisted upon a room. 'Any room would do,' you said. You were even willing to take a room in the process of being redecorated."

"I told Mr. Wimberly that I wasn't choosy. Who cares if there are only newspapers on the windows?" Grace watched the sergeant's jaw tighten. She was a woman who cared about such things and he obviously knew it. But Grace soldiered on. "I was tired of driving. Is that a crime?"

"Number two." Sergeant Harper held up a second finger then paused.

"Which is?" The stare-down was tiring Grace. She narrowed her eyes. Damn that cop. He didn't even blink.

"He didn't have any clothes." Harper leaned back and studied her.

"I know that!" Grace said. "I explained it. You have a nasty mind, Sergeant. I was not sleeping with that man. I'm a married woman." The pious sound of her voice was a big mistake, she knew. But so what? If he could find out that her marriage was on the rocks he could also find the problems weren't caused by *her* infidelity.

Harper raised an eyebrow. His expression told Grace he would be rich if he had a dollar for every married woman who had slept with someone besides her husband, and then lied about it.

"It'll be easier on everyone if you just told me his name."

"John Doe." Grace gave him the icy stare that Charlie always said made her look like a society woman. Poised and self-confident, he said. Not that she ever felt that way. She was forty-nine but usually felt an insecure sixteen even when she had done something smart. But the sergeant wouldn't know that. She kept her gaze locked to his.

"You can forget your cliché solution. I didn't know the man."

"I'm afraid that won't wash," Harper said. "You had to know him. The point isn't that he was naked. The point is that he doesn't seem to have any clothes—no clothes at all. Not on the floor, not on a chair, not in the closet, not on the cutesy hooks behind the door. Not even in the bushes outside the window."

Chapter 2

Sergeant Harper studied the odd assortment of people gathered in the upstairs sitting room. He had quizzed this group for over two hours and was tired of the hassle. The smart, good-looking blonde was most likely his murderer and that annoyed him. Interesting women were hard to meet.

He had done some quick research by telephone and learned that Wimberly Place was called a bed and breakfast but in reality served as a sort of residential hotel for people who liked to hang out in the commercial sea town of Port Ortega, where the rates were more affordable. He had just finished his speech about staying in town until further notice when the little fat lady took over. He sighed. This bunch was going to be hell to control.

"My dear Sergeant, Pansy and I will be here for sure. You just take all of the time you need to clear up this little problem." She smiled at Harper as if he were one of her more promising students and would likely do well on his ACT scores.

Harper wanted a Camel. He hadn't smoked in three years but this woman made him reach into his pocket for a non-existent pack. He fingered a pack of breath mints and forged ahead.

"From the register I know Ms Sydney Davenport and Mr. Erwin Quick are staying on the third floor..."

"Their rooms are adjoining," Pansy piped in. "Sydney's in the Robert Lewis Stevenson Suite. Charming room, yellow striped wallpaper and flounced drapes. Tulle everywhere." The small woman turned toward Grace as if entertaining at a tea party. "Interesting couple. Have you met them?"

Grace opened her mouth but Sergeant Harper interrupted.

"All of the guests were supposed to be in this area." He raised his voice and scowled. "Is anyone else missing?"

Grace bit her lip. Harper knew she was laughing at him and scowled at the entire group.

"Now, now, Sergeant, let's not lose our tempers." Theodora glanced toward the stairway. "Here are Ms Davenport and Mr. Quick now."

Harper studied the couple. The woman was at least six feet tall and sported two hundred pounds of solid muscle. Her hair was a dazzling white, maybe bleached from gray. She wore red slacks and a long, full, purple blouse. She seemed a mountain of color to him.

Mr. Quick was tiny, elderly, and frail, the antithesis of his name. He leaned on Ms Davenport's arm and walked with a surprisingly spry step. Somewhere in his early eighties, he was dressed entirely in neutral colors. Invisible in plain sight, Harper thought.

"Come and sit on the sofa with me." Theodora moved to make room then extended her hand, swirling a colorful chiffon sleeve. "You remember me, I'm Theodora Westmacott."

"Of course," Sydney clasped Theodora's hand with what looked like a death-grip to Harper. "Careful, Erwin, remember this little rug here." She spoke in a deep bass and shot a toothy smile at the group. "I do so love this charming old mansion." She spoke in the chummy way that fellow guests confide in one other. "I adore Victorian houses. Bed and breakfasts are so much nicer than hotels, don't you think? Like a home, actually," she lowered her voice to a whisper. "And a murder! It's all so very Agatha Christie."

"Isn't Sydney a wonderful woman?" Mr. Quick said. He shook Theodora's hand but his eyes scarcely left his companion. "Just wonderful," his voice quavered. "And afraid of nothing, always takes her walks, doesn't care if it's day or the dead of night." He poised his scrawny hips over the sofa and dropped his weight, making no effort to lower himself gently. The sofa shook even under his slight frame.

Harper was glad that Davenport was fit enough to lower herself downward between Quick and Theodora else the sofa might have collapsed.

A tall, silver-haired man in late-middle age spoke with a German accent. "What was the name of the victim? Was he a paying guest or someone's visitor?"

"Perhaps Ms Cassidy could tell us," Harper said, deliberately putting her on the spot.

Eyes turned toward Grace.

Harper could tell that it took every ounce of self-control she could muster to keep from squirming. But somehow the woman managed a smile.

"I didn't know him from Adam." She shrugged with an annoyingly innocent smile.

"His misfortune," the German gave a small European bow.

Grace grinned and Harper's temper flared. This guy was too handsome to suit him. Odd too that he was dressed in a gray three-piece suit at this hour, especially in California. Definitely not a tourist, so what was he up to?

Harper checked his notes then looked up. "You must be Mendelsohn. I'll be speaking to each of you privately later on." Harper paused a minute. What he really wanted was to see how well they knew each other. He frowned, not liking the way Mendelsohn eyed Grace Cassidy.

"Mr. Mendelsohn is staying in the Algernon Charles Swinburne Suite, right on this floor," Theodora explained to the room at large, then laughed. "How Mrs. Wimberly does love her Victorian writers but I understand that your taste runs more to painters, Mr. Mendelsohn?"

Harper saw an expression flick across Mendelsohn's face. Was it fear, annoyance, surprise? The look was masked so quickly he wasn't certain.

"Are you in town to collect art?" Harper asked.

"I'm in Port Ortega on other business, although I do collect art," Mendelsohn said.

"How long is this inquisition going to take?" A middle-aged woman with a strident voice asked. "I'm exhausted and my nerves have been destroyed. A person was murdered right across the hall from my room. Who knows which of us might be next? The least you could do is allow me a cup of tea."

Harper eyed the fiftyish woman. Her brown hair, twisted into an unbecoming bun and pulled straight back from her face, was just starting to gray. She wore a floor length floral housecoat and the no-nonsense expression of a woman accustomed to getting her own way in life. He immediately disliked her. The fact that she reminded him of his first wife,

who had accused him of being in love with his job and then
left him to marry a plumber, didn't help.

Harper swept his arm toward the sink. "Help yourself."

But it was Grace Cassidy who rose gracefully and walked
to the sink.

"I'll get you a cup of tea, Mrs....?"

"Blenkensop. Martha Blenkensop. And make it peppermint tea. I must have peppermint. It's the only thing that
doesn't upset my stomach. My nerves have destroyed my
digestive tract. Let me describe my symptoms..."

"Oh, my poor dear," Theodora cut in smoothly. "How
dreadful for you, perhaps you'd be happier in another establishment?"

Martha glared at her. "I've already suggested that to
George, but he refuses to leave." She nodded toward a nondescript man sitting beside her, frowned and then glanced at
Harper. "My husband says he's too busy." She pursed her
lips. "George is very famous in the computer world, you
know."

Blenkensop sighed wearily but said nothing. Could a man
that henpecked murder anyone, Harper wondered? He also
noticed that Blenkensop kept glancing at the older blonde
named Pansy. Harper took a second look at Pansy who was
perched demurely on a footstool. Humm, a bit long in the
tooth, but still there was something timeless and fascinating
about her, something very sexy. He might even be interested
himself if Grace Cassidy wasn't on the scene.

Harper leafed through his notes on the Blenkensops. The
dull looking man really was a guru in the technical world.

"Do you always accompany your husband when he comes
here to teach?" He asked Mrs. Blenkensop.

"Of course, George is simply lost without me around to
look after him."

An annoyed look from George denied this claim. He ignored his wife and spoke to Harper. "Who was this man and
how was he killed?"

Harper made eye contact with Blenkensop and deliberately ignored the questions. It took one second for the man
to drop his gaze and Harper almost grinned. Pushover, he
thought. The fact that the victim's neck had been snapped

would soon be known, but he had no intention of leaking any information tonight.

It would be tomorrow before he could get full background checks on everyone. He especially wanted to know more about Grace Cassidy. Also, there were the owners of the place, a Beth and Wilbur Wimberly to interview. Harper had decided to leave those two isolated in their own apartment on the first floor until later. He tapped his pen against his teeth.

There were others, the maid who had Down Syndrome— mentally challenged was the way Mrs. Wimberly had phrased it—and a gardener who lived downstairs, a geezer with a drinking problem. A couple of other old folks, or senior citizens according to Beth Wimberly's politically correct lingo, also permanently resided in the basement. Each person needed to be questioned.

Tomorrow would be time enough to quiz the others. They may have seen something, but the problem would be getting them to talk. The pensioners in the basement would either be dyed-in-the-wool law abiding citizens or totally suspicious of cops.

Grace Cassidy carried a fancy cup to the woman in the ugly robe, and the slight sway of her hips captured his attention. What he wanted to do with Grace Cassidy had nothing at all to do with this case.

Chapter 3

The night had been long and restless. Grace had never been so glad in her life to see morning's light. She stared into the mirror and asked herself a question.

"Who was the dead guy? Why my room?" Grace suspended her mascara wand mid-air. Why would anyone wander into her room, take off his clothes, and lie down? What could be the reason? Not looking for a nice place to be murdered, for sure. And what happened to his clothes?

The episode had all the earmarks of a sophomoric college joke that her son Brand and his friends might play on someone, using a borrowed body from a local funeral home. Only Brand was passing the summer somewhere in Germany with friends he had met on the Internet. Anyway, he would never have picked his own mother for the patsy. Would he? Grace frowned then gave the question honest consideration. No, never, she decided.

She brushed mascara across her lashes and accidentally smeared some beneath her eye. She glared at her hand.

"Quit shaking!" she ordered, then reached for a *Q-Tip*. "The people around here think I'm weird enough without looking like a hollowed-eyed zombie." She licked the cotton swap and wiped away the smudge.

Weird was probably too kind as a description Grace decided. After Harper had dismissed the group last night, Mr. Wimberly had come upstairs to take his turn blaming her for the world's problems.

"Wimberly Place always had a spotless reputation until you arrived," the pompous jackass had said.

"Then anyone unlucky enough to find a dead body in her bed should get free rent," Grace had snapped back and then watched Wimberly's lips disappear. Her assignment to this cubbyhole in the attic was payback for her smart mouth.

She didn't mind the room being shabby and small. She didn't care where she slept as long as the place had a closet, a reasonably soft bed, and no dead bodies. Grace smiled with grim satisfaction. This tiny room with its sparse collection of mix-matched furniture, circa 1940, wasn't half bad. A bit cozy, actually. The patina of use was the least of her problems.

It worried her that she couldn't locate Charlie. He seemed to have disappeared. For sure he was angry since she had just threatened divorce. Not that Charlie would mind being rid of her, but where she went, the family business—Charlie's little cash cow—followed. She closed her eyes and thanked the memory of her business-savvy father who years ago had written an ironclad business agreement into the founding of *C & G Collection Agency*. Dad could do that because his money had backed the venture. At the time Grace was a starry-eyed twenty and thought the document stating that in case of divorce the business belonged to her, was foolish and unnecessary. Now she thanked God for Dad's wisdom.

Grace took a deep breath, exhaled slowly then applied mascara with a steadier hand. Better, she thought. Not even a smear that time. Now at least I look normal. When your heart's the heaviest, put on a little extra rouge, Mama used to say.

A twinge of nostalgia swept through Grace. She smiled, picked up a long handled brush and added extra blusher. For you, Mama, she thought.

When the knock sounded she jumped. Could it be Charlie? No. More than likely it was that wretched policeman asking another million questions while his eyes said he already knew the answers. Just as well, though. Maybe he'd let her get the rest of her things. Sleeping naked was okay, but she couldn't wear this outfit forever. She smoothed the wrinkled silk shirt, walked to the door and opened it. The maid stood in the hall looking worried.

"Hello there, did you come to clean my room?" Grace spoke automatically, but the conflicting emotions of relief and disappointment swept through her. Dealing with her husband's lies and betrayal needed to be delayed until a better time, but the fact that he cared so little for her welfare still hurt.

The maid twisted the tail of her yellow blouse into a knot, bunching it against a hot-pink gathered skirt. She wore gray socks and what looked like ancient yellow PF Flyers. Wisps of dark blond hair framed the plain lines of her face.

"My name is Grace, what's yours?" The young woman looked terrified, so Grace smiled.

"I'm Maxie, and I'm not here to clean, Missus. I'm never supposed to knock about cleaning. I'm just supposed to wait until the room's empty." Maxie paused, frowned. "I came up because Mr. Wimberly needs to see you."

"See me? Do you have any idea why?"

"Nuh uh, but he's real mad about something, so you'd better hurry."

"Why is he angry?" She'd stall Maxie, ask her questions and learn a few things. A maid might have seen something that could help determine who the dead man might be.

"I don't know why you're in trouble. Lots of people get mad at Maxie, though." Tears welled in the maid's guileless blue eyes. "Maxie doesn't mean to make folks mad, but it's hard to know what people want me to say."

A sudden rush of pity swept through Grace. "Oh Maxie, don't worry about what people want to hear. You're as good as they are. Just tell the truth."

"I did that with the Dark Man, but he got mad anyway. Now I got to go." Maxie edged away, her expression anxious.

"Dark man? You mean Sergeant Harper, the policeman?" Grace was impressed. Dark man, it summed up the sergeant pretty well. Maxie noticed things.

"I got to go. I've got to clean Miss Pansy's room and help her move in with Miss Theodora. We got newlyweds coming today. Miss Pansy says she'll medicate and give Wimberly Place back good caramel."

"Medicate? Caramel?" Grace thought a minute then smiled. "You mean meditate and give good karma."

"Maybe, I hope." Maxie turned and almost flew downstairs.

"Me too," Grace said softly. "Me too."

Being summoned annoyed Grace, but she wanted to finish with Wimberly, so she grabbed her room key and steeled herself for the ordeal. Maybe afterwards she'd walk back down to the beach and breathe the ocean air. She crept down the narrow stairs to the third floor and opened a tiny door. She ducked her head in order to step out into the hall used by regular tenants. Her old room was still blocked with yellow tape. The sight stopped her dead in her tracks. One end was taped to the brass plaque that read, "John Stuart Mills Suite." A shiver slid down her spine. She hurried on, trailing her fingers on the banister. Polish and potpourri and years past mingled together, and the fragrance comforted her.

On the second floor Maxie's singsong voice floated out from the open door of The Robert Browning Suite.

"Make the bed. Don't change the sheets. Put out pretty towels." The words echoed like a chant.

Grace stopped a minute and listened to the litany. It was almost singing, a sort of running dialogue of directions spoken as if to friendly spirits from an earlier age. Delightful, she decided, definitely one of the nicer things about Wimberly Place.

She ran on down the stairs and into what Mr. Wimberly pompously referred to as the withdrawing room. A parlor really, Grace thought, barely glancing at the Oriental rugs covering the hardwood floors. The room was sparsely furnished as if to discourage people from using the street floor. Perhaps that was why guests seemed to prefer the smaller second-story sitting room where Theodora and Pansy had force-fed her tea and Harper had carried on his group inquisition the evening before.

Grace walked into the formal dining room still cluttered with breakfast dishes, then past the massive Victorian furniture. Earlier she had thought it charming, now it seemed dark and foreboding. Toward the back of the first floor Grace stepped into a small office, the same one where she had been questioned privately.

Wimberly sat behind his desk. A bland, ordinary looking man, Grace thought, gray hair, gray eyes, gray shirt. In the near past she wouldn't have given him a second glance. Today she had no choice.

"Good afternoon." She knew instantly that her bored sounding tone was wrong—where was that wretched charm when you needed it? She made herself smile, felt her effort cardboard and phony on her lips. "You wanted to see me?"

"Your check is no good." Wimberly waved the document at her. "I hand-carried your check to the bank this morning and insisted they verify the funds, but there weren't any. Your account was emptied yesterday afternoon."

"Emptied?" Shock stunned Grace. "The bank said my account had been emptied?" Only Charlie could have taken money from the account. Dear God, was he that angry? Had his indifference turned into hatred? She saw Wimberly's contemptuous expression and wanted to kill the courier.

"I can understand your annoyance, Mr. Wimberly." Grace spoke with a forced calmness, drawing from her childhood training. A lady never shows anger, Mama had said. Grace wasn't sure that she qualified as a lady, but she figured she could convince Wimberly that she was the closest facsimile he had ever seen. "Please don't be concerned. You'll get your money."

"Since your check bounced I'll need cash." Wimberly pushed back from his desk and crossed his arms.

"Cash? Don't be ridiculous. Do I look foolish enough to carry large amounts of money around with me?"

"I've been very generous with you, Mrs. Cassidy. I've let you remain here after that... that... person's death. I gave you a bed in the attic." Wimberly's face turned affable, his smile hungry. "I don't want to put you out the door. I'm a reasonable man, and you're obviously a sophisticated woman. Perhaps something can be worked out." His glance swept down Grace's body.

It was a minute before Grace could speak.

"You think I was having a weekender with the murdered guy, and since he's dead that I'll jump into the sack with you to pay my room rent?" Forget being a lady, Grace thought. Mama never met Wimberly.

"I know whose guest he was." Wimberly moved around the desk toward Grace. His foul breath almost choked her. She resisted an urge to step backwards. "But I have no desire to be your enemy, Mrs. Cassidy. Your protector perhaps?"

Grace blinked. His speech pattern had turned as Victorian as the room where they stood. He leered at her like a villain from an old melodrama. She could have sworn he twirled a nonexistent mustache.

"I'm not a man without feelings. I could perhaps be persuaded to be generous to a beautiful woman left stranded in a strange town without any means of her own."

"I'm not a woman without means." The phrase sounded stupid, but he'd said it first. "I'll bring you a credit card."

Wimberly looked stunned, as if for a minute he had forgotten credit cards existed. He stepped away from Grace. "Of course," he said. "A credit card would be fine."

"I'll be back." She turned on her heel and walked out of the room feeling Wimberly's gaze focused on her butt. Anger pounded blood against her temples. When she located Charlie there was a good chance the police would find a second dead body. This one would be badly maimed but fully clothed.

Grace ran through the house and up the stairs. On the second floor a bedroom door flew open and Theodora breezed into the passage. Today she was dressed in flowing black chiffon with strands of jet beads cascading down her bosom. The older woman's warm smile stopped Grace. Dear God. How she needed a friend!

"Good morning, Theodora. Did you sleep well?"

"Very well, thank you dear. I missed you at breakfast. I'm so glad to run into you, something important has happened."

"You've learned who the dead man was? Or how he died?" Grace's heartbeat quickened.

"Oh. Him. No, dear. That nice efficient sergeant isn't telling anyone anything. My news is about Mrs. Smith."

"Mrs. Smith? I don't remember seeing her in the sitting room last night. Is she a guest here?"

"No, she's the inn sitter who was coming to run the bed and breakfast while Mrs. Wimberly took her vacation to Hawaii. The poor woman slipped and broke her hip. Mrs. Wimberly will have to find a replacement or cancel her trip." She lowered her voice to a conspiratorial whisper. "And believe me dear, she needs to get away from that husband of hers. He's a trial to live with."

"That's the understatement of the year, but my life might be simpler if she stayed around."

"Tsk, tsk. Has that man made a pass at you?"

"He offered me free room rent for sex, all in a very genteel, Victorian manner. Nothing nasty actually put into words, of course."

"That's our Wimberly. He's spent years trying to get into Pansy's knickers. Of course our Pansy is very discriminating about her lovers."

Grace tried to picture the chaste looking Pansy as a sex-pot and failed. She grinned. Sweet old things, probably hadn't had so much as a kiss for years but liked to think about past conquests.

"With my luck Mrs. Wimberly will easily get someone to sub while she takes her trip and we'll all be stuck with her husband for a host."

"My dear, you just don't know, it's next to impossible. Running a bed and breakfast is like being chained to the house. Mrs. Smith's services are booked up a year in advance. I doubt there's anyone available."

"Then Wimberly himself may be forced to do some actual work." A picture of the self-important man stirring muffins in the kitchen, his clothes dusted with flour, a look of panic freezing his face while hungry residents watched, flashed through Grace's mind. She grinned, instantly cheered. "I've got to run my credit card down to Wimberly, then let's have a cup of tea and a chat." Her walk could wait until later, Grace decided.

"Gleaning for information?" Theodora asked, her eyes twinkling.

"Partly, mostly I'm just lonesome. You and Pansy seem to be the only people around here that I don't scare."

"I face hordes of seventh-graders every day and endeavor to teach them to write complete sentences. Nothing frightens me."

"Tea in fifteen minutes, then." Grace laughed and rushed up two flights of stairs and into her room.

She found her purse, pulled out her wallet and flipped through an assortment of credit cards. She had no idea what the account balances might be. God help me if I pick a card that's over limit, she thought. She glanced at the back of a card and using a phone snagged from the withdrawing room, began the number punching journey through automated telephone information.

An hour later Grace held her last credit card; the others had been tossed into the trash. The only cards left in her wallet were her driver's license, Triple A, telephone calling card, voter registration, library card, a Blockbuster Video membership card, and a yellow card from Big Al's in Tulsa, with three punches toward a free sandwich.

"What do you mean it's been stolen?" Grace yelled into the telephone. "It's my card and I'm holding the wretched thing in my hand right now."

Screaming didn't help her cause. The bored sounding voice threatened to hang up.

"No, please! Don't hang up. It took twenty-five minutes of elevator music and my mother's maiden name to get you. I apologize. Please help me." She struggled for control. "Someone's playing a horrible trick on me. I've called about all of my credit cards, and have gotten the same story on each of them."

"I'm sorry, ma'am, but there's nothing I can do." The voice was female and foreign.

"Can you tell me who reported the card as stolen?"

"The card was reported stolen by a Charles Cassidy. Evidently someone took his wallet. His secretary phoned in the theft for him, but she had all of the correct verifying information."

"Of course she had all of the information," Grace screamed into the receiver. "She's his secretary and his mistress. She knows more about him than I do."

The voice cleared her throat. "Thank you for calling. Have a nice day." A click sounded in Grace's ear.

"Don't tell me what kind of a day to have!" Grace shouted into the dead phone. Rage surged through her, followed by fear. What was she going to do? She grabbed her wallet and counted the cash. Ninety-seven dollars was all she had in the world.

Wait! That's not true! Grace took a deep breath. She owned a thriving collection agency and could very well run it herself, thank you very much. She found her calling card and punched in numbers. Grace was relieved when the office manager answered, a sensible woman who could be counted on to help sort through financial problems.

After a thirty minute phone call Grace sat immobile on the bed, dazed and paralyzed with fear. There was no solution for her, no way out.

A knock sounded at the door.

"Grace?" Theodora's commanding voice pierced through the solid oak. "It's been almost two hours. I was worried and decided to bring tea to you."

Grace stood on shaking legs, walked to the door and opened it.

"Why my dear child, what on earth is wrong? You're pale as a ghost." Theodora juggled a tea tray and studied Grace with a worried look.

Grace said the first words that came into her mind.

"I'm a woman without means."

Chapter 4

"A woman without means?" Theodora looked up at Grace, a small frown puckering her forehead. "That's quite an old fashioned phrase, my dear."

"The phrase was Wimberly's and I plead temporary insanity for repeating it." Grace stepped back and waved Theodora into the room. "There's something about this house that puts me straight back into the 1890's." She shivered. A goose walked over her grave, Mama would have said.

"Yes." Theodora peered at Grace. "Pansy said this morning that you seem to belong to Wimberly Place." The older woman turned and set the tea tray on the scarred surface of Grace's dresser. "Now suddenly you're without means." She cast a glance up and down Grace's body. "And that silk designer ensemble tells me this is something new for you. Perhaps you'd like to talk about it?"

Talk? Grace longed to lay her head on Theodora's full breasts and bawl like a baby, right into the woman's strands of jet beads. That, Grace mused, might render even Theodora speechless.

"It's sweet of you to offer, but I don't think I could talk about it without coming apart," Grace managed to say. "Besides, I won't be staying here much longer." She swallowed. Where would she go? She saw herself pushing a stolen grocery cart down a dark street. Alone.

"I think you need something stronger than tea. Come with me, dear." Theodora took Grace by the hand and pulled her through the door and down the narrow stairs. Instead of stepping into the third floor hall Theodora opened a small door that Grace hadn't noticed. Theodora stepped carefully down onto a narrow flight of stairs.

"Hey, it's like a secret door. Where does it lead?" Grace breathed in the musty odor of years past feeling a bit like Nancy Drew.

"These stairs lead outside. From there we'll go down to the basement, that's where the day people live." Theodora said.

THE DAY PEOPLE? The capitalized words flashed through Grace's mind, causing her to hesitate at the top of the narrow passageway that led downward.

"That's right, the day people. Now, be careful, these stairs are very steep." Theodora stepped carefully past a clutter of cleaning supplies left on the stairs. "Now watch this junk Maxie must have left."

"Maxie left cleaning supplies on the stairs?" Grace glanced down at a plastic carry-all filled with cleaners, furniture polish and what appeared to be a spray can of potpourri. "That surprises me, she seems to try so hard to do the right thing."

"Usually she's very careful, but as you can see the supplies are here. I'll pick them up as I go back. Whatever you do, don't mention it to Wimberly. He'd scold Maxie, and she's very sensitive. The man constantly hurts her feelings."

"The jerk, I think she's charming," Grace said. "She talks to herself while she works, and she chants. Or maybe she's singing."

Theodora stopped short and Grace touched the wall for balance.

"Are you all right?" Grace asked.

"Yes, yes, quite all right. Just slightly out of breath. I don't know how many doctors have told me I should lose weight. Can you imagine? As if that were some brilliant new idea I might leap at if only the thought were to enter my head."

"Sounds about as useful as some of the parenting advice my childless pediatrician used to offer." Grace glanced back up the steep stairs. "Do any of the other guests use this entrance?" she asked.

"No. At least not that I'm aware of and I imagine that we're not supposed to, either. I've never asked permission." Theodora moved downward again. "The outside door is almost hidden by shrubbery. Interesting, don't you think?"

"Very," Grace agreed.

"Almost there," Theodora sang out gaily.

Grace saw a solid door at the bottom, fastened securely with a dead-bolt lock and a chain.

"Here's the back door," Theodora said.

Grace stared at the dead bolt. No way that the murdered man could have gotten through that burglar-proof setup without inside help.

Without hesitation Theodora twisted the heavy bolt, un-hitched the chain and pushed the door open. She didn't re-lock the door and Grace followed her into a wildly tangled flower garden.

"Oh!" Grace said.

Color and fragrance blitzed Grace. At first sight the area seemed neglected, but upon closer scrutiny she realized the effect was the result of careful labor. Magical scents from exotic flowers wafted through the air. Coral blossoms punc-tuated yellow and purple blooms amongst thick greenery and Grace wished she knew the names of these exotic flowers. The unleashed artistic impressionism filled her with delight.

"What a wonderful place!" Grace said. "I had no idea this was here." A standing swing was almost hidden in a cluster of red blooming bushes. Visions of lovers secretly meeting here flashed into her mind.

"It is lovely. Walter, one of the day people, serves as gar-dener to pay for his rent." Theodora smiled. "He's a rather charming fellow, but he tipples a bit too much." She lowered her voice to a hoarse whisper. "I believe he might have a sort of crush on me."

"His taste is faultless. Perhaps we could sit here and chat." Grace wanted to stay forever. She closed her eyes and almost heard the rustle of silken tea gowns from another century. "It's enchanting."

"Perhaps later, now we must get on. What with finding dead bodies and being without means you're going to need all the help you can get."

"And these Day People can help? How?"

"A simple principle, when you're in a battle, take advice from fellow soldiers," Theodora said.

"Fellow soldiers?"

"Others who are down on their luck, struggling with a bad hand dealt them by life."

"And that's supposed cheer me up?" Grace teased, trying for a joke. Lame at best, she decided when Theodora shot her a hard look.

"Who are these Day People?" Grace asked in an apologetic tone. "I have this mental picture of people with faces glowing from some Inner Light. They sound wonderfully special."

"Do you often see things like that?" Theodora asked, "Pictures that flash through your head?"

"Since I was a child, shameful confession that it is." Grace grinned.

"Fascinating," Theodora stopped and turned, lifted her head to stare up at Grace. "Absolutely fascinating, I would never have expected that. You seem so... so..."

"Boring?" Grace offered.

"Not at all, I was going to say sophisticated, but you were asking me who the day people were. It's quite simple, actually. The day people live in the basement every day." Theodora paused a minute seeming to ponder her words with a new interest. "They live here at night too, of course, but it would sound a bit ridiculous to call them the day and night people."

"Oh. They're just ordinary people?" Grace knew that the disappointment she felt was absurd. There was no magic.

Amusement flickered across Theodora's face. "You thought maybe they were elves?" Her dimples flashed. "They're not magical, but they are special. They avoid all tourists except Pansy and me. We became acquainted with them years ago because Pansy—oh well, you'll see for yourself."

Theodora stepped gingerly around the side of the house and walked toward steps leading down to the basement.

"This is their home. They aren't tourists." She knocked, a hollow, echoing sound. "No breakfast, no artsy-craftsy decor, just a plain bed and a small kitchenette, at an almost affordable price. Mr. Wimberly pretends they don't exist except on the first of the month when he comes down for their rent."

The door was opened by a tall, well-built man in his mid-seventies who scowled down at them. The first thing Grace noticed was that he had notes of various sizes pinned to the front of his clothing. Then she saw the shirt. It was made of exceptionally fine linen and the initials AMM were stitched on one cuff. Frayed she noted, but immaculately clean. Classy, she thought. Discreetly classy.

His gaze focused on Theodora and the scowl disappeared. A smile transformed his weathered face.

"Come in, come in." He stepped back, bowed slightly, gestured them inward.

Debonair, Grace thought, again drifting back into the atmosphere of another era. He has the manner of a man who just stepped out of the nineteenth century. Even with those silly pieces of paper pinned all over him, he looked courtly. She half expected him to kiss her fingertips.

"Hello Drew. So sorry to intrude, but it's a bit of an emergency." Theodora walked into the dark hallway and headed toward an open door leading into what was obviously Drew's private apartment. "My friend needs a drink for medicinal purposes. Brandy if you have it."

"I have Everclear," he said, his tone purposefully even.

Grace saw him watching her, studying her clothes, judging the price. Instinctively she knew her fellow tourists had treated him badly. Grace seldom drank and had no idea what Everclear was, but she wanted this man to think well of her.

"Pour it." Grace stepped inside, then stopped, nonplussed when she saw Pansy sitting on a shabby green sofa buttoning her blouse.

"Hello, you two." Pansy smiled, completely unruffled, as calm as if she were sipping tea.

"Sorry to interrupt," Theodora said again, bustling toward the worn sofa. "But this is something of an emergency. Grace needs a drink most desperately."

"Something else has happened." Pansy sat soldier straight, her eyes closed then reopened to focus on Grace. "I knew something else was going to happen to you, something dark. I felt an aura of dampness this morning while we breakfasted and I was focusing on your empty chair."

The small blond woman now had her blouse buttoned demurely to the neck, sleeves to her wrists, prim as a pilgrim.

"Aura of dampness?" Grace echoed. A picture flashed into her mind. She sat at the Victorian table where breakfast was served; a small black cloud drizzled rain on her chair while the other guests basked in sunshine.

"Are you the woman with the naked corpse in her bed?" Drew asked. Grace knew she had his interest.

"That's me." Grace met his stare. "Pansy's wrong about the damp aura. It's an absolute downpour. Now where's my drink?" I'll drink that wretched stuff even if it straightens my hair, she thought.

He smiled his wonderful smile again, reminding Grace that sex appeal had nothing to do with age.

"Actually I have some sherry," he said. "It's not top quality such as I used to get, but you'll like it better than Everclear. Besides, that rot-gut belongs to my friend Walter and he'd get a bit testy if we consumed it." He smiled. "I'm Andrew Martin Maynard. You can call me Drew."

"Grace Cassidy." She held out her hand and liked the feel of his firm handshake.

His apartment suited him, Grace decided. One fine piece of furniture had been intermingled with someone's cast-offs. A magnificent roll-top desk stuffed with papers and assorted junk sat directly under a tiny high-up window, catching the only natural light. In front of it was a chair from the chrome and yellow plastic dinette set that took most of the left side of the room. A brown leather chair and matching footstool were in one corner, with an exceptionally fine painting positioned directly across from the sofa. Did Drew sleep on his couch or was there a Murphy bed hidden from sight? She wondered.

"I love your room," Grace said, "And that painting! It's magnificent."

The image of Drew settled into the chair's roomy comfort while studying the picture filled Grace's mind. The thought softened the ugliness of the blue lamp behind the chair, the lamp's bowl suspended by plastic poles, efficient but unsightly.

It was a minute before Drew answered.

"You really mean that, don't you?" His voice was gentle.

"Absolutely, it's wonderful. You have books everywhere. I could live forever in this kind of place."

The walls were lined with shelves made from boards and cinder-blocks, and volumes of all sizes and color were wedged tightly together. More books were stacked in one corner forming a triple column that almost reached the ceiling. Yet everything seemed somehow tidy. The room reminded her of her childhood, her father's study. Happiness. She moved closer.

The painting looked like a Winslow Homer, either an original or a very good copy. She longed to examine it more closely. If it were an original it would be worth well into seven figures. What was this poverty-stricken gentleman doing with a million-dollar piece of art in his basement apartment?

"Is that a real Homer?" Grace asked.

The two women in the painting, one young, one middle-aged wore the bathing garb of the late 1800's and the New England Sea behind them was alive with the waves of high tide. At the bottom left was written W. Homer and a date.

"Are you familiar with Victorian art?" He answered her question with a question and a pleased smile, neither admitting nor denying.

"Not really," Grace said, "But I've always liked Homer and that picture is quite lovely, breathtaking, actually."

"Yes." Drew studied the picture a minute then turned back to Grace. "But I'm forgetting my manners. You came for a drink." Drew walked to the desk, found a bottle and three glasses then poured the wine. "Would you care for tea?" he asked Theodora who waved the invitation away with an airy gesture and a shake of her head.

Grace looked at the picture again. It couldn't possibly be authentic, but it was a wonderful copy. Perhaps Drew liked to pretend it was real.

"For you my dear," Drew handed a glass to Grace and another to Pansy before picking up his own. "Cheers," he said.

Grace raised her glass and took a healthy swallow. The sherry burned a path down her esophagus and her eyes teared. She struggled not to embarrass herself by coughing and showing what an inexperienced drinker she was. Then warmth flowed into her stomach.

"Have a bit more," Drew moved to top off her glass. She tried to catch a glimpse of what was written on the pieces of paper he wore, but the flamboyant penmanship foiled her. He grinned, replaced the bottle, and walked toward an electric pot sitting on the cluttered desk. "And Theodora, I insist you have tea."

He shuffled through papers on the desk, unearthed a crumpled looking tea bag and dropped it into a cup, knocking a photo onto the floor in the process. It floated through the air and landed almost at Grace's feet. She picked up the black and white print and briefly studied two young sailors from years ago.

"My housekeeping leaves a lot to be desired." Drew laughed, taking the photo from Grace and pinning it to a bulletin board hanging beside his desk. "Too much old junk hanging around to keep everything shipshape."

"No, no," Grace protested. "Your apartment seems perfect to me."

"Thanks for the kind words." He waved a hand toward Theodora. "This lady's a tee-totaler." He grinned at Grace. "The pun, of course, is intended. A drop of alcohol has never passed her lips." He poured steaming water from the pot and Grace watched vapor rise.

"A promise I made to my mother some years ago." Theodora accepted the cup offered to her and gave a sassy smile. "Her lectures were reinforced because Daddy was a sot, a charming sot but a sot none the less. But enough about me, what we need to do now is help Grace."

Grace felt three pairs of eyes peer expectantly at her. She wanted to squirm.

"Now tell me dear, what is all this about? It has a great deal to do with that rascal of a husband of yours I expect?"

"How did you know about Charlie?" Grace asked.

"Oh, my dear child," Theodora said. "With a woman like you, there's always a man like Charlie."

Chapter 5

Maxie couldn't stop worrying. She flipped the duster over the dresser, put all of Miss Pansy's pretty little bottles and boxes in a nice neat row beside Miss Theodora's makeup, then moved to make the twin beds. But the worry thoughts wouldn't stop.

Attic Missus was nice. Not pretend nice, with lips stretched into a funny looking smile, but really nice. Missus' smile made Maxie feel warm and happy inside. Like when she played with a kitten and Maxie hadn't been nice back to Missus. Missus might be mad. The thought made Maxie unhappy. Maybe she should go back upstairs and tell Missus what she was worried about. Yes. That was what she would do.

She remembered the can of cleaner left in the bathroom. "Mustn't lose anymore supplies," Mr. Wimberly would yell. She went into the bath, picked up the can, and patted the apple green towels she had left on the racks. All nice just like Mrs. Wimberly had showed her. The big one first then the little one with the cloth on top. She liked her work. Better than the other job with all of the people sick. Maxie smiled and walked back into the bedroom, put the can into the little yellow box with a handle. She liked yellow. It was pretty, like sunshine. She made sure the door lock snapped on her way out.

Maxie turned and saw the Question Man walking toward her with an armful of clothes on hangers. She wanted to run, but he blocked her way.

"I have Mrs. Cassidy's things," the question man said. "She'll need them. Could you take them up to her room?"

Maxie nodded, shifted her supplies to her left hand and took the heavy load. She was scared of this man. He could look right into your soul. Maxie didn't like that.

"Can you manage all of that?"

His voice sounded kind, but Maxie still didn't trust him. She nodded again and backed away, scuttling up the stairs as quickly as possible. When she reached the attic she shifted her burden and knocked.

"Missus? Are you in there Missus?" She knocked again, puzzled because there wasn't any answer. She knew Missus had gone downstairs to see Mr. Wimberly then come back up. She had heard her.

"Maxie has good ears," she muttered. "Maxie hears everything, and Missus sure didn't come back down again." She drew a quick breath. "Unless she used the bad stairs," Maxie shivered then opened the door with her special key. "Missus?" she asked, her tone uncertain.

""You here?" Maxie looked around. "No. Room's empty. Maxie will hang up your clothes and tidy your ugly little room so it looks real nice." She liked the word tidy. It was one that Mrs. Wimberly had taught her. When she was done maybe she could wait for Missus. She laid the clothes on the narrow bed, set the yellow carrier on the floor and began to sing.

Grace still glowed from the sherry. Usually she distrusted an alcohol buzz, but today she welcomed the escape, and that worried her. Nothing could be solved if she were smashed, tempting as the thought might be. She still had to go upstairs and face Wimberly. Drew had been right in putting away the bottle.

Her new found friends sat politely, as if at some long ago tea party waiting for her to describe last night's ball. The warmth from the sherry further blended the present and the past. They should all be wearing bustles, Grace decided. Except for Drew, who should be balancing a top hat on his knee, Grace pulled herself back into the present. They were all still looking at her.

"Thanks for the drink." She smiled, feeling uncomfortable, hoping someone would speak and take the spotlight off her. No one did. Pansy offered an encouraging smile. Theodora set her cup down and waited. Drew grinned.

"Just say what's on your mind, Grace. You're among friends," Drew said.

"There's a line in one of Tennessee William's plays about the kindness of strangers." Grace stalled.

"Oh, you're wrong. We're not strangers," Pansy said. "The minute I met you, I knew you from somewhere."

"Perhaps you've been to Oklahoma?" Grace asked politely, knowing she had never set eyes on Pansy before. Pansy she would have remembered.

"Not Oklahoma. Quite a lovely state, I hear, but I've never been there. I remember you from another life. I'm quite sure of it. You have a lovely blue aura, did you realize that?"

Blue aura? Grace blinked, wondering if she had heard correctly.

"I feel we're kindred souls." Pansy's gaze seemed focused on some distant object. "I sense that you're an old spirit, and perhaps this is your last time to pass through the testing of life on earth."

"I hope so," Grace said, amused by Pansy's charming candor.

"I'm accustomed to disbelief," Pansy said, crossing her ankles.

"Oh, I'm so sorry," Grace said. "I didn't mean—it's just that..."

Pansy waved Grace's embarrassment away. "I never take offense when none is intended. Now tell us how you came to be in such distress."

Pansy and Theodora settled themselves back, their faces expectant.

"You're talking to three battle-scarred veterans." Drew smiled. "And I'm not referring to my youth in service as a SEAL. Pansy survived an abusive husband, Theodora's Ex traded her in for a twenty-five year old, and I've been fighting the big C. It's taken all of my money and left me with a colostomy." He smiled his wonderful smile. "There now, I've dumped on you. It's your turn."

Dear God, Grace thought, how could he tell something like that? A colostomy! Surely he must hate having people know.

"It could have been worse," Drew said, seeming to read her mind. "It could have been my penis."

Grace laughed. "That's a great way to look at it," she said.

"It was the only way I could bear it."

"Oh, for goodness sake, Drew," Pansy said. "What's the big deal? I don't even notice that thing taped to your stomach just a little crinkly sound during love making. Nothing to worry about."

As long as it doesn't leak, Grace thought. She felt Drew's gaze on her, forced herself to look at him. He was grinning, watching her reaction. She decided to level with this good man.

"I don't have any money," she said.

"No money?" Drew mused. "You put on a good appearance. Is this new broke or old broke?"

"About noon yesterday, Charlie wire transferred all of our cash to an account in his name only. He left twenty dollars, just enough to keep the accounts open." She glanced down at her fingers laced tightly together in her lap. "In addition to that, all of our credit cards were reported stolen and closed."

"Charlie did what?" Drew leaned forward and narrowed his eyes. His whole demeanor spoke of how he would deal with Charlie if he could find him. Just like daddy, Grace thought then swallowed to clear the lump in her throat.

"Cutting off your credit doesn't even make any sense, if he just wants to disappear from sight. The man must be both cruel and vicious, he must want to destroy you," Theodora boomed.

Grace shook her head. "Charlie wouldn't have bothered calling about the cards. He didn't care enough to be vindictive. That bit of mischief was done by his secretary and current girl friend. He probably told her to cut-up the plastic since using credit would leave a paper trail. My husband didn't care enough about me to be vindictive. He just wanted the money."

She glanced down at the faded blue linoleum, then back up. She told them everything. The bad marriage, Charlie's many affairs—the latest with Clover McBride—and how the business became hers in case of a divorce. Explaining the rest would be harder. She took a deep breath and tried.

"I never gave much thought to the fact that most of our assets could be liquidated at a moment's notice."

"But you said that the business will belong to you." Drew set his glass on a battered metal TV tray. "I can help you call the bank and get a loan using your company for collateral. You're not in as much trouble as you think."

"I've already called them," Grace said. "Believe me, there are no assets."

The silence deafened Grace.

"What kind of business are you and Charlie in?" Drew asked, his brows drawn together.

Grace took a deep breath. She hated telling him, mostly because of his medically induced poverty.

"We own a collection agency."

Drew raised an eyebrow then crossed his arms and leaned backwards.

"It wasn't one of the sleazy agencies," Grace said.

"No one is accusing you, we only want to help." Pansy soothed.

"I don't think Grace has finished yet," Theodora said. "Please tell us the rest, dear. Charlie's done more than just steal *your* money, hasn't he?"

"Yes, Charlie absconded with client funds." Grace's voice broke and she cleared her throat in order to continue. "The major assets of a collection agency are the clients and their good will. With their money stolen, I've lost both."

"Oh, dear," Pansy said. "He turned criminal and flew the coop."

Drew dropped his gaze to Pansy's face and his eyes filled with tender adoration. Grace would have given five years of her life to have a good man look at her with that same expression.

Drew moved his focus back to Grace. "Tell me how a collection agency works," he said.

She thought about his question for a minute. The system seemed a bit complicated even to her.

"Charlie and my signatures were good on three bank accounts: a personal one, the company account used for all business expenses and payroll, and what I always called 'the biggie.' All money collected by the agency staff was accumulated in this special account until the end of the month. At that time the clients are paid their part and the agency's portion is transferred into the business account."

Drew began to unpin notes from his shirt. His simple movements struck Grace as ominous, and she wasn't sure why. She forced herself to continue.

"The agency keeps forty to sixty percent of whatever is collected, depending on the specific client contract. Charlie receives a salary from the collection company and that's deposited into our personal account."

Grace hugged herself. She could tell by the trio's expression they already knew where she was headed.

"Money from the special account can't be mingled with regular funds or used in any way, else we'd be operating on client funds. That's unethical and illegal. All checks drawn on that account are written to clients, and of course, one to our collection agency. That is only cut after the client's portion has already been paid."

"How much money was in this account?" Drew asked.

Grace studied her re-knotted fists, then forced herself to meet Drew's gaze. "We had an unusually good month, according to the office manager. This month the account held almost five hundred thousand dollars."

Both Pansy and Theodora caught their breath. Drew closed his eyes. Somehow Grace managed to continue speaking.

"Only about 45 percent of that sum would have been transferred to the business. And a large part of the agency portion was earmarked to pay agent commissions, office rent, clerical salaries, vendor bills, and of course to support our lifestyle." She watched Drew doing the math in his head.

"The bastard!" He muttered.

"Rascal," Theodora agreed.

"Another black-hearted cur," Pansy's eyes teared.

Grace's heart warmed. It had been years since she had her own private cheering section. Not since Mama and Daddy died. It now seemed easier to continue.

"As soon as the bank president came back from lunch, his assistant informed him the accounts had been closed. He then called the CEO of our largest client, St. Martin's Hospital, who happened to be a golfing buddy. The man's lawyer immediately put a lien on all corporate assets." Rehashing the catastrophe sobered Grace instantly. She bit her lip and considered begging for another glass of wine.

"What about your house? Since the business was a corporation, your personal property would be exempt," Drew said.

"And jewelry," Theodora said. "Most philandering husbands ease their conscience by giving jewelry."

"Not mine. I have some nice pieces that belonged to my mother, but I'd live in a cardboard box before I sold those.

Selling the house wouldn't help. Charlie talked me into refinancing our home a year ago. He said we'd get a better rate. Then he invested the equity."

"And I suppose that's gone, too," Drew said.

"Yes, it seems that after closing the bank accounts Charlie called our broker and sold all of our stocks and mutual funds, then wire transferred the money to his new bank in San Francisco."

"Have you reported this to the police? Maybe an attachment can be put on that account," Drew said.

"It's too late. Charlie has already moved the money to the Cayman Islands and then on to another bank somewhere else."

"And no one can find Charlie, I suppose?" Theodora asked.

"He appears to have disappeared, along with sweet Clover McBride. It seems that all of the help have walked off the job at the agency, because there's no money for payroll. The collection agency office manager had been trying to reach me, but didn't know where I was until I called her this morning."

"Much as I hate the sons of bitches it sounds like you need your lawyer," Drew said.

"I called him. He agreed to do what he could, but his parting phrase was, 'It looks like you've been royally screwed'."

"That's a lot of help," Drew said.

"Yes, and to think I paid for that brilliant statement. Or not paying, as it will probably turn out to be." Grace swallowed hard. "I'm even terrified to return my rental car. I must do it today, but fear they'll call the police because my credit card isn't good."

"Let Theodora return it. I can follow her in my car and bring her back," Pansy suggested. "No one ever dares challenge our Theodora. She can park the car and just hand them the keys, say she's doing the renter a favor."

A rush of gratitude warmed Grace. "That would be a huge help. I need to spend my time and energy figuring out where in the world I'm going to live. According to the police I can't leave Port Ortega. Sergeant Harper seems to think I'm the murderer, or at least connected with it in some manner. I can't go, but I don't have the money to stay either."

She looked around, loving the untidy coziness.

"Are there any of these basement rooms available? Maybe I could move down here." She rubbed a hand across her eyes. "I haven't mentioned that Wimberly offered me my attic room rent free, in exchange for 'favors'."

"That louse." Drew snorted.

"Good grief." Pansy seemed to shift to a practical mode. "If you're that desperate you can do better than a room in a bed and breakfast."

Grace gaped at her.

"Don't be alarmed by Pansy's pragmatic side." Theodora smiled reassuringly at Grace. "I have a terrifically better idea for you than selling your body."

Chapter 6

"Let's hear your terrifically better idea, Theodora. I'd prefer to put the body-selling off for a bit." Grace grinned at Pansy. "I'll make that plan C. Right after stealing a grocery cart and residing at the bus terminal in plan B. For Plan A I'm game for anything that doesn't include Wimberly."

"I'm so sorry, dear, but I'm afraid it does." Theodora's laugh swelled and filled the room. "Only not in the way he wants. If you'll remember, there's a job opening here."

"Of course!" Pansy trilled, clapping her hands. "Mrs. Smith! You can fill in for Mrs. Smith."

"Mrs. Smith?" The name seemed somehow familiar, but Grace couldn't place it immediately.

"You remember, I told you about her earlier," Theodora said. "She's the inn sitter who fell and broke her hip."

"The inn sitter?" Grace blinked, decided she must have another tiny swallow of sherry; handed her empty glass to Drew hoping he would refill it. Instead he just held it and grinned.

"A superb idea, Theodora," he said. "Poor Mrs. Wimberly will get to take her trip to Hawaii and Grace will have a job. At least for three weeks." He set Grace's empty glass on the lamp stand. "Enough liquid courage, however, you'll need your wits about you to handle Wimberly."

"Grace can handle Wimberly," Theodora said. "And if she needs help, we're here."

"And Grace being in charge will give us time to find out why a naked man was killed in her room," Pansy said. "We must do that. It's the only way Wimberly Place can be cleared of the dark aura of violence. And I do so love Wimberly Place."

"I seriously doubt that the police want our help." Drew patted her leg.

"Wimberly isn't going to hire me anyway," Grace said. "Not unless I'm willing to cooperate with his intentions, which I'm not."

"You won't apply to Mr. Wimberly, you'll apply to Mrs. Wimberly. She's desperate and desperate makes for quick decisions," Theodora said.

"But I don't know squat about running a bed and breakfast," Grace protested. "I haven't even cooked much the last couple of years."

"Oh, pooh," Theodora waved away the problem of inn keeping with a graceful movement. "Cooking is like riding a bicycle. Once you know how, you never forget. Pansy and I spend most of our summers living here. There's nothing we don't know, and we'll teach you."

Grace opened her mouth to ask how two public school teachers could afford to spend so much time living in expensive resorts then she closed it. Maybe they saved for years and now were blowing their nest egg, or maybe they had won the state lottery. What difference did it make? People only told you what they wanted you to know and she wasn't in the position to challenge any offer of a job.

"Should I change to a dress for the interview? I have a couple with me."

Pansy's laugh was musical, Theodora's robust. Drew seemed to be the only one who took the question seriously.

"That's not necessary in California," he said. "What you have on is all right to approach Mrs. Wimberly, but not for the daily grind. Are all of your clothes casual-elegant?"

Grace thought a minute. When she had packed for the convention, housework hadn't entered the equation.

"I suppose so," she said, running through a mental list of what she had with her. "I'll admit to being partial to silk, but I have a few casual things along, including shorts and jeans of course."

"Dress as casual as possible," Drew said. "You'll have to work like a donkey. Wimberly doesn't cut anyone any slack without a reason."

"So now," Grace smoothed her silk shirt, "I'm a burro."

Grace ran up the stairs, adrenaline pumping, heart pounding. She had the job! Mrs. Wimberly had first been surprised, then delighted. It was just as Theodora had promised, desperate people don't ask many questions. Grace was to change her clothes and hurry back down for instructions. There were only two hours available for training.

The old fashioned bedroom door, painted a homey white, looked wonderfully solid, safe almost. Hope surged. She would survive. She always did. Grace inserted her key, twisted it, and pushed open the door. She stopped dead. Disbelief washed through her.

"Maxie. What are you doing? You're wearing my dress!"

Maxie stood rooted to the floor, eyes wide with fear, mouth gaping. Her straw-colored hair stood in spikes, mussed by changing clothes.

"I'm sorry Missus. I'll take it off. Don't tell Mr. Wimberly." Maxie's fingers plucked frantically at the tight-bodiced, slim-skirted dress.

Grace noticed the waist was a bit tight, but except for that, the dress was a perfect fit.

"Take it easy, Maxie," she said. "Let me help you." She reached out to stop Maxie's fingers from tearing the fabric. "Don't panic. I'm not going to tell anyone."

Maxie went limp, her expression pathetically grateful. "You won't tell?"

"Of course not, but you mustn't try on the guests clothing, it's a wrong thing to do. People won't like it." She opened her mouth to say more then stopped. Mrs. Wimberly wanted to be the one to tell Maxie that Grace would be in charge, not Mrs. Smith. It would save confusion, she had said.

"I know that, Missus. But this was so pretty. It's yellow." Maxie's simple expression softened and then intensified with longing. "I just love yellow."

Something in Maxie's expression shot to Grace's heart. The look of desperate need for something unattainable mirrored Grace's own inner longing when she caught a happily married couple surreptitiously sharing an intimate glance.

"Me too," she said hoarsely then cleared her throat. "Yellow is my favorite color, too." She helped Maxie pull the dress over her head. When it was off Maxie sniffled, standing helpless and pitiful in a white cotton slip.

"Oh Missus, I'm so sorry. I been bad. I didn't mean to be bad, but I was. I'm so sorry."

"Oh, Maxie, you haven't been bad. Not really. You just made a mistake. We all make mistakes."

"No, Missus. I've been really bad. I want to tell." She began crying again, tears spilling down her cheeks.

"Now, now Maxie," Grace said. "It's not that important. It's all over now." Grace fished a clean tissue out of her pocket, offered it to Maxie, and patted her shoulder.

"All over?" Maxie looked at her through the tears, her face hopeful.

"Of course, you mustn't worry about it anymore." Grace watched relief sweep over Maxie's face. "Now put on your own clothes and go back to your work." Grace held Maxie's shirt so the young woman could slip her arms into the sleeves.

"You're sure it didn't matter?" Maxie asked.

"It didn't matter." Grace would have said anything to erase that scared look from Maxie's face. She reached for Maxie's skirt, urgently needing to protect the woman from exposure, from indignity.

"Not even..." Maxie began just before Grace plopped the maid's skirt over her head and gently pulled downward. Maxie's words were muffled by the fabric.

"...and I won't ever do it again, I promise." Maxie finished, pulling free from the tangle of cloth, pushing hair from her eyes, tugging her skirt straight.

"Of course not, just get along with your work and don't worry," Grace said, eager to be alone so she could change and run back downstairs to Mrs. Wimberly.

Maxie's face brightened. She picked up her container of supplies and tools and shuffled toward the door. The rubber soles of her tennis shoes squeaked against the hard wood floor. Maxie looked down. "Step lightly," she said, then picked up her feet and walked out.

Grace stood for a moment, the yellow sheath draped over her arm.

"I've got my hands full now," Grace muttered, walking to the closet to hang up the dress.

"I've got to run this inn with the help of two senior citizens and a child-woman." She reached for an ivory colored cotton shirt. "And in my spare time I need to find Charlie and maybe solve a murder to clear myself." She pulled on black jeans. "Of course, I have three whole weeks to pull off the miracle."

Chapter 7

Mrs. Wimberly met Grace at the bottom of the stairs with a long list and a big smile. "Grace, dear, I know you're going to do splendidly. After all, Pansy and Theodora recommended you and they've been customers for years."

She took a happy breath and handed Grace a sheaf of papers. "I have everything written out—I always leave a full set of instructions for Mrs. Smith." She picked up her purse and backed toward the door. "My bags are in the car."

"But my training? You said we had a couple of hours, and that seemed little enough."

"Everything you need to know is on the list." Mrs. Wimberly beamed and reached for the doorknob. "So good of Theodora to tell me how much background in inn-keeping you already had."

"Background?" Grace pattered behind, conscious that she seemed an inept echo. "But..."

"Don't forget to bake cookies, Grace. For the guests' afternoon tea."

"Cookies?" Grace watched the door slam. "What kind of cookies?"

Grace hugged herself. The kitchen was wonderful. Artfully disguised to appear Victorian, it was as modern as next week's computer. Glass-enclosed cabinets stretched on every side of the large room and were filled with a mismatched clutter of charming antique china. Copper pots hung around a large work island in the center of the room. A small white table with chairs sat before a bay window and plants were everywhere.

"Cookies," Grace took a deep breath and reached for a cookbook in a nearby rack. "It's been awhile."

The ringing of the front door bell startled her. Were the newlyweds early? Mrs. Wimberly's notes said that Pansy had moved in with Theodora this morning to make room for a young couple. Excitement surged. Her first new customer!

Inn-keeping might be fun. Grace ran to the entry hall with a dishtowel still in her hand and pulled open the door.

Her heart sank. It was that dark souled policeman. He'd exchanged his rumpled navy suit for rumpled gray slacks. The top button of his navy shirt was unfastened and a black and maroon striped tie hung loosely knotted just below the opening. The man was either single or his wife hated him. Grace took a deep breath.

"Can I help you?" She saw him glance at the dishtowel where red poppies flamed against a black background. He looked a bit perplexed, then just as quickly he masked his expression.

"I'd like to ask you a few more questions." He peered over her shoulder into the back of the house.

"Of course, would you mind coming to the kitchen? I'm baking cookies." Grace flipped the dishtowel over her shoulder and grinned at Harper's gaping mouth. This time he made no pretense of hiding his surprise. "Chocolate-chip with pecans, not native Oklahoma pecans, of course, but your California ones aren't a bad substitute." He raised an eyebrow and she grinned. Let him profile a murderer who baked cookies.

The oven buzzer sounded behind her.

"They're ready." She turned and darted toward the kitchen. "Follow me."

Grace wondered if he could sense her composure, her happiness. Baking cookies had been pure therapy, taking her back to a time when she and Charlie had been happy together. And Grace knew what the catharsis had been. It wasn't the gathering together of the ingredients, or the pure pleasure of creaming butter and sugar, nor the plopping of happy spoonfuls of dough onto the baking sheet. No. It had been the smell, the enchanting fragrance of baking cookies that had swelled and seemed to fill some sort of imaginary but colorful balloon in the cheerful kitchen. A balloon that rested happily over her head, chasing away the gloom and doom and thoughts of murder.

That same aroma of baking cookies had taken her back to Brand's childhood, to hectic afternoons of laughter and her child's flour smudged cheeks and wonderful spicy smells. For a brief moment she felt twenty-something and sexy and totally in charge of her life. Maybe she could bake cookies for a living when these three weeks were over. Her options seemed endless.

She pulled open the oven door and a wave of heat swept over her. She breathed cookie smell, smiled, wrapped the dishtowel several times around her hand and pulled the pan of cookies from the oven.

"They're perfect," she said. "Almost done but not quite, the heat from the cookies themselves will finish the baking." She grinned up at an astonished Harper. "That's the secret of perfect cookies. Most people over-cook them, make them hard as bricks." She set the pan on a pad and began lifting cookies out to cool, setting them on a baking rack.

Harper watched her, frowning. He'd overcome his initial surprise and Grace couldn't read his expression.

"Want one?" she asked.

"Humph..." He leaned back against the center island, cocked his head, scowled. Grace took it for a yes.

"Here," she pulled a chair away from the table, grabbed a saucer from a shelf to her left and dumped some cookies on it. "I have fresh coffee, too," she said, moving to get a cup.

Harper hesitated, then walked to the table and sat down. "Does Wimberly know you're in his kitchen?" He blew on the hot cookie for a minute then bit off half and chewed.

Grace watched his expression mellow as he chewed. She grinned. Darned right, she thought. I haven't lost my touch. Always did make the best cookies in the state of Oklahoma.

"I hope so." Grace reached for the coffeepot, poured Harper a cup, pushed a matching cut-glass cream pitcher and sugar bowl toward him. "He's paying me for it. Or at least, Mrs. Wimberly is." She shot him a quick glance without mentioning she was working for little more than minimum wage. "I'm the new inn sitter." She watched his mouth drop open, full of cookies and all.

"The what?"

"Inn sitter." She still felt twenty-five and cocky. She knew it was the cookie-smell, but her mouth wouldn't stay shut.

"An inn, according to Webster, is an establishment providing food, drink and bedrooms for travelers. A sitter is one who sits but it doesn't look as if I'm going to be doing much of that." She spooned fresh cookie dough onto the baking sheet.

Harper poured cream into his coffee, added a couple of spoonfuls of sugar, stirred. His eyes never left her.

"Thanks for the lesson," he said with a straight face, then reached for another cookie. He chewed, took another swallow of coffee. "What's in this stuff?" he asked, studying his cup.

"Mixture of Colombian and French roast with just a pinch of cinnamon. Like it?" She grinned. It was weird, him sitting there eating her cookies, asking about the coffee, his face deadpan. For a minute she almost liked him.

"It's okay," Harper took another bite of cookie, swallowed some coffee. "I could do without the cinnamon. The cookies are great, though. Next time you make some with Oklahoma nuts let me know. I'd like to see if I could tell the difference."

Grace wondered how he could keep his eyes locked to hers and still make her suspect he was scrutinizing her breasts.

"I don't intend to be here that long," she said coolly.

"Don't leave town just yet." His gaze shifted back to his coffee cup. "While I'm here I'll take down that tape we left upstairs. We're through in your former bedroom."

The cookie-balloon burst. Suddenly Grace felt forty-nine again, maybe fifty-nine.

"Have you found out who he was?" she asked. "Or how he died?"

Harper drained his cup, leaned back, studied her. "Got any more coffee?" he asked.

"Sure." She picked up the pot and poured him a cup. Her hand shook. She could see that and so could the detective.

"When did you say your husband was coming to join you?"

She felt his gaze burning into her face and suddenly felt the need to study her French pedicure.

"He won't be joining me." She forced herself to look at him. His face was still expressionless. "But you already knew that, didn't you, Sergeant?"

"I made a few calls." He doctored his coffee and then took a sip. "I've asked the San Francisco police to keep an eye open for him at airports. If I hear anything I'll let you know."

"Then you already know that he's a thief. But you're wasting your time if you think he had anything to do with this murder."

"Humm," Harper said.

Chapter 8

Grace glowered at Harper before dropping the last spoon of cookie dough onto the baking sheet and popping it into the oven. The warm glow of happiness she had experienced earlier vaporized into a feeling of dread. The colorful balloon filled with cookie smells had turned into a mushroom cloud toxic with despair.

She longed for someone who liked her to be standing between her and Harper. Where were Theodora and Pansy? She liked having them underfoot, trying to run her life, telling well-meant lies on her behalf. A character reference from a self-assured schoolteacher who wasn't restrained by the truth or even an outrageous lie would be appropriate about now, Grace thought.

She knew Harper's eyes never left her for a second. Even with her back to him she felt his stare. Grace turned to face him but couldn't think of a word to say.

He stood and opened the glass-encased cabinet then plucked a cup and saucer off the shelf. He filled the cup with surprisingly efficient movements.

"Break time," he said. His eyes swept the length of her body with no attempt to hide his frank appraisal.

"Well." Grace embarrassed herself by blushing. "Do I pass or fail?"

Harper grinned.

"Sit and relax a minute while I ask you a few questions." He pulled out a chair and set the cup before her.

Relax? In this guy's presence? He had to be kidding. Grace's first impulse was to refuse. Then she realized how silly that would be. Dumb too. Why cross the man for no good reason? Yet when she opened her mouth her foot just seemed to slide inside.

"Am I still your prime suspect?" She walked to the table and sat down, pulling the cup toward her. "If so, I'd like to know the name of whomever it is I'm supposed to have killed."

Harper's expression turned pointedly bland.

"You can forget the Baby Huey dumb look," Grace said. "I'm gullible, not brain-dead."

"The Baby Huey dumb look?"

"Baby Huey the duck. A cartoon starring an oversized baby duck with a minute brain." She didn't add that the duck with his guileless innocence always outwitted the bad guy.

"That who I remind you of?" Harper grinned again. The humor softened his face, made him seem somehow vulnerable. Grace steeled herself against the sudden impact of unexpected charm.

"No," she answered honestly. "But that expression you just assumed reminded me of him." She grinned. "My son Brand, used to pretend to be Huey when he was about five. He had this game he played called Who Am I? When he was Huey he could slip that same expression onto his face. That was when I knew to watch him like a hawk."

Harper grinned openly. "The Who Am I game, huh?" he asked.

"Right," Grace took a sip of coffee, hot and black and bitter. She craved the richness of cream and decided to worry about the calories later. She picked up the pitcher, poured a healthy slug into her cup and drank deeply. Pure heaven.

"If you think that's dumb," she said. "You should have had to play the silly game."

"Maybe I have." Harper laughed, sat down and leaned back in his chair; his expression more appealing than Grace wanted it to be.

"Don't laugh. It was a tough game." Grace stirred her coffee, loving the color, the aroma. Missing her son! A sudden need to see Brand washed through Grace. Adult and distant as he had grown, she wanted him with her. The emotion was urgent and frantic and desperately homesick. She needed the feel and the boyish smell of him and he was wandering through Europe, God knew where.

"You surprise me, Mrs. Cassidy."

"Why?" Grace asked. "Because I raised a child and can bake cookies or because you think I murdered some guy, stripped him naked and burned his clothes in the fireplace?"

"I know you didn't burn his clothes," Harper said with a straight face. "I've already checked."

"You checked?" The spoon stopped in the cup. It was a minute before she could speak. "Why would I have wanted to burn his clothes? It wasn't a cold day and there was no need for a fire." She set the spoon on the Havilland saucer, lifted the cup to her lips, sipped and swallowed. Her throat hurt.

"That's true." Harper's voice held a forced serious tone.

Grace grinned in spite of herself. She took a cookie, bit into it. The chewy sweetness comforted her. She waited for Harper to speak.

"You're also too smart to think it would keep us from identifying the victim. But perhaps you had another reason, one I haven't figured out yet?"

"Do you know who he is?" Grace studied the pattern on her cup.

"Have you ever hired a private detective?" he asked.

"Private detective? Of course not."

"You're sure?" Harper asked.

"Like I might hire one and then forget it?" she snapped.

"Like you might hire one and not want to tell me."

Grace rolled her eyes. "Day before yesterday I didn't even know that I needed an investigator. But even if I had, I would never have done such a thing." She met his gaze with a level look. "There's just something in me that would never invite a stranger to probe my family's secrets."

Harper sat in silence, his eyes intent on her face. The Baby Huey look was gone.

"What was the victim's name?" she finally asked.

"His name was Arnold Huxley," Harper said.

"Arnold Huxley." A picture of the corpse flashed through her mind, gray as concrete. She remembered seeing dark circles around his eyes. She forced the thoughts to the back of her mind. A name made him become a real person. She swallowed.

"What was a California private detective doing in my room?" She pushed her coffee cup away, folded her hands in her lap.

"I was hoping you would tell me." Harper's expression reverted to bland and harmless, but Grace wasn't fooled.

"What company did he work for?"

"He seems to have been a loner. Worked for the highest bidder, and didn't seem to mind changing to a new boss whenever the price was better."

"He was disreputable?" Grace asked.

Harper took his time answering.

"I suspect he wasn't above blackmailing his customers, but no charges were ever filed." He pinned Grace with his eyes. "Is there any chance he was blackmailing you, Mrs. Cassidy?"

"Certainly not!"

Harper sat without speaking. Grace tolerated the silence for as long as she could bear.

"What exactly killed Arnold Huxley?"

"His neck was broken. That's what caused the raccoon eyes." Harper paused a minute. "Was your husband ever in the armed services?"

"I'm sure you already know that Charlie spent a few years in the Oklahoma National Guard." Grace met the sergeant's gaze.

"When you hear from him, I want to know about it immediately."

"I can pretty much guarantee you that my husband isn't going to be calling me."

"Then he's a damned fool," Harper said, and Grace caught her breath.

Theodora swept into the kitchen with a burst of color and a rush of movement. She had changed clothes and wore a long flowing dress made of some kind of homespun fabric, swirled with rainbow colors. Joseph's coat, Grace thought wanting to throw herself into the woman's outstretched psychedelic arms.

"Grace, darling, how is everything going? I've finished my afternoon stroll and have come to assist you."

Harper stood and glared down at Theodora. He towered over her by more than a foot.

"This is a private conversation, ma'am." His tone would have stopped George Patton.

"Sergeant Harper, how delightful to see you." Theodora stepped to the table, again spreading her arms, this time as if staking her territory. Each hand rested on a separate chair.

"Pansy and I were just discussing you, and how proud your mother must be of producing such a masterful son."

Grace watched Harper's reaction and grinned. He had expected anger and resentment. Charm, he didn't quite know how to handle.

"Please, ma'am. I'd appreciate it if you'd just go back upstairs to your room, or outside, or anywhere else but this kitchen for a few minutes."

"Are you conducting an official police interrogation?" Theodora asked with exaggerated politeness.

"No." Harper bit off the word.

"I thought not." Theodora's pink tongue swept across her red lips, like a Persian cat, Grace thought, a very self-confident and flamboyant Persian cat.

Harper tried to stare Theodora down and failed. He turned instead to Grace.

"As I mentioned before, our technicians are through with the room upstairs. I'll take down the tape."

"Then, it's okay for me to rent it out?" Grace asked.

Harper raised an eyebrow. "It'll take quite a bit of cleaning. Fingerprint powder makes one hell of a mess. But yeah, it's okay to rent." He paused a minute. "Are you going to tell your walk-ins that someone was murdered there?"

"Why not? That shouldn't daunt the type of guest we seem to attract." Grace smiled at Theodora who almost purred.

"Humph." Harper shifted his massive shoulders. "Thanks for the coffee," he said before striding out of the kitchen.

"Well, well," Theodora said in a knowing undertone. "You seem to have made a conquest."

"Don't be absurd," Grace said. "The man hates me."

Theodora's whoop of laughter somehow made Grace feel not only young but also beautiful.

Grace remembered Maxie the exact same moment the doorbell rang. She hadn't seen the young woman since morning, and worried that in the excitement of departure, Mrs. Wimberly might have forgotten to tell Maxie that she would be in charge.

She pulled open the door, and her heart twisted at the sight of a young couple. Had she ever looked that young and that happy? The honeymooners, who according to Mrs. Wimberly's notes were due to arrive from Fresno, stood on the front porch. The woman was about twenty-five. Curly red hair cascaded down her shoulders and she looked lovely even in jeans and T-shirt. The man was perhaps five years older, slender and scholarly looking with gold-rimmed glasses. He wore walking shorts and a green sweatshirt.

"Welcome to Wimberly Place," Grace said.

The usual platitudes were exchanged while she ushered them in, registered them as Mike and Ashley Blake, and showed them to the Robert Browning Suite next to the upstairs sitting room. The couple couldn't keep their hands off each other. Ashley smiled up at Mike, her eyes making promises soon to be kept. Mike cupped her hip, pulling her against him. Grace grinned. Entertaining these two would not be a problem. She could search for Maxie without worry of interruptions from them.

The hall clock chimed three when Grace walked back past the guest's sitting room. Martha Blenkensop sat straight-backed in the ivory colored Queen Anne chair working on counted cross-stitch. An over-sized magnifying glass was hooked around her neck.

"Good afternoon, Mrs. Blenkensop." Grace smiled. "Have you seen Maxie?"

"Maxie?" Martha slewed her eyes upward, her gaze cold and bored.

"She's the maid," Grace said.

"I'm hardly on a first-name basis with the maid," Martha Blenkensop said coldly, "But I haven't seen her."

"If you see her, please tell her I need to talk to her." *Witch*, Grace added silently and then smiled. Witch was a good word for the woman—only one letter wrong.

"I hope afternoon tea won't be late," Martha said.

"Of course not."

Grace ran down the main stairs and through the house to the back office where she almost collided with Wimberly.

"Whoops." She backed away.

"Grace." He beamed his delight.

"I'm looking for Maxie." She forced a bright smile. "I suppose you know I'm your new inn sitter."

"And much more decorative than Mrs. Smith." Wimberly moved toward her, his breath as foul as ever. "I want you to know that I'm always available to supervise whenever you need me."

"How kind of you," Grace used the phrase Theodora had suggested. Darted out of the darkened office and toward the front hall where Erwin Quick was being helped down the stairs by his ladylove.

"I hear you're our new concierge." Sydney flashed her toothy smile. "I wonder if we could have more towels? Dear Erwin so loves his hot showers."

"Certainly, I don't suppose you've seen Maxie, our maid?"

Sydney seemed startled by the question, and the affable Mr. Quick looked sad.

"I'm afraid not. I'm afraid that Maxie avoids me," Mr. Quick said, his breath coming in short gasps. "And now we're going to take a short constitutional before tea."

Grace wondered how much more exercise the already winded man could endure then saw that Sydney was getting the best workout by supporting him.

Grace frowned. Why would the maid avoid this seemingly harmless couple, she wondered?

"Enjoy your walk," she said, and then rushed upstairs to locate the linen closet and replenish Mr. Quick's towels. The old man's bathroom was a rumpled, steam-filled mess. Grace grabbed a damp towel and wiped down the sink, tile walls and tub. She gathered the sodden bundle, placed fresh towels on the bars and put extras on the shelves. That should keep Erwin happy. It was a relief to see the bed was made. Perhaps he slept in Sydney's room?

If Sydney and Erwin knew she was in charge, Maxie probably did too. Would that have rattled the young woman and caused her to leave her job early? Might she quit?

Grace spiffed up Sydney's room then quick-stepped through the house, peeking in shared bathrooms, alcoves and the back stairs. She avoided her old room until last, then walked to the door and stopped, key in hand. True to Harper's promise the tape was gone. She took a deep breath. Life seemed a series of hard things and Grace didn't figure it was going to get any easier. She unlocked the door and stepped inside.

The bed was stripped but an image of the dead man was vivid in Grace's memory. She steadied herself with a hand against the doorframe and concentrated on what she could control. Fingerprint powder blackened every surface. Harper was right, this room would be a challenge to clean. She would need to help Maxie.

Grace caught her reflection in the mirror. Every speck of makeup was gone. Maybe she should run upstairs and touch up her lipstick then check in the attic for Maxie? She shrugged. No one cares how I look, so why should I? She headed downstairs toward the kitchen.

Maxie must have decided to leave early, Grace thought. After tea she would find the young woman's home number and call her.

She met Pansy on the stairs.

"The aura of death is back," Pansy said.

Chapter 9

The aura of death? Pansy's words chilled Grace to the marrow of her bones. There was a deep-seated honesty in the woman that caused Grace to take the absurd phrase seriously. Pansy stood erect, like a fragile solider dressed in a white oxford cloth button-down shirt, olive-green canvas shorts and weathered athletic shoes. Two hundred years ago she might have been burned at the stake.

All of a sudden Grace needed to talk. She glanced at her watch and it was a little after four. Even a short visit might make that dratted tea time late, so she'd better not.

A door opened at the top of the stairs and Grace turned to see Theodora swing her ample rump out of the Elizabeth Barrett Browning suite.

"Grace dear, I know you'll think I'm daft, but I have this uneasy feeling that something is wrong." Theodora straightened the flowing lines of her bright multi-colored dress.

She looks exactly like some sort of exotic tropical fruit, Grace thought, smiling at her friend.

"Wonderful! Pansy just told me that the aura of death is back. The two of you are spooking me, but I'm hoping that you're both just having a panic attack." Grace glanced at Pansy who looked calm as a Hindu priest. "But maybe not. Do you think that Drew would mind if I ran down to the basement and talked to him for a minute?" She glanced at her watch. She would be pushing the time, but still wanted to talk to the older man. Somehow just being around him seemed to ground her.

"You want the opinion of someone without a uterus perhaps?" Theodora asked in a crisp tone.

"That sounds awful put like that." Grace bit her lip to keep from smiling. "But, yeah—I think that's what I mean."

"Honesty wins me over every time, we'll all go." Theodora headed toward the stairs.

"I'll catch up later," Pansy glanced at her watch. "It's my time to meditate."

"If you don't make it downstairs we'll see you at tea," Theodora called back in a strong voice before lowering her volume. "Grace, I appreciate it that you're not treating me as if I were some sort of busybody and trying to get rid of me. It would be such a waste of time, and I feel that time is valuable right now." Theodora picked up her pace.

"Theodora, I look on you as a gift from God and have no desire to be rid of you."

"You see me as one of those angels that are so popular on television, perhaps?" Theodora's laugh swelled, rich and full.

"It wasn't my first thought," Grace said with a smile. "But who knows?"

The rich sound of Theodora's laugh echoed in the narrow staircase.

They reached the street floor, walked outside then downstairs. Theodora knocked. Grace grinned. Even the woman's knock seemed self assured. The door swung open and Drew stood before them with his notes pinned once again to his shirt. Grace wondered if he had made any changes.

"Come in, come in." He waved toward his living room. "Walter's here too, he just got back from playing softball. But don't worry, if he doesn't behave himself I'll run him off."

"Like I'm not house-broken?" A sandpapery voice bellowed from Drew's apartment. "You'd just throw me out like some damned dog that peed on the rug?"

"No, please," Grace protested. "I've been eager to meet Walter." The old man wore a blue ball cap, white T-shirt and much-washed jeans with frayed knees. A softball bat and mitt lay beside him on the sofa.

"Walter Slovak!" Theodora strode past Grace and into the apartment, her face exuding charm. "How lovely to see you, those peppermint leaves you picked for my tea quite cured my indigestion."

A rush of affection warmed Grace. Theodora had an admirer. How wonderful that in the midst of murder and suspicion a flirtation between two older people might add a little sunshine to life.

"And you shall have more, dear lady." The stubble-faced Walter stood and walked to Theodora offering his arm with a gallant bow. "Let me escort you into my enchanted garden and pick the freshest and the best, just for you."

Theodora smiled like a cat with her bird sighted and charmed. She took Walter's arm and moved out of the apartment murmuring something. Grace noticed her speech didn't contain one single word about Walter's mother or how proud that worthy woman might have been of him. And Theodora's laugh was decidedly throaty.

"Let me move Walter's softball gear out of your way so you can sit down, Grace." Drew picked up the ball and bat and tossed them into a corner. "Walter's been a buddy of mine since we served time together in the Navy eons ago. I think the world of him, but it's still good that Theodora lured him away so that we can talk." Drew paused to study Grace. "I can tell by looking at your face that things are worse. What happened?"

"Very little on the surface," Grace said. "But both Pansy and Theodora sense something evil underfoot. And somehow I think they're right. I..." Grace bit her lip. The spirit of the man sitting beside her was so like her father that her voice broke.

"Come here, Honey." Drew put his arms around her, pulled her toward his chest.

"I'll get your notes all wet," Grace said. Then she put her head against his chest and bawled like a six-year-old. Whoever said you couldn't go home again had never met Andrew Maynard. Grace felt safe for the first time in days and she poured out her heart, even the things she had recounted earlier: the murder that surrounded her yet seemed to have nothing to do with her, Charlie's betrayal, the victim's name and manner of death, and most of all her homesickness for her son, Brand.

"Young men grow up fastest when they are given responsibility," Drew said. "It seems to me that Brand should be here, helping his mother to solve her problems."

Grace lifted her head and studied the weathered creases mapped across Drew's face and the strength in his gray eyes. It didn't matter that he was well into his seventies, she knew that beside her sat a real man.

"I never thought of asking Brand to help me," she said.

"Then I would advise you to give it some serious consideration. I've worked with hundreds of young fellows in the Navy, made good men out of quite a few of them, too."

Someone pounded on the door.

"You in there, Maynard?" the whisky voice of Walter Slovak rasped out. "We've gathered our herbs and it's made me damned thirsty."

"Why Walter, are you saying that you prefer Jack Daniel's company to mine." Theodora's voice also carried clearly through the thin panel.

Grace could hear Walter protest that no one enjoyed the company of a good looking woman more than he, then a surprised squeak from Theodora when Walter evidently emphasized his statement with some sort of affectionate gesture. Then the banging started again.

"Let them in." Grace laughed. "I've got to go anyway, I'm almost late. I still have to earn my board and keep."

"Just as well, it's hopeless to argue with Walter when he's thirsty." Drew walked to the door and pulled it open. "What's wrong with you, Walter? Don't you have any manners?"

Theodora bustled in rubbing her right buttock, her face pink. "Absolutely none," she said with a pleased smile.

Walter followed, carrying a much-used basket filled with green leaves. His gaze was on Theodora and his smile took years from his grizzled face.

"Just testing to see if it was ripe," he said.

Grace laughed then extended her hand toward Walter. "I don't think anyone gave you my name, I'm Grace Cassidy."

"You're the little gal with the naked dead guy in her bed." Walter shook her hand with an enthusiastic pumping motion. "Pleased to meet you, you gave us something to talk about downstairs besides when our social security checks will arrive."

"Walter!" Drew said.

"It's all right," Grace grinned at Walter. "So you're retired, too."

"Semi-retired," Walter corrected. "I still work some."

"That's right Theodora told me you keep this magnificent garden."

"Yeah, I know all about plants," Walter said. "You need something to make you sleep better? I'm the man to see." He winked. "I've got all sorts of herbs and a few unmentionable plants that could make someone sleep permanently."

"Walter!" Theodora scolded. "Don't be naughty." She cast a glance in Grace's direction.

"Don't worry, Walter, I like honesty." Grace laughed, "But I must get back upstairs, Mrs. Blenkensop will have my head for not serving afternoon tea right on time."

Grace left Theodora to make last minute good-byes to Walter, and walked back to the kitchen. Too late she remembered the seascape and wished that she had taken a minute to study the picture. She shrugged. She would go back later, look at the picture and maybe quiz Walter about anything he might have seen on that ill-fated afternoon. A gardener is always outside and might notice something others would miss.

She and Brand would survive all of this. And maybe Drew was right. It would be wonderful to have her son with her. But how could she manage a ticket, even from Tulsa? She hadn't brought any of her jewelry along to hock. But having Brand here and asking him for moral support was a new thought. She liked it.

The homey kitchen reminded Grace that she was supposed to be running the inn. She hoped Maxie had cleaned all of the bedrooms and done her other duties. She would help the maid scrub the room where the murder had taken place tomorrow morning, going through it carefully, looking for clues. There might be something the police had missed.

First things first, tea would probably take about an hour. She would serve those wretched cookies and make small talk with the guests, learn something maybe. Grace glanced at her watch. She needed to hurry.

Grace rummaged for tea things. She chose a hand-painted platter from the antique breakfront for the cookies, and a cut-glass bowl for some strawberries she had spotted earlier in the refrigerator. She removed a damp dish towel from sandwiches she'd made earlier and put everything on an ornate silver tray, along with a small pitcher of cream and a bowl of sugar before juggling the heavy load through the dining room. She stopped in the vestibule, shifted the cumbersome weight to a more comfortable position and walked slowly up the stairs to the guests' sitting room. By that time her arms were aching from the heavy burden. Maybe all of this physical labor would firm up her muscle tone. There should be a few small perks with all of the misery.

The area was designed for comfort, eclectic with artistic, homey, clutter. Grace set the tray on the coffee table. According to her watch it was 5:10 and Mrs. Blenkensop was nowhere in sight. She sighed and took a minute to glance around. Mrs. Wimberly had put a great deal of thought into decorating the room.

A crimson velvet Victorian sofa sat against one wall, framed under a collage of pictures. Tastefully mismatched chairs sat on either side of windows facing the street, and the Queen Anne chair created a balance in the far corner. A half-finished jigsaw puzzle of what seemed to be a medieval castle lay on a game table situated in a small alcove by the window, its jumble of pieces strewn around the half-finished mosaic. Books, comfortably faded with age, lined the shelves, or if a guest preferred there was an assortment of newer magazines spilling from a large wicker basket beside the sofa. It was a room where you could sit back, relax, and think or plan a murder, perhaps, Grace thought.

She went to the sink and saw dirty cups. Grace frowned. One of Maxie's duties was to wash up. Had the young woman missed cleaning the guests' rooms also? Wimberly would have a fit.

She filled the sink with soapy water and quickly washed and dried the fragile patterned teacups. She spooned loose tea into a china pot, inhaled the fragrance, and paused, holding the lid mid-air.

She needed a plan to help sort out her fragmented thoughts. Mama had always said to write down what's worrying you and then you don't have to think about it. The list is always there. You won't forget anything, so you can afford to take a worry-vacation.

Grace walked to the coffee table, picked up a scratch pad and a black pen and sat down. She paused a minute then began writing.

1. Locate Brand and tell him where she was.

2. Study Drew's seascape. It looked valuable. Could the painting be the reason the murdered man was in the inn?

3. Ask Walter if he remembered seeing anyone out of the way yesterday.

4. Learn as much as possible about the guests staying in Wimberly Place when Arnold Huxley was murdered.

5. Find out exactly what span of time Maxie was here on the day of the murder and whether she heard or saw anything.

6. Were there any others who might have been here on that day? Delivery people? The postman? Repairmen?

7. Ask questions of everyone.

Grace underlined the last resolution. She paused a minute and chewed her pen. The guests were all given a key to the front door so strangers couldn't just walk in from the street, anyone else had to ring the bell. Of course someone might come in through one of the back entrances but that would require inside help.

Then she remembered something that had been bothering her and wrote down:

8. Ask Maxie why she left supplies on the back stairs.

Grace was deep in thought when Theodora's rich contralto voice startled her.

"Grace, I rushed back upstairs to help you with tea."

Grace jumped. "You scared me half to death!" She forced a smile and hid her list under a magazine, like a kid caught with her hand in the cookie jar. I'm suspecting people who have tried to be helpful to me, she thought. But her mind picked up the other side of the debate.

Too helpful perhaps?

She hadn't heard so much as the rustle of movement as Theodora came up the stairs. Was that deliberate? How could someone as full-figured as Theodora move so softly without making an intentional effort? Like a sleek, self-confident cat, she appeared underfoot at unexpected moments. Always observing.

Theodora smiled and licked her lips, then brushed something invisible from her cheek. Canary feathers, perhaps? Grace wondered.

Chapter 10

"I didn't mean to startle you," Theodora said in a tone spun from silk. She glanced at the tray and her face registered approval. "Ah, the cookies that our Sergeant Harper so admired look lovely on that platter. It's evident that you're a woman who entertains with flair." She moved closer and her eyes sparkled. "Yummy, the strawberries look so luscious they seem decadent."

Silver-tipped fingernails swept over the tea tray and a fluttering of teal and rose chiffon floated through the air. Theodora had found time to again change. The woman was a clothes horse.

Grace smoothed her ivory T-shirt. Why were so many of her clothes in neutral colors? Theodora made her feel as if she were a wren entertaining a South American cockatiel.

"I knew you'd appreciate the strawberries," Grace said. "I brought them especially for you since I've heard you mention that you don't care for pastries." She grinned knowingly. "I'm surprised you could pull yourself away from the charming Walter."

"My dear! Leaving Walter is always a sacrifice but very necessary. I adore romance, but I consider marriage a disease, and was long ago immunized by one serious and painful bout. However, if I hang around Walter too long, I sometimes find myself forgetting my vow to stay single."

"Maybe you should let go and just enjoy the romance-ride." Grace slipped her list out from under the Town and Country magazine and folded it into a small square, her gaze on Theodora. "If you find yourself reaching for the gold ring, call me and I'll tell you war stories that would scare even a veteran like yourself." She slipped the paper into her pocket.

Theodora smiled but said nothing. She reached down for a berry and bit into it, uttering a sensual groan.

"Delicious. Absolutely wonderful. Let me get my cup of tea and we can visit."

"I have a pot ready to brew," Grace said. "I was just waiting for everyone to gather." She rose to her feet and stepped toward the sink.

"Lovely," Theodora said. She sank into the sofa and settled herself like a cat preparing a napping nest, then reached
for another strawberry. "Pansy should be here in a minute."

"Tell me everything you know about the other guests
while I work." Grace held the teapot up to the tap of instant
boiling water. "Knowing about them will help me be able to
make small talk."

"And perhaps decide if one of them committed murder?"
Theodora smiled and then crossed her ankles. "Were you
able to get much information out of Sergeant Harper when
you talked to him earlier today?"

"He told me the name and occupation of the dead man,
but not much else."

"Oh? Who was the poor man?" Theodora's hand halted
halfway toward the strawberries. "Did you recognize his
name?" The transparent sleeves rippled slightly.

"No, I had never heard of him." Grace glanced at
Theodora. "His name was Arnold Huxley and it seems he was
a private detective who sometimes blackmailed his clients."

A muscle tightened in Theodora's jaw. "How appalling,"
she said after a minute's pause. "Whatever could he have
been doing at Wimberly Place?"

"I have no idea. Everyone has secrets, though, so tell me
the gossip about this bunch."

"Gladly, but don't you also want my thoughts about
them?" Theodora cocked her head to one side, thinking. "One
can't help but surmise."

"Great. Surmise away," Grace said.

"Martha Blenkensop, who you'll notice is late, goes on
and on about how clever George is," Theodora said. "It makes
one wonder if she isn't trying to convince herself he isn't also
crushingly boring. But he is famous for creating some
exceptional sort of software and has developed a method for
teaching it. That's why he and Martha stay here so often, he
comes to Port Ortega to teach special classes."

"I thought cutting-edge software was written by younger
guys," Grace said.

Theodora paused a minute, glanced around then lowered
her voice to a whisper. "There was a rumor a few years ago
about Blenkensop giving a huge scholarship to a neighbor-

hood high school kid. That seemed a very uncharacteristic action, and gave me considerable pause."

"Pay-off money?" Grace asked.

"That's one scenario that would explain why Martha never brags about George's philanthropy."

"Has that software made them wealthy?" Grace asked.

"I suspect so. I often wonder if George could have stolen the software that makes him so famous in certain circles. And that thought brings blackmail to mind." Theodora picked up the magazine from the coffee table and fanned herself. Grace thanked God that she had moved her list.

"It could be a reason for either of them to hire a killer." A sudden picture of the matronly Martha sneaking down a backstreet, seeking out a killer-for-hire, flashed through Grace's mind. She grinned. It was easier to imagine the respectable-looking woman breaking someone's neck.

"George seems too weak to be a killer, but Martha strikes me as the type who would do anything to protect her respectability and status as the wife of a successful man. Tell me about the other guests."

"Now let me see." Theodora paused a minute, thinking. "You saw all of them the night of the murder, so you no doubt have already formed some kind of impression of each person."

"Of course, and I've studied the guest register. Everyone seems to be a regular customer."

"That's true. All of us use Wimberly Place as our regular watering hole."

"Ms. Sydney Davenport and Mr. Erwin Quick are a most unusual couple."

"That would be an understatement, I think, but they're a devoted couple. Each one seems to be protective of the other. I find it charming." Her black eyes met Grace's with a surprising seriousness. "Don't be fooled by Erwin. He appears very fragile, and so he may be, from the neck down. Don't underestimate him from the neck up."

"Are you trying to tell me that harmless-looking little man might be our murderer? I'd be more likely to suspect the stalwart Sydney."

"If I were you, I'd suspect everyone who was in the building yesterday afternoon." Theodora glanced behind her. "And here are Ms Davenport and Mr. Quick now."

Grace turned, disappointed she hadn't had time to ask if Theodora knew why Maxie was afraid of Erwin. But she was now in charge of a tea party so she smiled and extended her hand to Sydney.

"How nice to see the both of you. Do sit down."

"Grace, dear. What a lovely tea you've prepared. So sorry we're late. That's something that never happens, but we were watching the gulls." Sydney said. "Careful, Erwin, you always forget this little rug." Ms Davenport spoke in her deep bass before shooting a toothy smile. She clasped Grace's hand with her usual death-grip. "Here, Erwin, sit on the sofa beside Theodora."

"Isn't she a wonderful woman?" Mr. Quick's voice swelled with praise. "Just wonderful." He patted Sydney on the hand. Grace couldn't help noticing how small his hand looked in comparison to his companion's.

"Is there anything left to eat?" Gustav Mendelsohn ran up the stairs, not even breathing hard. He was wearing a lightweight wool navy blazer with gray slacks. His cotton maroon turtleneck added the perfect touch of color.

"We've just started." Grace smiled. "I don't know if anyone has told you, but I'm your new inn sitter."

"Wonderful news, please call me Gustav and I'll call you Grace." His hand was soft and his gaze admiring. Grace enjoyed his obvious admiration. It cheered her to think that in spite of Charlie's indifference, some men still found her attractive.

"Pansy should be right down, Gustav," Theodora said, her face purposely straight, her eyes naughty.

Grace saw an expression flick across his face. Was it amusement? Annoyance? Surprise? It was masked so quickly she wasn't sure.

"Is my tea ready?"

Grace turned toward the strident voice that could only belong to Martha Blenkensop.

"You're late today, Mrs. Blenkensop," Theodora said. "But we haven't started without you."

"Come in and sit down, Mrs. Blankensop, I've just made tea," Grace said.

"Make mine peppermint tea, I must have peppermint, it's the only thing that doesn't upset my stomach." Mrs. Blankensop sat in one of the side chairs indifferent to the fact that she was adding to Grace's work by requesting a special tea. "And my nerves have been destroyed by that awful murder."

"Oh, my poor dear," Theodora said sweetly. "How dreadful for you. Have you given any more thought to moving to another establishment? I'd keep trying to persuade George if I were you."

Martha snorted. "I've begged that husband of mine to leave but he refuses. He keeps insisting that the murder has nothing to do with us, and he hasn't the time to move." She preened slightly. "My husband works for Vantech Imports, you know."

"Yes, we know," Theodora said in a dry tone, accepting a cup of tea from Grace.

Running steps pounded up the staircase, and a winded Pansy rushed into the room.

"So sorry I'm late," Pansy said, her face flushed and her usually immaculate slacks slightly wrinkled. "I was out for my walk, and picked up the afternoon newspaper. The headlines are just horrible."

"Yes, I heard the news just now on the radio," Gustav said. "It seems that there is a Mexican sweatshop operating right here in Port Ortega. Mexicans are being slipped across the border and driven up the coast to work here for almost nothing in some sort of textile factory. The working conditions are said to be deplorable."

There was a crash and Grace turned to see Theodora mopping tea stains from her dress.

"I'm so sorry," she said. "So very, very sorry."

Chapter 11

Grace scanned Maxie's personnel file for a phone number and found the word "none." Maxie's prior employer had been Halcyon Nursing Home where she worked for three years as a nurse tech, and then been laid off. That was nine months ago. At that time, and upon Erwin Quick's recommendation, Mrs. Wimberly had hired her as a maid.

Humm. Why then would Maxie avoid Mr. Quick, Grace wondered? It didn't make any sense. She frowned and kept reading.

There was a number for a social worker, but Grace feared that bothering the official might make trouble for Maxie. She replaced the folder and walked to the kitchen.

First thing in the morning she would have a long talk with the young woman, both about work duties and about the sequence of yesterday's events. Also she would ask Maxie why Erwin Quick made her nervous. She would choose her words carefully in order not to alarm the young woman.

"Oh, there you are," Theodora rushed into the kitchen. She had changed into a free-flowing red tunic printed with yellow Aztec designs and matching red slacks. "I left my clothes soaking in the bathtub. Tea stains are so hard to remove. Now, how can I assist you in your duties? After all, I did promise to help you in this little adventure of inn sitting."

"That's very nice of you, considering you're paying to be pampered." Grace opened the refrigerator door and took out two cartons of eggs, Monterey Jack cheese, milk, and butter, setting each item on the table. "What will Mr. Wimberly say if he catches you in here?"

"Who cares?" Theodora shrugged her flamboyant shoulders, ran fingers through her short, curly hair. "Anyway, as you said, I'm a guest. I should be allowed to do anything I please."

"So you should." Grace snagged jalapeno peppers and tomatoes from the produce drawer and then used her hip to slam shut the refrigerator door. "Would you mind rummaging through the cabinets and finding a large casserole dish? I'm making eggs ala Grace for breakfast in the morning."

"I love any excuse to snoop." Theodora laughed, pulling open doors and shifting through various kitchenware. "Ah. Here's just what we need." She took out an oversized Pyrex baking dish.

"Perfect." Grace began cracking eggs into a large bowl, then glanced at Theodora. "I'm going to mix up a breakfast casserole and let it marinate over night in the refrigerator. I'll pop it into the oven first thing in the morning."

"Sounds yummy," Theodora moved to the sink and began rinsing dirty cups. "Did you ever find Maxie?"

"No, and I'm concerned because she never checked in with me today. Do you think she could be upset because I'm taking over as inn-keeper?"

"I doubt it. Maxie's a good soul and quite reliable. She'll be here to help in the morning."

"I certainly hope so." Grace shrugged and changed the subject. "Is there something wrong with Pansy?" She pulled a whisk from a cluster of utensils. "She seemed almost distraught over your little mishap during tea. For some reason she seemed to blame herself. It was a good thing Mendelsohn was there to comfort her."

"Oh, Mendelsohn loves comforting Pansy although he'd like to do a great deal more." Theodora laughed. "I do hope that Pansy can resist his charms. Pansy is my oldest and dearest friend, but I'm afraid she lets herself get involved. With men, I mean. Then she suffers a guilt attack."

"Guilt? I don't understand. She didn't act a bit guilty to me when we caught her half undressed with Drew."

"Certainly not. That was with Drew. They're in love, of course. Pansy would never feel guilty about Drew."

"You mean there are others? But, Pansy is so..." Grace caught herself just in time, but Theodora laughed anyway.

"Old?" Theodora suggested.

Grace's cheeks grew hot. To hide her confusion she grabbed the cheese grater from a drawer and began furiously grating cheese into the bowl of eggs.

"She's quite lovely." Grace stumbled, tried to recoup herself. "But one just never expects..." She shot another look at Theodora whose impervious stare further unnerved her. "Oh, well. I can't make this any worse, so I may as well admit you're right. Old, the word I avoided was *old*."

"The truth is always best, dear," Theodora said primly.

"It just never occurred to me that men would line up to sleep with a woman of what? Sixty? Not even when she's as great looking as Pansy."

"My dear, there's no age limit on that mystical and magical quality called sex appeal."

"I suppose not," Grace admitted, deciding that "it" was a commodity she had entirely missed when gifts were being handed out.

"I hope you're not one of those people who think that no one past sixty could enjoy a sex life?"

"Of course not," Grace set the cheese down and began pulling jars of herbs off of an open shelf. "When I'm that age, I intend to still enjoy sex myself."

Theodora stood holding the Pyrex, eyebrow lifted and a small teasing smile curved her lips. "Are you currently enjoying sex? At the very attractive age of what? Thirty-eight perhaps?"

"No. What I'm doing is making a terrible fool of myself." She held the whisk mid air and grinned back at Theodora. "And maybe it just makes me jealous that someone old enough to be a grandmother attracts more men that I do."

"Then please take a moment to think how I feel." Theodora whooped laughter.

"I can imagine. If she weren't such a sweetheart, you'd probably hate her." Grace began chopping jalapeno peppers. "What I don't understand is how men recognize these women? Pansy always looks so prim and proper, like one of our Pilgrim foremothers. Why, compared to her, you and I look like a couple of hookers."

"It's my aura." Pansy's voice sounded loud and clear from the doorway, "Your aura tells people around you more about you than your mode of dress."

"Pansy I'm so sorry." Grace felt her blush reach to the roots of her hair. "It was unpardonable for me to be gossiping about you. Can you ever forgive me?"

"For what?" Pansy walked to the table, picked up a knife, sliced off a piece of cheese and plopped it into her mouth.

"For being shamefully rude, you've been so sweet to me, and I've repaid you by gossiping."

"Nonsense," Theodora said. "There can be no gossip or scandal when there's no concealment. Pansy is always perfectly open about everything she does."

Pansy began choking on the bite of cheese she had just swallowed.

Grace dragged herself up the third flight of stairs. It had been a long day. Her body ached with fatigue starting with a pounding in her temples and spreading downward to the soles of her feet. All she wanted was to run a nice tub of hot water, pour in a generous amount of scented oil and soak until her body melted.

A disgusting stench reached her at the top of the landing and she saw that her door was ajar. Grace's heart pounded, echoing in her ears. She drew in a quick breath then walked to the heavy oak panel and pushed it open with a cautious finger.

"Oh, my God," Grace said.

A woman's body, dressed in Grace's favorite yellow dress, was sprawled face upward on the bed. Her neck was twisted to one side. Her work worn hands splayed out helplessly on the pink hand-sewn quilt. Her body waste fouled the bed.

"Maxie!" Grace shouted. "Oh dear God, it's Maxie." Grace backed out of the room and fled down the stairs. She heard herself screaming, but knew that even that shrill sound wasn't loud enough to distress Maxie.

Chapter 12

Grace fought hysterics until sirens sounded. She showed the first uniformed policemen Maxie's body, and then tried to answer their endless questions. Shock turned her world into a surrealistic sleep-walk, but she kept trying.

Hang on, she said to herself as if she were a small child on a spinning carnival ride. Hang on, hang on, hang on, else the universe will completely gyrate out of control. But the cops were hostile-eyed and she felt scared and alone.

Finally Theodora and Pansy pushed their way up the stairs and threw around Sergeant Harper's name until they managed to spirit Grace back down to the guests' sitting room.

A ragtag group of residents had gathered, and Wimberly, white faced and angst ridden, glared at Theodora and Pansy who ignored him.

"Now, now," Theodora soothed, plying Grace with a cup of Earl Grey as Pansy hovered nearby. "It won't help Maxie for you to make yourself sick. Knowing the victim renders it harder for all of us. After all, you didn't know the other person very well. Mr.... what was his name, now... the naked one?"

"I didn't know him at all, and tea isn't going to help. This was the place where I'm supposed to wake up, only the nightmare won't end." Tears stung Grace's eyes and she blinked hard to keep them from flowing down her cheeks.

"Perhaps not," Theodora said, cooing as if to a child. "But neither will it hurt."

Theodora handed the cup and saucer to Grace who obediently took it. What the heck, Grace thought, it was something to do. She took a sip and scalded her tongue.

"There, now," Theodora said. "Doesn't that make you feel better?" She gave her teacher-encouraging-a-promising-student smile.

"Nothing's going to make me feel better. Maxie's dead. Dear God! She died in my room. Two people in two days, am I some kind of a violence-carrier?"

Pansy sat down beside Grace and patted her hand. "How could the deaths be your fault? You haven't killed anyone. If you had I would sense it in your aura. It would be black, not the clear purple of sorrow."

Grace blinked then let this bit of Pansyism drift through her mind. Oddly enough she found it to be comforting. She took another sip of the hot liquid. Somehow it did seem to help and Grace found herself able to speak in a reasonable manner.

"Why would anyone want to kill Maxie? She was the most harmless person I ever met." Grace's voice wavered.

"Humm." Theodora cocked her head to one side, flounced her red tunic then settled herself down onto the sofa with Grace and Pansy. "Now that's what I call an interesting question. Are we sure it was Maxie they meant to kill?"

"What?" Grace straightened, sloshing tea into the saucer. Fear clutched her stomach. "What do you mean?"

"She was wearing your dress, Grace." Theodora gave Grace a hug. "It's dreadful of me to worry you further, dear. But I really do think you should start being very careful."

"Careful? You mean like quit hanging around with people who get themselves killed?"

"Now, now, there's no need for despair." Theodora paused a minute, thinking. "Pansy, why don't you run downstairs and fetch some wine from Drew to help calm Grace." Theodora leaned forward and dropped her voice to a whisper to keep the words from traveling to Wimberly who was pacing nearby. "Better still, bring Drew along. I don't care if it is against the rules of the house, Drew's like a mighty oak in a strong wind and he's taken quite a liking to our Grace."

"Leave it to me," Pansy whispered back, making a circle with her thumb and index finger. She jumped up and ran toward the stairs. She stopped and tossed a bit more information Grace's way. "Now don't worry about a thing, Grace. Everything is going to be all right. I checked your astrological sign first thing this morning and there are better days ahead." She dashed on down the steps.

"What are you women whispering about?" Wimberly demanded, pausing for a minute from pacing up and down the short space of the guest's sitting room. "And where the hell is that detective? The patrolmen who first showed up haven't done a thing." He ran his fingers through his thinning gray hair then shot a spiteful look at Grace. "This is going to ruin Wimberly Place. We never had a murder here until you came. Now we have two in a row. Two! Just think of it! And think of the shame of having my inn sitter arrested for murder."

"Really, Mr. Wimberly," Theodora said. "Grace isn't going to be arrested. It's not against the law to find a corpse."

"Two corpses!" Wimberly corrected, "And both times in her room."

The doorbell rang and Grace flinched.

"Oh, God," she muttered. "That will be Harper." She didn't move. She knew it was her job to open the door, but somehow she couldn't find the strength.

"I suppose I'll have to attend to this." Wimberly headed toward the stairs, his gait heavy. He glanced back at Grace as if he expected her to spring up and answer the door for him.

Grace sat without moving and listened first to the stairs creak from Wimberly's weight, then more distantly to the sounds of the door being unbolted and opened.

"Well it's about time, Sergeant. That woman from Oklahoma's found another body," Wimberly said, his loud voice rising up from the front door. Then his tone changed to angry indignation. "Hey Maynard, get out of here! People from the basement aren't allowed upstairs."

"Step aside Wimberly." Drew's deep voice boomed with authority.

"I'll need to talk to everyone," Harper said.

Grace noticed Harper's voice didn't sound bored anymore. Footsteps pounded upward. Pansy's fluted voice filled in details of the murder for Drew's benefit.

"Some monster has killed our Maxie. And in Grace's room. Such darkness! Ah, and here Grace is, the poor darling."

A duet of sympathy from Theodora and Pansy poured over Grace. Drew opened his arms at the top of the stairs, and Grace stood and walked into them. Her face brushed against the pieces of paper pinned to his shirt.

"I'll get your notes all wet again," she said.

"Go ahead and cry," he soothed, his arms warm and comforting around her. "Don't worry about my scribbling."

"Someone killed Maxie in my room." Grace felt the comfort of soft, well-washed linen and the sharpness of pins against her cheek. "Why are people being killed where I sleep?"

"The first thing you're going to do, young lady, is have some of this hooch I brought with me." He handed Theodora a bottle of sherry.

"Pour some of this into one of those damned china cups," he said to Theodora. "It has more muscle than tea."

"Use the Spode," Pansy piped up. "The Maritime Rose is quite lovely, and sure to make her feel much better."

"Yes," Wimberly said, his voice heavy with sarcasm. "Be sure to find the right pattern of china. That will make everything all right again."

Grace shivered. The only pattern she saw was death.

Chapter 13

Grace looked at the guests of Wimberly Place who were once again assembled in the small sitting room. Sergeant Harper and a uniformed policeman had gone up to survey the crime scene and left the somewhat uncomfortable group cooling their heels.

Grace felt as if she were protected by a stalwart German shepherd, a bulldog, and an attack poodle. Theodora, the bulldog on her right, sat forward and looked ready for battle, as if she expected a siege upon Grace.

Drew was on her left. His arm curved protectively around her shoulders. A no-nonsense look masked his usual affability. Tonight Grace saw a different side to the man, and she liked what she saw. This was the side that must have served him well in the Navy and later in business before his bout with cancer ended his career. His expression stated that he tolerated no nonsense from fools and not even Wimberly seemed willing to challenge him.

Pansy sat cross-legged at Grace's feet, unsmiling and serious mannered. An unusual state for Pansy, Grace thought. As if reading Grace's mind, Pansy reached up, patted Grace's leg and whispered something about a clearing atmosphere.

Even Walter had trooped bravely up the stairs into what must have seemed to him like enemy territory. He now sat straight and uncomfortable looking on the ivory satin Queen Anne chair across from a glaring Wimberly.

Walter winked at Grace then wiggled his eyebrows. She smiled back.

Grace felt loved and protected and a little bit like a child that no one trusted to behave properly. A picture flashed through her mind of herself dressed in a pinafore and Mary-Janes with puffy pink bows tied at the end of twin braids. She smiled, one Cinderella with four fairy godmothers.

"I'll have a little bit of that booze you brought." Walter lifted his cup toward Drew.

"I've told you once to keep your mouth shut," Wimberly snapped. "You're not even supposed to be up here. You're stinking up the place, too. My God, you smell like a brewery."

"I'd rather smell like a brewery than like that sissy crap you wear. Damned stuff smells like some fancy kind of disinfectant." Walter guffawed. "And you can't make me leave. That police fellow ordered me and Drew to hang around."

"Really, Wimberly," Theodora protested. "Can't you do all of us a favor and keep silent until the Sergeant returns from examining the body?"

Wimberly opened his mouth to protest but was stilled when the three sets of eyes from Grace's trio of protectors sent "shut up" messages. Pansy reached upward and patted Grace's leg once again, murmuring something soothing that again reminded Grace of her childhood. She studied Pansy and Theodora fondly. One small and demure, hiding her seething sexuality behind a calm facade of perfection. The other full-figured and flamboyant in flowing red and black. She loved their uniqueness. The opposites that complemented each other, making a perfectly unmatched set.

Grace took a deep breath and studied the rest of the cast, all of whom seemed no less extraordinary.

Erwin Quick had been hastily seated in a small bedroom chair carried into the crowded sitting room by his companion, the resolute Sydney Davenport. His thinning white hair stood in spikes and his eyes were bright as a bird's. He wore a hot-pink striped pajama top and gray sweat pants.

Ms Davenport loomed behind him, a chartreuse colossus in a rumpled silk jumpsuit that lengthened her already gargantuan stature. She stood arms akimbo, her face making no attempt to mask her excitement. Murder, Grace thought, seemed to agree with both of them. Grace smiled then remembered. A lump closed her throat. If only it hadn't been Maxie's death their excitement might almost have been amusing.

The newlyweds cuddled in a window seat behind the game table. Dressed hastily in terry cloth robes, their eyes were interlocked in a gaze that seemed almost sexual. She felt a momentary pang of envy. Her thoughts were interrupted by a jarring Mid-Western twang.

"To think I could have been murdered in my own bed!" Martha Blenkensop shrilled. "George, we're moving from this place of death first thing in the morning."

The matronly woman was seated in a gold velvet chair across from Grace and wore a knee length housecoat patterned with the dullest colored flowers Grace had ever seen. Her husband sat close by, looking oddly uncomfortable in bright green sweats. Grace felt he would have been more at ease in a three-piece suit.

Mrs. Blenkensop leaned back and patted her heart as if to calm its beating.

"I told you we should have left when that man was killed." She glared at her husband. "You will never listen to me."

"Making a fuss won't help, Martha," her husband answered in a bored tone.

Grace studied George Blenkensop and realized he was a man who would be hard to describe because he was so ordinary, so nondescript, so medium everything. He was someone who might go unnoticed with his thinning gray hair, his brown eyes, and his average looking features. He could be anyone's uncle. Her gaze shifted and she caught her breath. Harper had walked in so quietly no one had noticed, and he was studying George Blenkensop with a fixed expression.

"So, you teach software classes for Vantech Imports?" Harper said to Blenkensop.

"That's right." Blenkensop shifted uncomfortably. "I fly in from Austin to teach special classes on a regular basis."

"Why don't they use someone local? Wouldn't that be cheaper?"

"Cheaper isn't better. I developed this unique software to track the shipment of machine parts. It's the best in the world if I do say so myself." Blenkensop cleared his throat and reached up as if to straighten a non-existent tie. "People come from all over the world to take this course with me as the teacher, and the company wants it taught in Port Ortega."

"And you always stay at Wimberly Place?" Harper ran a hand through his salt and pepper hair. He blinked in what seemed to be an effort to rest his blood-shot eyes, and an unexpected sympathy surged through Grace.

"That's right. It's comfortable and convenient to the local Vantech offices where I teach my classes."

"Humm," Harper said. "I guess you copyrighted this software?" Harper pulled a notebook out of his pocket and began writing. Grace decided that this was just for show, she felt sure that nothing slipped the good sergeant's mind.

"Of course."

Grace leaned forward. A suspect other than me, she thought with a glimmer of hope.

Blenkensop cleared his throat. "Is there a point to these questions, Sergeant?" His eyes glittered with anger.

"Just routine inquiries," Harper scratched something on his pad then shifted his gaze. "And you Ms Davenport. What brings you to Port Ortega?"

"I'm a tourist." Sydney Davenport flashed her usual smile, but Grace noticed that the woman's hands trembled as she reached to pat Quick's bony shoulder. "Erwin and I have come to relax and enjoy ourselves."

"Humm," Harper said. "Port Ortega isn't a tourist town, it's a commercial sea port. Most of the tourists stop at San Francisco or Sausalito."

"Erwin and I are enchanted by the Victorian houses built by the early merchants and sea captains of the area, and Wimberly Place is one of these historic treasures." Sydney patted her long bleached hair.

"You're a registered nurse, aren't you?"

Sydney drew a sharp breath. "Yes," she said.

"And you, Mr. Quick. Are you retired?"

"Semi-retired," Mr. Quick retorted to everyone's surprise. "I still like to keep my fingers in the old corporate pie."

"And what pie might that be?" Harper asked.

"Why, the Vantech Corporation, of course. I'm a member of the board of directors."

Chapter 14

Grace watched Harper settle himself into a straight-backed chair that had been fetched from the kitchen by a uniformed policeman. He glanced around the small sitting room.

"Isn't there a guest missing?" Harper scanned the list in his hand. "Gustov Mendelsohn, isn't here."

"He hasn't come in yet," Theodora answered even though Harper was looking at Grace. "After Grace informed me of the tragedy, I knocked up all of the guests but Mr. Mendelsohn didn't answer. I took it for granted that he wasn't there." She smoothed the front of her red shirt.

"Knocked up?" Martha Blenkensop's mouth worked soundlessly for a minute. "Really," she finally articulated. "What a thing to say."

"It's a British expression. I can't help adopting that country's mode of speech. Everyone knows what an Anglophile I am. And "knocked up" simply means exactly what it says. In that sense it has nothing at all to do with sex or pregnancy." Theodora smiled smugly at Martha who sniffed and looked away with her nose in the air.

"It's something we say all the time downstairs," Walter said, grinning wickedly at Theodora.

"Really!" Martha shook her head in disdain.

Grace decided it was time to intervene.

"Everyone who lives in the building is here, including the day people." She noticed Harper's surprised look. "Er—I mean the people who live in the basement, Drew and Walter." She gestured toward them.

"There's one more of us," Walter piped in, seeming to enjoy the importance that came with being an on-site participant in a murder investigation. "A Mrs. Hortense Murphy, but she wouldn't come up and it wouldn't do any good to try and knock her up. She's ninety-eight, you know." He winked at Theodora and she smiled back.

I've met Mrs. Murphy," Harper said. "I'll talk to her in the morning."

"Good idea," Walter said. "The old lady goes to bed every evening at eight o'clock. I tried, knocked a few times, but she yelled for me to get the hell out. She gets up at five every morning and walks the beach looking for shells to sell to the tourists. That woman's older than the sea." Walter grinned at Theodora, as if celebrating the fact that they were both still young and vigorous. "Cantankerous happens to folks when they hit that age. I've seen it before."

Harper wiped a hand across his mouth, but not before Grace saw the twitch of a smile he was trying to hide.

"Thanks for the advice," Harper said.

"Any more help you need from me, you just holler," Walter said. "I'd be glad to pitch right in."

"Thanks," Harper said dryly. "Now does anyone know where Mendelsohn might be?"

Grace's memory kicked in.

"He's..." her voice faltered. She flushed, cleared her throat. "I believe he mentioned something about dinner in San Francisco."

"Really?" Harper asked. "Do your guests always tell you where they're going?"

"Only when they invite me to accompany them," Grace snapped back, immediately regretting giving Harper the information. His expression never changed, but Grace knew better than to trust that deadpan facade.

"What time was that?" Harper asked.

"About seven." She remembered Mendelsohn's invitation to have dinner with him. She'd almost accepted. The idea of a steak had made her mouth water. But she had needed to get things ready for breakfast and finish her other chores, so she had settled for peanut butter and honey on Triscuits from Wimberly's pantry.

Harper checked his watch and Grace glanced at the ornate clock sitting on the mantle.

"It's now ten o'clock. Mendelsohn should be back soon, unless he decided to take in a movie—or found other company." Harper shot Grace a look that made her want to stick out her tongue. She smiled instead, leaning back into her chair. Harper scowled before continuing.

"I want each of you to tell us exactly where you were to-day—say from three o'clock onwards. Officer Rosser will take your statement." He nodded toward a beefy man in a blue uniform.

Harper glanced at Grace. "I'd like to question you a little further, Mrs. Cassidy. I'm sure that Mr. Wimberly wouldn't mind if we use the office again."

It wasn't a question, but Wimberly acted as if it was.

"Not at all, Sergeant, I'll be glad to cooperate in every way possible. I hope you know that the inn is in no way re-sponsible for these horrible deaths."

Harper grunted then motioned Grace to precede him. She stood, immediately missing the comfort of her friends. Almost as if sensing Grace's reaction, Drew and Theodora rose in unison.

"I'd be glad to tag along," Drew said. "Mrs. Cassidy has had quite a shock. It might do her good to have a friend present."

"Or I could come." Theodora moved gracefully toward the stairs, a billowing cloud of red. "I'll be quiet as a church mouse—never interfere one iota."

Harper grinned.

"I'm sure you have never interfered one iota, ma'am. I can't imagine you doing anything that wasn't on some sort of a grand scale."

Theodora opened her mouth to reply, but Grace felt Harper grasp her elbow and propel her toward the stairs. She glanced backwards to see her friends looking much like parents bereft of a small child. Pansy, still seated on the floor, lifted her hand and fluttered her fingers.

"They've been wonderful to me," Grace said over her shoulder to Harper.

"They're a pain in the butt," Harper responded, making no effort to lower his voice.

They walked down the stairs, trailing through the parlor, the dining room and back into the tiny room that served as an office. Harper switched on a light then walked to the desk and pushed the only comfortable chair from behind the desk and rolled it toward Grace.

"Sit down." Harper lowered his weight onto a cane-bottomed chair, across from her. "Have you heard from your husband yet? Or are you still struggling through this mess alone?"

"What?" It wasn't the question Grace expected.

"Have you heard from..."

"No, I haven't." She answered honestly. No excuses, no explanations. Harper's unexpected kindness unnerved her.

Harper shifted his wide shoulders then reached into his pocket for a notebook. Grace frowned. This is the question he cares about, she thought. The other was bait.

"Are you okay?" Harper asked.

Surprise shot through Grace a second time. That was the wrong question. But she liked it.

"As okay as you might expect under the circumstances." But she wasn't. She wanted to lean her head against his solid-looking chest and cry. "Why would anyone want to kill Maxie?"

"I don't even know why she was in your room wearing your dress. Maybe you could answer that?"

"I don't know. She probably came up to clean and then stayed for reasons of her own." Shards of an earlier conversation filtered through Grace's mind. "It's possible that she wanted to tell me something. I think she tried to earlier, but I misunderstood and didn't listen."

Harper moved closer.

"What did she say to make you think that?"

"She said she had done something bad." Grace swallowed, glanced at her hands. "I thought she was talking about trying on my clothes. I'd caught her wearing the dress she was later killed in and was helping her get back into her own things." Tears stung her eyes and she blinked. "I told her that what she had done wasn't bad and just not to do it again."

"Now you think she was talking about something besides the dress?"

"Yes. Hindsight is always twenty-twenty. She was too relieved for it to simply be the dress. I misjudged her because..."

"Because she was retarded?"

"Yes." Grace wiped away a tear with her fingers.

Harper reached backwards, grabbed a box of Kleenex, pulled out a handful of tissues and handed them to Grace.

"Normal thing to do," he said in a gruff voice.

"Maybe, but that doesn't help Maxie." She blew her nose and threw the used tissue into a wicker wastebasket. I must look like hell warmed over, she thought and then felt ashamed of herself for caring.

"So she went back to your room and put on the yellow dress again." It wasn't a question. Harper spoke in a musing tone, thinking about what he'd said. "When was the last time you were in your room?"

"About eleven o'clock this morning when I changed into my working clothes and became the new inn sitter. It's been a busy day. Once I thought about putting on some lipstick, but blew it off. Part of the time I spent looking for Maxie, but it never occurred to me to look in my own room."

"There's another possibility as to why she was killed," Harper said.

"What could that be?"

"If her back was to the door, someone might have thought it was you."

Chapter 15

"My dear, you must be exhausted." Theodora took the still-warm muffins Grace offered, chose one, and then passed the basket to Pansy. "And sleeping on that short sofa in the office last night must have been torture."

"The sofa wasn't too bad." Grace picked up raspberry preserves from the buffet and handed the small cut-glass pot to Pansy. She smiled at the three women still seated at breakfast. "But you're right, I didn't get much sleep since Mr. Wimberly looked in on me every few hours—to make sure I was safe, he said." She remembered the lecherous face leering over her at regular intervals until she finally threatened him with the poker she snitched from the withdrawing room fireplace.

"Such a considerate man," Martha Blenkensop said. "I really would insist on George moving us to another inn after these terrible murders, if it weren't for the character of Mr. Wimberly." She smoothed the blue ruffle at her neckline and let her hand drop to caress her large, solid, one-piece bosom. "Mr. Wimberly just keeps this house squared away."

Pansy choked on her fresh fruit compote, then coughed into her napkin.

Martha Blenkensop scowled at the little blonde.

Grace bit her lip to stop a smile. "Would you like me to pour you another cup of peppermint tea, Mrs. Blenkensop?" Grace asked.

"Yes, indeed. I must drink plenty of peppermint tea for my digestion," Mrs. Blenkensop said. "My nerves are absolutely destroyed. How I can manage to eat a bite after two wicked murders is a miracle." She took another muffin then reached a second time for the egg casserole.

"How wise of you to fortify yourself, do have another slice of bacon." Theodora's eyes twinkled when she passed the antique floral platter to Mrs. Blenkensop. "Now Grace, we must think of a more suitable room for you. You can't continue camping out in the office." She cleared her throat. "We mustn't strain Mr. Wimberly's kindness."

Grace smiled at Theodora's droll tone.

"Oh, dear me no, and we must do something quickly." Pansy closed her eyes then placed a hand over her heart. "Black clouds are thickening overhead. I feel the oppression."

"Thank you, Pansy," Theodora said, an annoyed edge to her voice. "Grace should find that most helpful."

Grace was still thinking of Pansy's words when she hung the last of her clothes in the room where Arnold Huxley had been murdered. Somehow Pansy's eccentric speech had brought the memory of her mother's face into sharp focus.

Anyone can behave well when things are pleasant and nothing is distressing you, Mama had always said. You find out what a person is made of during a crisis.

And Mama had shown what she was made of during her fight with cancer.

Grace looked at the bed, remembered the victim's body and shuddered. Was she really going to be able to sleep there? She sighed, knowing that she must.

"Okay, Mama. Now we'll see what I'm made of." She took a deep breath and began scrubbing the finger print powder off of the dresser.

Crass and uncaring as it seemed, Grace still had to arrange to replace Maxie. When her room was clean she made a quick call to a local temporary agency and learned a maid couldn't be sent out until the next day. She closed her eyes in frustration and reached for the broom and the basket of supplies that Maxie had used for cleaning the guest's rooms.

"I guess I'm it," she muttered and felt glad she was still wearing the wrinkled shirt and jeans from the night before. "No use getting anything else dirty. I'll bathe and change afterward."

Grace thought about Arnold Huxley while she moved through the inn, making beds and dusting. She didn't know him, but did he know her?

She finished Gustav Mendelsohn's room and moved down toward Pansy's when Mrs. Blenkensop came bustling up the stairs, her face flushed, her jaws working.

"Mrs. Cassidy—Mrs. Cassidy!" She rushed over to Grace. Her blue polyester bosom heaved in a righteous sigh. She took another deep breath. "I've been looking everywhere for you. You simply have to do something to make them quit."

The words stopped Grace dead in her tracks. What now? She wondered.

"Make who quit what?" she asked.

"Make *them* quit!" The woman's cheeks turned an even darker red. "You know—the newlyweds—they're doing it— again. And everyone can hear."

"I beg your pardon?" Grace said.

"Oh, never mind," Mrs. Blenkensop said. "Just come with me and listen. Then you'll understand." She bustled down the stairs motioning Grace to follow.

At the foot of the stairs the unmistakable sounds of lovemaking reached Grace's ears. The sounds were echoing through the walls, loud and uncontrolled. Pansy and Theodora sat in the guest's sitting room, their faces set in that neutral expression certain women assume when they're determined to act like ladies and pretend nothing untoward is happening.

"A perfectly normal occurrence," Pansy looked up and smiled. "Why shouldn't people enjoy themselves on their honeymoon?"

"A bit distracting," Theodora twisted the long strands of coral beads that draped her peacock blue caftan. "I hate to admit that Martha might be right, but I suppose that perhaps Grace should advise them of the thinness of the inn's walls. It might not have occurred to them that we could hear."

I can't believe you expect me to interfere, Grace wanted to shout at the women's expectant faces, but didn't because she knew it was her job to keep the inn quiet.

"I can't believe you just sat and listened," she said instead.

"Apart from leaving the Inn, we can not *not* listen," Theodora smiled. "I really am afraid that you'll have to do something, Grace dear."

"How long has this been going on?" Grace asked, stalling for time.

"Pretty much since they arrived," Pansy said. "But you've been busy and it really didn't bother me. Then today, when Mrs. Blenkensop wanted to join us in the sitting room— well—she heard and thought she should fetch you."

The ecstatic cries increased. Grace walked uncertainly to the Robert Browning Suite, hesitated, and then knocked gingerly.

"Err, folks?" She struggled for the names of the couple. "Mr. Blake? Mrs. Blake? Are you in there folks?" She blushed. What a stupid question. She took a deep breath then began again, raising her voice. "Mr. Blake, I'm afraid your noise is disturbing the other guests." There. That sounded better.

"Ohhhh—" Young Mrs. Blake's voice came through the door. "We're sooooo sorryeeeeee. We'll be quieeeeet." Then a feminine scream split the air.

"It's all right, Grace," Theodora said. "They'll be quiet for a while now."

"Oh," Grace said.

"Well!" Mrs. Blenkensop said, "I never!"

I'll just bet you haven't, Grace thought. But she noticed that the woman's eyes were brighter than usual.

At three o'clock Grace, bathed and dressed in a pale green denim skirt and matching cotton sweater and then carried a cup of tea out to the garden where she found Walter working in a flower bed. Drew sat in the bench swing, his elegant legs crossed. He stood, motioning with a flourish for her to join him.

"It's so wonderful out here," Grace said. The instant she sat down she felt transported back to the nineteenth century and Drew seemed to her very much a gentleman of the time. "It's like a secret garden, wild and wonderful." She looked down at Walter. "You're a gifted artist, and this garden is your canvas."

"It is how I pay the rent," Walter said pretending to shrug off the compliment, but Grace saw a flush of pleasure creep up his neck. He returned to his weeding.

"Why don't you take a short break and stop to chat with Drew and me? I could run back inside and grab a couple of *Cokes*, or make a pitcher of iced tea."

"Don't put yourself out on my account," Walter said. "I bring my refreshment with me." He pulled a bottle of *Wild Turkey* from its hiding place behind a clump of purple irises and unscrewed the lid, taking a swig then wiping his mouth on the back of his hand.

"You're going through that bottle even faster than usual, Walter," Drew said. "Maybe iced tea would be a good change." Drew gave his friend a concerned look.

"Don't need you giving me orders," Walter snapped, and then tipped his bottle again. "We're not in the Navy anymore."

"Suit yourself." Drew said. "Grace should relax a minute anyway. I expect she's been double-timing it all day." He leaned back rumpling the notes pinned to the front of his shirt when he crossed his arms.

"Please tell me what those notes are," Grace said with a laugh. "I've been trying to read the wretched things since I first met you."

"Research my dear. I'm writing a book on naval history during the eighteen hundreds. Very dull stuff to most folk, but I've always loved the sea. I kept losing my notes and spent all of my time searching for something lost until I hit on the idea of pinning everything to myself. At night I fasten them to my curtain or stick them on the bulletin board. Works like a charm." Drew chuckled and unpinned a note, handing it to Grace.

"You're writing about the Navy, huh? I remember the exquisite seascape hanging in your apartment. I don't know very much about art, but it looked like the real thing to me." Grace tried unsuccessfully to read the note then handed back the scrap of paper.

Drew repinned the paper to his shirt.

"If I don't keep the damned things on me, I lose them. The memory's the first thing to go, you know," he chuckled, tapping his forehead. "So you like my painting?"

"Very much," Grace took a deep breath. "Is it real?"

"Somehow, I don't think you came out here to talk about the decor of my apartment."

"You're right. I spotted you both from the kitchen window and I wanted to bounce some ideas off you. Thoughts about the murders actually, and questions about anything unusual you might have noticed on the day either of the murders took place."

"That sounds like you're planning on playing detective," Drew said.

Grace sat silent for a minute. Her voice was soft when she spoke.

"Yes, I may as well be honest. I do plan on playing detective."

"Hold on there a minute." Walter seemed to sober up instantly. "Snooping around sounds like a bad idea for anyone, especially a woman, maybe we'd all better chip in and collect enough money to send you back to Tulsa where you'll be safe."

"I'm not sure the police would let me go since Sergeant Harper considers me a suspect. The only way to clear my name is to get to the bottom of what's happening." In spite of her protest, Grace relished the warm feeling that washed through her body at their concern. These sweet old men were trying to look after her.

"I don't like this, Grace," Drew said. "It's a really bad idea."

"He's right." Walter took another long swig, glanced at Drew, then screwed on the lid and stuck the bottle in his pocket. "This house has turned into a dangerous place and asking questions might get you into big troubled, killed even."

Grace shivered. "I think I may already be in trouble. Maxie was wearing my dress when she was murdered. If she stood with her back to the door she might have looked very like me." She swallowed hard. "Harper thinks her death may have been an accident and that I was the intended victim. What do you think?"

"I think it proves that you need to clear out of California and go somewhere safe. Staying here might make you the next victim."

Grace felt the blood drain from her face.

"You're scaring the poor girl to death, Walter," Drew said.

"I'm trying to help, that's all." He scowled and shot a wistful glance at his whiskey bottle. "You always think that I don't know nothing."

The embarrassed silence that followed seemed to incense the old man into further justifying himself.

"I know that the guy who turned up naked and dead sneaked into the house on the day of the murder."

"That's what I figure too," Drew said.

Grace watched Walter's face darken with annoyance.

"But did you see the guy sneak in?"

Chapter 16

"You saw the man before he was murdered? Saw him when he slipped into Wimberly Place?" Grace rushed on before Walter had time to answer. "Which door did he use, and what kind of clothes was he wearing?" She took a deep breath, inhaling the exotic fragrance of the tangled garden. Her head almost seemed to spin with the new information the old man had blurted out. She glanced at Drew and he looked equally surprised.

Walter ignored her questions. He rested on his knees and busied himself with digging. His trowel turned over fresh earth with such speed that he seemed more like a machine than a man.

"Please answer me," Grace said.

"Didn't mean to say that," Walter's expression tightened.

Grace didn't know if Walter was scared of getting involved in a dangerous crime, or if he had just lied about seeing the murderer.

"You're sure you saw Huxley?" Grace caught Drew's eye and noted that his skepticism matched her own.

"Come on, Walter. You never pay any attention to the people from the inn." Drew spoke softly, but with a thin edge of impatience. "You brag about not even seeing them, saying that except for Theodora and Pansy they're cardboard cutouts and you wouldn't waste your time looking at make believe people. Now you're telling us that you noticed this fellow?" Drew shook his head in disbelief. "Don't make up stuff just to sound important."

"Why do you always think I'm all mixed up?" Walter rubbed his hand across the stubble on his chin. "I did see the guy. I noticed him because he wasn't invisible."

"Invisible? Grace asked.

"Yeah, invisible. Most tourists wear uniforms. You know, like the postman or the UPS man. I don't notice regular tourists because they all wear uniforms. They're invisible to me. I just look right through them."

Grace lifted an eyebrow.

"Okay, so they aren't *identical* uniforms, but they're uniforms all the same. It doesn't matter if it's some gaudy T-shirt or those expensive "all natural" duds that look like hell but cost the earth, they're still the tourist uniform, and that uniform makes them all invisible. Sometimes it's even an expensive suit."

Walter threw down his trowel, retrieved the bottle of Wild Turkey from his back pocket, and took a swig.

"Go easy on that stuff," Drew said.

"None of your business how much I drink. I know that sometimes I like to make up a good story just to liven things up but this time I'm telling God's own truth." He set his bottle carefully on the ground, rubbed sweat from his hands onto the legs of his khaki pants then reached for the trowel. "I don't care if you believe me or not, but the fat bald guy who got hisself killed while he was buck naked, went up those steps wearing a white shirt with a weird mustard-colored tie and shiny-seated brown britches. Guess he spent most of his time on his butt."

"You noticed the color of his tie?" Drew stopped swinging.

"Yeah. It was different. I remember thinking the guy looked sort of like a hamburger. Brown pants, white shirt, mustard tie." Walter laughed at his own joke, bouncing on his heels.

"How did he get into the house?" Grace asked.

"Through the back door, same way Pansy comes and goes." Walter's face changed expressions when he heard his own words, frowning as if they had somehow come out wrong. "Only Pansy wasn't here that day. It was one of those afternoons she and Theodora do that damn fool Chinese exercise thing."

"Tai Chi," Drew said in reply to Grace's questioning look.

"You saw him go inside?" Grace asked. "Did you see anyone else? Anything else?"

"Nope," Walter began turning rich soil, removing tiny weeds as he worked with deft movements. "It was about the time of day I always finish my bottle, so I went back downstairs and took myself a little nap. Same as always, you can ask Mrs. Murphy if you want. She saw me."

"Did she see this man go inside?" Drew asked, leaning forward.

"Nope, she came out just afterwards," Walter said.

"It didn't occur to you to stop a strange man from walking into Wimberly Place? You just let a stranger enter the house uninvited?" Grace asked.

"How did I know he was uninvited? And what was I supposed to do? Someone must have opened the door for him. I figured it was probably Wimberly who let him in. The guy looked like a creep. I figured they had business together. Anyway, I've lived to be this ripe old age by minding my own business." Walter paid careful attention to a small petunia that seemed out of place in a collection of exotic flowers, lifting the delicate plant with his trowel, and setting it aside for what Grace supposed would be transplanting.

"Then you didn't tell Sergeant Harper?" Drew asked.

"Nope, I didn't tell." Walter paused from his digging and scowled at them. "Didn't tell him about Maxie neither."

"What about Maxie?" Drew and Grace spoke in unison.

"Damn it, Walter. Why the hell wouldn't you tell me if you saw something important like that?" Drew asked.

"Everybody thinks I have "loose lips," but I don't tell everything I know. Walter threw down his trowel and took a drink from his dwindling whiskey.

"Tell us about Maxie," Grace said.

Walter sat quietly for a couple of minutes, as if debating on whether or not to trust his friends. Finally he gave a deep sigh and then spoke. "Just after the guy went inside Maxie poked her head out the door. She was crying."

"Did you ask her what she was crying about?" Drew snapped.

"Naw, she ducked back inside and slammed the door. Didn't look to me like she wanted anyone asking her questions. Sort of like me now." Walter scowled. "If I'd of known she was going to get herself bumped off I'd have asked her a bunch of stuff."

"You don't have to explain yourself to me," Grace said with a wry smile. "I didn't ask questions when I should have, either. What else did you see?"

"You wouldn't believe me if I told you." Walter set his face in a stubborn expression.

"Which means he didn't see anything," Drew said, winking at Grace.

"Is that right? Are you just messing with us?" Grace wouldn't have put it past the man to make up a tale just for the attention it created.

"You two are worse than Harper." Walter scooted to his right and continued weeding. "At least he takes notes while he gives me the third degree."

"I'm sorry, Walter," Grace said. "I'm not very good at asking questions. Please tell what else you saw."

"Don't let him put a guilt-trip on you," Drew said, grinning. "If he knew anything he'd be quick to spit it out."

"Humph." Walter pulled himself to a standing position and stretched. "I've said all I'm going to say to the two of you."

"See?" Drew laughed.

"Oh Walter, I didn't mean to hurt your feelings." Grace smiled up at the old man until she saw him grin back. She sipped from the almost-forgotten cup of lukewarm tea, balanced in a saucer on her lap, and pondered the new information her sleuthing had unearthed.

Perhaps that was when Maxie left the cleaning supplies on the stairs, Grace mused, setting the rose-covered cup back onto its fragile saucer. She needed to know more about Maxie. Tomorrow she'd find time to snoop into the maid's past.

Early the next afternoon Grace walked through the long winding neighborhood of Victorian houses and checked street numbers against the address she held in her hand. Thank God the nursing home where Maxie had once worked was near enough to reach on foot. She pulled a folding cart pilfered from the hall closet behind her, the kind senior citizens carried onto buses. After her sleuthing she would pick up supplies for tomorrow's breakfast at a nearby shopping center. Tucked into the pocket of a multi-colored print skirt was a credit card which Mrs. Wimberly had left for her to purchase supplies.

Am I organized or what? She asked herself. And it was lucky that she was, because the employee agency still hadn't sent her a maid. It seemed that no one in Port Ortega needed a job. Grace paused when she spotted a classy looking sign that said "Halcyon Nursing Home" in elaborate script. The facility had been revamped from a Victorian mansion into a plush home for the sick and aged. If a person had to be old and sick, this would be the place to do it, Grace thought.

She stopped at the foot of the steps, dreading the chore ahead. Only the reward she had promised herself, strong coffee and a cheese Danish, kept her from running away like a jack-rabbit. She walked up the steps, bumping her cart behind her and pushed through the door. The nursing home was plush enough not to have the usual offensive odor, reinforcing Grace's belief that the place must be unbelievably expensive. Memories of her mother's final illness flooded her mind. She stood hesitantly in the foyer.

An overweight woman of about twenty, wearing a too-tight pink and orange flowered T-shirt, sat at the reception desk. Grace knew she should contrive some story about why she deserved the information she was about to ask for, but somehow she couldn't come up with any plausible fabrication. She decided the woman was about her son Brand's age so she assumed her mother-in-authority look.

"A woman named Maxie Davis used to work here. Did you know her? If not, I need to speak to someone who did." Grace spoke as if there wasn't a doubt that her command would be obeyed.

Four minutes later she found herself seated in front of the head nurse on duty.

"Call me Nurse Nancy," the woman said and Grace's eyebrows shot up. "Yeah, yeah." Nurse Nancy smiled. "I know. It's a bad joke, but my name really is Nancy, and somehow the moniker got stuck on me, so I decided to be a good sport about it."

"I remember that name from one of my son's books when he was a little boy," Grace said with a smile.

"What can I say?" Nurse Nancy shrugged. "Now, how can I help you, Mrs. Cassidy?"

The woman was about fifty, so Grace knew the mother thing wouldn't work. She switched to a 'business-woman in charge' mode.

"I understand that Maxie Davis used to work here?" Grace said.

"And what's your connection to Maxie?" Nurse Nancy wore green hospital scrubs and a tired expression. She looked pointedly at Grace's shopping cart. "The police have already been here asking questions."

"I'm the innkeeper at Wimberly Place, and Maxie worked there as a maid. Her employment application didn't list anyone except a social worker for me to contact. I called but she couldn't work me into her schedule."

Actually, the woman had refused to see her as a possible violation of privacy, but that was a minor detail that Grace decided to skip. She smiled then continued. "I thought perhaps Maxie might have friends here at the nursing home who would want to know what had happened." Grace belatedly thought about funeral services and felt ashamed that she hadn't asked Harper who would plan that sad event. She added that to a mental list of to-dos.

"Maxie didn't have any real friends that I know of, even though everyone was fond of her. She was dependable, but different if you know what I mean."

"Everyone has some sort of a friend at work," Grace persisted, "even if it's just a pal to chat with during break. There must have been someone."

"Not really." Nancy shifted the papers on her desk, as if uncomfortable and needed something to busy her hands. "I trained her. It took patience, but once she understood what I expected she followed orders to the last detail. Which is different from most of my employees, I was surprised by how good she was at proceeding without supervision."

"Do you know why she decided to leave?"

"I really can't discuss employee matters." Nancy's friendly manner vanished. She pushed her chair back and stood.

Grace narrowed her eyes at the woman's reaction. "Was she asked to leave?"

"I didn't say that." Nancy walked to the door and held it open. "I'm afraid I must get on with my work."

Grace sat nonplussed for a minute. "I'm being thrown out?"

A flurry of movement sounded in the hall and a wild-eyed attendant wearing scrubs, stuck his head in the door.

"We've got a code-blue in room one-oh-six," he said.

"See yourself out," Nancy yelled before she sprinted from the room.

Grace stood and glanced around the room. Her gaze fell on a row of putty colored file cabinets. Did she dare? Snooping in other people's things would be new for her. She walked forward and fingered a drawer. What was Nurse Nancy going to do? Calling the police would be too much publicity.

Grace read labels printed in neat, twenty-four point Times New Roman font. The 3rd down said 'personnel'. She pulled it open and riffled through folders until she found Maxie's. On top was a form marked "Terminated with Cause," which stated that Maxie had been fired for trying on a patient's yellow gown. The patient had been a Doreen Quick and the complaint had been made by her husband, Erwin.

Chapter 17

Grace found nothing else unusual in Maxie's file. She shut the drawer and cast a guilty look around the room, feeling a bit like a child pilfering in her mother's purse. She snagged her cart and walked into the hall.

Sober-eyed employees hurried down the corridor. A skinny blond in her early twenties with frizzy hair and blue fingernails plodded after them shaking her head and grumbling.

"This is a gross job," the blonde said to Grace. "If you applied for the new opening, you'd better think it over. A person would be better off working at that Mexican sweatshop we're hearing so much about. I'm looking for something else myself. I heard that the Taco Bell is taking applications."

"Hard work, huh?" Grace asked, delighted at the opening.

"You'd better believe it. And the worst is the nasty stuff, if you know what I mean?"

"Uh, I'm not sure. But perhaps you knew a friend of mine who used to work here? Maxie Davis was her name."

"Sure," the woman said. "And I wish she was here now, she could help me with this mess."

"My name is Grace Cassidy." Grace held out her hand. The young woman looked surprised, as if she weren't accustomed to shaking hands.

"Sandy Walker," she said. Her grip was limp and uncertain.

"Were the two of you friends?" Grace asked. "Did you happen to be working here when she was terminated?"

"You mean when old deep-pockets got her fired?"

"Deep Pockets?"

"Yeah, the old guy who talked his company into funding the new occupational therapy room on the east end. His bitchy wife got pissed at Maxie about something and the next thing I knew she was out the door."

"What did Maxie do to make her so angry?" Grace glanced down the empty hall and hoped her good luck held.

"She was caught trying on a fancy gown when her majesty walked in on her. The old lady was supposed to be in therapy, but left early. It was a stupid thing for Maxie to do, but she had this thing about yellow stuff."

"Is his wife still a patient here?" Grace asked.

"Oh, no, she died." Sandy lowered her voice. "When the old lady kicked the bucket, the old guy, her husband, took off with the private nurse he'd hired after the run-in with Maxie."

"No kidding?"

"Yeah, he had buckets of money, and you can guess what that nurse was after. You can bet it wasn't for his ability in bed." Sandy snickered. "His name was Quick and I figure that probably described him in the sack."

Grace kept her face expressionless to conceal her annoyance with the crass Sandy.

"I suppose the nurse was pretty?" Grace fished.

"No way, she was a big butch of a woman with a toothy smile that made you want to gag."

"Then you've worked here a long time?"

"Started evenings before I graduated high school but I'm looking for something else, now. I'm sick of this place."

The head nurse stepped out of a room at the end of the hall and strode toward them.

"Whoops," Sandy said. "Here comes Nurse Nasty. I'd better get moving or I'll get a butt-chewing. See you." She walked toward Nancy.

Grace headed toward the foyer to avoid Nurse Nancy and pushed open the door, escaping with her cart into the sunshine.

Well, well, Grace thought. Erwin Quick had evidently been badgered by his wife to have Maxie dismissed, but he'd gone behind the old woman's back and secured the girl another job at Wimberly Place. But why did Maxie avoid him? Was it simple embarrassment or something more?

Grace walked toward the mall mulling over what she'd learned, then she stopped, propped her cart against her left leg, rifled through her purse and found the to-do list she had written earlier. She crossed through "Ask questions at Halcyon."

She needed more information. She looked about as suspicious as anyone else. It was no wonder that Harper put her name at the top of his list. Of course it may have slipped down a few notches since he now thought she herself might have been an intended victim. Not that that fact made her feel any better.

She shoved the paper into her pocket and squinted through the sunshine. The mall loomed ahead and she strode toward the small cluster of attractive buildings. She was sick of murder and needed distraction. It seemed years since she had done something ordinary like window shopping.

She strolled along and allowed herself to be charmed by everything she saw: the children's shop featuring antique toys, a small window with nothing but music boxes, a boutique with an assortment of summer shorts. Another pair of shorts is just what I need for my job, Grace thought. Then her eyes fell on a price tag. She swallowed hard. A week ago I'd have bought that without hesitation, she thought and walked on.

Tucked in between a bookstore and an old-world looking pharmacy was a tiny resale shop run by the local animal aid society. Delight surged through Grace as if she had found a gold mine. She pushed through the doors with the zeal of a prospector panning for gold. New age music played softly in the background and the store smelled of scented candles. An intelligent looking clerk wearing a tie-dyed T-shirt looked up from the book she was reading.

"Are you seeking anything special?" the woman asked.

"Shorts, size ten." Grace grinned. "And I'm working with a very limited budget."

"Back of the shop," the woman nodded toward the rear.

Grace walked past racks of dresses toward a table stacked with shorts. The merchandise was sorted by size and Grace felt as if she had hit pay dirt. She sifted through the stacks and found a pair of navy denim shorts marked down from ten to three dollars. She longingly fingered a designer set of peach-colored linen shorts with a matching top, saw the twenty-dollar price tag, and backed away.

"Where could I try on these shorts?" she called to the clerk.

"There's a work room in the rear," the clerk answered without looking up from her book. "A little cluttered, but it's all we have."

"Thanks." Grace propped her cart against a table and walked into the small room. She lifted her skirt and pulled on the shorts without removing her shoes. The fit was perfect. She slipped them off, being careful not to snag her sandals, and was headed back to the front when her gaze fell on a table cluttered with clothing in the process of being sorted. In the middle of a blaze of bright colors was a streak of mustard.

Grace's heart stopped beating. She snared the drab cloth between two fingers, and snaked out a wrinkled tie.

Chapter 18

Grace stared at the mustard colored tie draped over her fingers. It was a minute before she could walk to the front of the store.

"Could you tell me where you got this tie?" she asked the clerk.

"That's not ready to sell." The clerk peered at the tie over half-lens glasses. "It hasn't been inventoried and priced." She cast a longing glance toward her book.

"I just need to know who donated it," Grace said.

The clerk lowered her book reluctantly. "But I'm not going to tell you. It's against our rules."

Grace resisted the urge to grab the woman's book and use it to smack her. She took a deep breath, and tried again.

"I have no intention of making problems for anyone. It's hard to explain, but I really need to know about this tie."

"Sorry, rules are rules." The woman looked toward the door.

I've alarmed her, Grace thought. She's hoping someone will come in and distract the crazy woman who obsesses over ugly ties. She wanted to scream at the woman. Instead she smiled.

"Of course, rules are rules but aren't they made to be broken?" Grace intensified her smile. Maybe a little charm would work.

"If I start breaking rules, people might quit donating their used items." The clerk put a grocery slip in her book to mark her spot and laid it on the counter. "Did you want to buy the shorts?"

So much for charm, Grace thought.

"Yeah. Sure. I'll take the shorts and the tie. No need to do anything special to it for me." Grace hoped she had enough cash.

"Oh. Okay." The clerk glanced down. "I guess that would be okay. Three dollars for the shorts, and ummh, I guess about three would be right for the tie, too.

"How about two for the tie?" Grace pulled a five-dollar bill from her pocket.

"It's for charity," the clerk said in a strained tone.

"Five is all I have." Grace looked at the clerk feeling embarrassed and vulnerable. Being broke sucked, as her son Brand would have said.

The woman's look softened. She smiled then dropped both items into a used grocery sack. "Five will be fine," she said. Grace laid her money on the counter and sighed. So much for the coffee and Danish, she thought.

The food market with its lush fruits and vegetables mesmerized Grace. She breathed in the heady fragrance of ripe fruit and fresh cut flowers, fingered Wimberly's credit card, and flew into a buying frenzy.

She grabbed red bell peppers, flat-leaf Italian parsley, beefsteak tomatoes, and leeks to use in an omelet, reminding herself she needed extra eggs to begin her plan of using mostly egg whites in an attempt to save Theodora from herself.

Wimberly had ordered her to plan for variety so she bought whole-wheat flour with the thought of her mother's herbed whole-wheat popovers and dried cherries and cranberries for different kinds of muffins. If that isn't enough variety I can always make Grandma's chocolate gravy and orange self-rising biscuits, Grace thought. That should different enough even for Wimberly.

She saved the fruit section for last. Once again she fingered the credit card then completely lost control. She chose succulent blackberries, ripe yellow cantaloupe, and luscious looking mangos for a fancy fruit parfait. Large Bosc pears would be perfect to sprinkle with cinnamon and bake, and Golden Delicious apples would keep a few days for Dutch apple pancakes. There was no need to shop every day. She had a murder to solve. She checked out and grinned wickedly at the amount of her receipt.

On the trip home the mustard tie hit her conscience with the weight of concrete. Should she call Harper immediately and tell him about her find? If that tie was Huxley's as she suspected, and it was found in her possession, she'd look as guilty as Satan. Still, it would have been unthinkable not to buy the thing. It was a clue, for goodness sake but the closer she got to Wimberly Place, the more frightened she became by what she had done.

Grace headed for the only place she felt safe—the kitchen. She hid the tie in a brown paper sack and stashed it in the vegetable crisper between the parsley and the tomatoes. She put away the groceries then continued unnecessary puttering about, delaying the time when she would have to go upstairs and face the ghost of Arnold Huxley. She had just about decided to bake a fresh apple cake when a masculine throat cleared, causing her to start.

"Oh!" She turned and saw Gustov Mendelsohn, natty in a blue and white seersucker suit and blue tie the exact color of his eyes. "Mr. Mendelsohn? I had no idea you were there."

"Sorry if I alarmed you." He ran fingers through his perfectly cut silver hair then held up paper sacks decorated with a golden arch. "I thought you might be hungry."

He smiled a boyish smile and Grace wondered if the smile was practiced. Did it reach into those blue eyes? She wasn't sure.

"Everyone laughs at me, but I must confess to a weakness for your American hamburger."

His German accent made the words seem romantic, and against her better judgment Grace felt his seductiveness wash over her.

"Yummy," she said with what she used to think of as her flirtatious smile. "But that sack looks like enough for the whole inn."

"I sometimes tend to be intemperate. Perhaps some of the other guests might like to join us?" He moved toward Grace, masculine sensuality oozing from every pore.

Grace enjoyed the exchange. It had been such a long time. This is some ladies man, she thought, remembering her earlier suspicion that Gustav was having a fling with Pansy.

"Why don't we go up to the sitting room and see? I can make tea up there." English tea and Quarter Pounders, Grace thought with a smile, only in California.

They found Theodora, clad in a black flowing pants suit with innumerable strands of white beads, snapping pieces into the framework of a jigsaw puzzle.

"Pansy had other plans," she answered to their question, waving a hand heavenward in a vague gesture, and Grace suspected Pansy was with Drew. "What do we have here?" Theodora looked hopefully at the sacks, now blotted with streaks of grease.

"Mr. Mendelsohn has brought us hamburgers. Are you hungry?" Grace handed Theodora the food.

"I'd love to." Theodora peered into the sack. "My goodness, what a lot of food, are others coming?"

Grace walked to the sink and busied herself with the ritual of tea while Theodora made small talk with Mendelsohn. She glanced up at the mention of her name.

"Grace's son is spending the summer in Germany," Theodora said. "She seems to have momentarily lost track of him, do you have any suggestions about how she might contact the boy?"

Grace set down the pot for a minute. Mendelsohn was an international traveler. Perhaps he could help.

"I assume you want to tell him about the murders and your new job, but you should consider one thing. Sometimes young men don't want their mothers to find them."

The thought almost stopped Grace's heart.

Chapter 19

"Brand wouldn't deliberately avoid me." Grace crossed her fingers, hoping the statement was true. "His summer adventure in Europe was planned last Christmas. I didn't expect to hear from him for a couple of months." She glanced over her shoulder at Mendelsohn then poured steaming water into the cups. There was no way she was going to explain about Charlie to a suave German.

Grace doubted that her and Charlie's divorce would come as a shock to Brand, but she dreaded telling him none the less. She especially dreaded informing her only child that he no longer had a home base from which to operate. Grace carried teacups to the coffee table and sat down. Her defensive reaction had piqued her friends' attention, and their inquisitive gazes made her want to squirm.

A picture flashed though her mind of a spotlight dazzling her eyes while two ruthless detectives—looking exactly like Theodora and Gustav—grilled her without mercy. She blinked to clear the image.

"Please Grace," Mendelsohn smiled appealingly at her. "Don't be distressed. I'm sure you had nothing to do with the death of that unfortunate man." He handed her a Big Mac and a package of fries. "Enjoy your hamburger and let's discuss how to contact your son. Does he carry a laptop? Most young people do nowadays."

Grace halted a French fry half way to her mouth. "But of course, how stupid of me. I hate techy things so ignore any suggestion of email. I like to think that I'm too young to be called a dinosaur, but the truth is I've never made a successful entry into cyberspace. I haven't even memorized Brand's email address, but it's written down in the address book I carry in my purse."

"It isn't as if you had nothing on your mind," Gustav said in her defense. "And I'm delighted that the solution is simple."

"My dear Grace, you're not the only computer-illiterate person in the world." Theodora had made short order of her own bag of fries and reached for a second. Even though the rotund woman disliked sweets, Grace now understood her friend's struggle with a weight problem.

"Do you dislike computers, too?" Grace asked.

"Oh no, Pansy taught me enough so that I can prepare tests and keep track of my investments." Drippings from her hamburger landed on Theodora's bosom. "Oh, dear, I've made a mess. She dabbed at the grease spot with her napkin.

"Can I get you some club soda?" Grace grabbed the extra napkins lying on the coffee table and handed them to Theodora.

"No, no. This is fine." Theodora waved the suggestion away. "Let's not get sidetracked from finding your son. I'm surprised *he* didn't teach you about computers."

"Brand offered to teach me, but I kept finding excuses." Grace shrugged. "I can't help it—the things scare me to death."

"Computer phobia," Theodora nodded her head. "Unreasonable fears are very hard to overcome. I can see that we're going to have to drag you kicking and screaming into the twenty-first century. But your son is no doubt a whiz."

"True," Grace said. "You can't separate Brand from his laptop."

"We can send your boy a message on my computer after we eat. All we need is his email address."

"That would be wonderful! Thanks so much."

Grace really wanted to throw the sandwiches into the trash and drag Mendelsohn to his room immediately. Instead she forced herself to chat about inconsequential things until everyone had their fill of fat and cholesterol. Finally, Mendelsohn stood and brushed imaginary crumbs from his seersucker pants.

"We'll contact your son now, but please give me a few minutes to tidy up my room." He smiled suggestively at Grace and then walked toward the door. "I'll expect you in about five minutes."

The look he gave Grace over his shoulder before leaving the room made it obvious that Theodora wasn't invited. The older woman studied him with an amused smile and lifted one eyebrow.

"Isn't this wonderful?" Theodora gushed, ignoring the slight. "Seeing Gustav's room will be an interesting experience, I'm sure." She chuckled.

"I'm so glad your feelings aren't hurt," Grace said.

"A woman of a certain age must learn to hear what suits her purpose," Theodora said with a naughty smile. "Old women and cats do as they please."

Grace laughed. "Theodora, you're priceless. It was almost worth losing every cent I owned to meet you."

"Friends are important. Drew asked me just this morning about your son. He seems to think it's critical that the boy come to help you. He thinks it necessary in order to build Brand's character."

"I could never come up with the money to fly Brand to California." Grace wrapped paper around what was left of her Big Mac and stood. "I'm flat broke."

"But my dear, at the end of the summer he'll have to come here anyway. Do you think you'll have more money by then?"

"I have no idea." Grace tossed her trash into a container near the sink. "In fact, I've been deliberately putting that question out of my mind."

"Don't worry, we'll figure out something. Husbands and money come and go, but children and friends are forever," Theodora said with a wise look on her face.

Grace thought for a minute. Theodora was right. Any problem that could be solved by throwing money at it could somehow be overcome. She straightened her spine.

"Brand will come here," Grace said. "His home is wherever I happen to be. But now I must run up to my room and get Brand's email address, then I'll meet you in Gustav's room. He's so looking forward to *our* company." She shot Theodora a wicked grin.

Her friend's laughter followed her up the stairs.

Five minutes later Grace knocked on Gustav's door. When he opened it she saw Theodora already seated in a chair near the window, as comfortable and self-assured as the cat she had mentioned earlier. Grace bit her lower lip to keep from smiling.

"Everything is ready." Gustav had taken off his coat and tie. He had unbuttoned his shirt half-way to his waist but if the suave man was annoyed by the older woman's presence, he didn't show it. "Step over to this small table I use for a desk and I will relay your message for you."

Grace considered his offer for a minute. She wasn't sure what she was going to write, but whatever it was she didn't want to share.

"Show me how and I'll try and act like a grownup. I actually learned to type in high school." She smiled.

Gustav gestured toward a chair in front of the laptop.

"It's all set up, just start keyboarding." He returned her smile with a flirtatious one of his own.

Keyboarding? No one must type anymore, Grace thought. I'm going to have to upgrade my jargon into the 21st century or I'll seem hopelessly dated.

"Thank you." She seated herself in front of the computer feeling awkward and scrutinized. The position of the keys seemed foreign to her touch, almost like the toy typewriter she'd had as a child. There was so much she wanted to say to her son, where on earth could she begin? Disjointed sentences flashed through her mind, and none of them seemed appropriate to the occasion.

Grace leaned forward and stared at the blank screen. Her fingers shook and she could hardly keep them on the keys. She took a deep breath and began to type.

Brand, I have some bad news. Your father and I are getting a divorce. She paused a minute and swallowed. This was the wrong way for anyone to learn such a thing.

"How do I get rid of what I've written and start over?" she asked.

Gustov reached down and punched the backspace.

"Like that," he said.

Grace cleared the page and began over.

Brand, I need to talk to you. I'm in California, call me immediately. She added the number for Wimberly Place and rechecked it for accuracy. She wanted to close by saying she missed him so much her heart felt hollow to her legs, but that would terrify him. So she simply typed *Love, Mama.*

"I'm done," she said to Mendelsohn, blinking hard to fight the tears that stung her eyes.

Mendelsohn stepped close and did something with the mouse.

"Your letter is on its way," he said.

"When will he get the message?"

"Immediately," Mendelsohn said. "I'll let you know as soon as I receive an answer."

Brand cried somewhere in the darkness. Grace ran forward, arms reaching through black fog, flailing blindly.

"Brand!" she cried. "Brand, I'm here." Suddenly she saw him standing at the edge of a cliff. He faced her direction looking young and helpless.

"Don't move!" She tried to run, but her legs wouldn't work. "I'm coming. Don't move," she shouted just as Brand took a step backwards.

Grace awoke with a hard knot of fear in her chest, almost like a physical pain.

She looked at the clock and realized with a start that she had forgotten to set the alarm and should already be in the shower. It was 5:15 and soon would be time to start breakfast. She stretched her legs and focused on the darkness, the stillness. Mama used to meditate when she awoke, and had encouraged Grace to do the same.

"Take a few moments to express your gratitude," Mama had said. "And then ask for guidance in your daily life." Mama, a good Baptist, had always spoken of God as a close personal friend, and Grace now wished she hadn't neglected her advice.

Grace had admired her mother's unique strength of character, but had never practiced her faith. Suddenly, she felt the need for all the help she could get. But how did she start?

With honesty, Grace thought. So she did her best.

"Good morning, Father," she said as Mama had instructed all those years ago. "This is Grace, and I'm in what my son would call a shit-load of trouble. Sorry for the language, but I'm speaking my unedited thoughts, as Mama said to do.

"I know you've been helping me, because I have a new job. Thanks. Please help me with the rest of this mess, and bring Brand back safely to me. Amen."

Like email, it was a new way to communicate. Grace sighed and shrugged. She would see.

***

"What do you mean the maid won't be coming until to-morrow?" Grace balanced the teapot with one hand and held the phone in the other. "You've been promising me someone for six days."

She listened to the woman's excuses then punched the off button harder than was necessary.

"What's wrong with these people?" she muttered, reaching to pour Pansy another cup of tea. It was impossible to cook, play hostess, make beds, clean, *and* find time to solve murders. The dining room and sitting rooms were covered with a film of dust. Of course Wimberly had been raising Cain.

"Not to worry," Theodora said from the breakfast table, flouncing her tangerine and gold muumuu. Grace squinted, perusing the figures on her friend's garment. *Whatever were those people doing?*

"Pansy and I will be glad to pitch in and help. After all, it was our suggestion that got you into this situation."

"That seems so much to ask," Grace protested, hoping Theodora would continue to insist, knowing that she couldn't do all the work alone.

"Nonsense," Theodora neatly folded her white damask napkin and pushed her chair away from the table. "I'll just fetch my boombox and enrapture myself with music as I vacuum.

"It will be fun." Pansy stood and brushed an imaginary thread from her immaculate pink shirt. "We actually feel as though Wimberly Place is our home. Caring for it will seem perfectly natural." Her expression transfixed. "These rooms need a special cleansing. I will meditate as I dust, with every movement calculated to cleanse both the surfaces and the atmosphere."

Grace sighed. Whatever worked.

Grace finished preparing a breakfast tray for the Blakes. She had begun doing so after Theodora had left the remaining cold hamburgers in front of the self-sequestered new-lywed's door. "The lovers will think elves have left them," Theodora had said with a laugh.

That was four days ago, the day she had emailed Brand. Grace swallowed hard. The thought of her son caused an arrow of sadness to pierce her heart. Her son's answer to her desperate message had been short and seemed to be without concern for her welfare.

Mama, I called and the phone number was busy. I'll get in touch soon. Love, Brand.

He didn't care about what she needed. He wasn't a boy any longer. Had she raised her son to be selfish and indifferent to another's needs? Guilt added its weight to her burdens. Would a second email make any difference?

Wimberly walked through the door and Grace forced herself to smile. He returned her effort with a scowl. Business as usual, Grace thought, steeling herself against his onslaught of anger.

"Guests cleaning? What are you thinking? And all that racket! The little blonde is chanting something while she polishes furniture in the withdrawing room. Why the hell is she doing that?"

"It's called a mantra I believe, and its purpose is to cleanse the atmosphere," Grace watched her boss' mood darken.

"The only thing that needs cleansing is the furniture surfaces, and not by a paying guest. It makes the inn look bad. Cleaning is part of your job."

"The maid from the temporary agency hasn't shown up, and Pansy and Theodora offered to help, so in desperation I accepted, but if you'd care to pitch in then I can tell them they're not needed."

Wimberly stopped complaining long enough to cast an appreciative glance at her legs. Maybe the thrift store shorts weren't such a good idea, Grace thought. His hand roved toward her hip. "That's not the help I need," she said sidestepping Wimberly's hand.

Wimberly scowled, whether from her words or from her moving away from him, Grace wasn't sure.

"There's too damn much noise! The one upstairs has some kind of Cuban music blaring, and this one is playing that new age crap. And she's burning something in a silver pot, incense I think or some kind of candle. Why the hell did you tell her she could burn stuff in my inn?"

"I didn't tell her anything. I just handed her a dust cloth and a bottle of lemon oil and let her do it her own way. She said she'd make it fun." Grace added salt and pepper shakers to the breakfast tray then picked it up.

"Fun? Fun? You think running this place is fun?" Wimberly's cheeks puffed out. "Let me tell you that running an inn isn't fun, it's work. Hard work."

"I know," Grace said. "That's why when they offered to help I let them. Like I said, the employment agency said no one could come until tomorrow."

"You mean that no one *would* come," Wimberly's temper won over his lust. "Everyone is afraid to come to an inn where people are murdered. We're going to be out of business, thanks to you." His face purpled. "Soon all of the rooms will all be named after murder victims instead of Victorian authors. The first one you slept in can be called the Arnold Huxley Room."

"Oh, no," Grace said evenly. "The guests are calling it *The Naked Dead Guy's Room.*"

Wimberly gave her an evil look, turned on his heel and stalked away. Then a sudden fear pierced Grace's heart. The man she had cavalierly insulted might very well be a dangerous murderer.

Chapter 20

Grace carried the breakfast tray upstairs, paused in front of the Blake's' door to listen for any embarrassing noises then knocked.

"Hello, in there," she called out. "I've brought your breakfast. I'll leave it in front of your door, but you'll want to eat before it gets cold." She knelt to set the tray down just as the door opened.

"Hey there," Mike Blake grinned down at her. He wore the inn's white terry cloth robe and had pillow marks on his cheek. "We love this TLC."

"My pleasure," she stood and handed Mike the tray. Ashley's red head popped through the door beside her husband.

"Oh, yummy," Ashley reached for a strawberry. "I'm starving and this looks wonderful. One of these days we're actually going to make it to breakfast. Gustav says you're the best cook ever."

"So you know Mr. Mendelsohn?" Grace asked.

"I met him about two months ago when I first interviewed at Vantech Corporation," Mike said. "Ashley didn't meet him until later, after I'd decided for certain to change jobs."

"You're starting work at Vantech?" Grace asked. "What a coincidence, almost everyone in this inn seems to be connected with Vantech Corporation."

"Not too surprising," Mike said. "I was told the company always uses this place to house official visitors."

Grace took the tray from Mike with a quick movement. "I'll set this up on that nice little table in front of your window. Newlyweds should be waited on." She walked forward with an air that tolerated no argument. "You don't want these eggs to get cold."

"That's awfully nice of you," Mike said in an uncertain tone.

Grace began removing plates and cups from the tray and setting them on the mauve colored linen tablecloth.

"Both of you just sit down and dig in while I tidy things up a bit."

"It's really not necessary," Mike said, but his wife was already moving toward the table.

"Ummmm," Ashley sat down and put a forkful of vegetable omelet into her mouth. "Oh, wow. This is great."

"We sure appreciate this." Mike bent to kiss the top of his wife's head, then sat down and buttered a muffin.

"Just doing my job," Grace moved to the bed, threw back the rumpled covers and began to smooth the sheets. "So, Mr. Mendelsohn is also employed by Vantech?"

"Indirectly," Mike salted and peppered his eggs. "He's the overseas connection for selling the company's software packages in Europe. I'll be working closely with him in my new position as marketing manager."

"He was the one who told Mike about this inn." Ashley licked butter prettily from her fingers. "He just went on and on about it, even mentioned the old man in the basement with the Homer Winslow painting. It seems that Gustov wants to buy the thing, but the old guy won't sell."

"He wants to buy Drew's painting?" Grace paused from spreading the comforter across the bed. "He told you that?"

"Did he ever? He went on and on. He was thoroughly miffed because the old guy wouldn't budge. Said he'd offered him a fortune." Mike frowned at his fruit cup, took a tiny bite as if testing for poison, then grinned. "Hey, this stuff is great."

"Thanks, glad you like my cooking." Grace plumped a pillow then shot Mike a quick look. "So Mendelsohn was upset over not being able to buy the painting?"

"Yeah. It's kind of funny to see someone like Gustav not getting what he wants. He's not used to that." Mike held a piece of bacon for Ashley to taste. She took a tiny nibble then wrinkled her nose at him.

"Gustov told us he had a new plan to snare the picture," Ashley said. "That was when he took us out to dinner about a week before our wedding."

"Must not have worked out, though." Mike took a huge bite, finishing off his eggs. "Ashley asked him about it when we were sitting in the lounge waiting for the police and he acted as if he didn't know what she was talking about."

"I was very discreet." Ashley took a sip of coffee then smiled. "In fact I was the soul of discretion. I didn't mention so much as a word about the painting, I just asked him how his new plan had worked out. He turned red then muttered something about it not being the time to discuss business." Ashley drained her cup.

"The soul of discretion, darling?" Mike laughed. "You were being naughty, and you know it." He fed Ashley the last bite of muffin and she kissed his fingers. He leaned forward to nibble her neck then seemed to remember that Grace was in the room.

"Well, Mrs. Cassidy, we certainly scarfed down your delicious breakfast in a hurry. Thanks a million." Mike smiled a charming smile.

"I think that's my cue to leave." Grace laughed, gave the bed a final pat then gathered the dishes back onto the tray. Mike held the door for her. "Goodbye, you two," she called over her shoulder.

"See you later," the couple answered in unison.

Grace spotted Theodora in the guest's sitting room pretending to flick the furniture with a feather duster. The door had barely closed when the duster was cast aside.

A sense of urgency put wings to Grace's feet. The dirty breakfast dishes rattled all the way downstairs. Her mind was awash with wild speculation and the soft pattering noise of Theodora's footsteps tracking dead behind didn't help her concentration.

"What did you learn from that sweet little couple?" Theodora asked, her supposed whisper projecting with such force that Grace shot a glance upwards.

"Hush, Theodora, the Blakes will hear you. Wait until we're in the kitchen."

"Ohhh," Theodora's tone was amused. "Little miss junior league is finally losing her manners." She chuckled, "And about time, too. This is serious business."

"That's an understatement." Grace walked into the kitchen, dumped the tray on the counter top with a clatter, and glanced around her. "Gustav Mendelsohn is connected with Vantech Corporation," she said.

"Of course, practically everyone in this inn is connected with Vantech," Theodora answered. "That's no big surprise. The place has been used by Vantech for years."

"There's more. Mendelsohn wants to buy Drew's painting." Grace paused for effect, but Theodora didn't look impressed.

"Oh pooh, lots of people want to buy Drew's painting. He won't sell. It's one of those male testosterone things. Part of his manhood ritual. You know how that sort of thing works." Theodora plopped herself down on one of the kitchen chairs and smoothed her tangerine and gold muu-muu. "Tell me what else our newlyweds said."

"That's about it, but I think you're wrong about what I learned. I think everyone being connected with Vantech is an important clue. We already know that George and Martha Blenkensop may have had a motive, and he works for Vantech." Grace moved pink floral china from the tray to the sink.

"I don't see how Vantech Corporation could be of any importance." Theodora toyed with the multicolored beads that cascaded down her bosom.

"Mr. Quick is on the board of directors, and Gustov Mendelsohn sells their software overseas, Blenkensop wrote their software—it seems like too much of a coincidence." She rinsed a china cup under a stream of hot water and set it in the dishwasher.

"That's all true, but what about Martha?" Theodora cocked her head to one side and smiled. "Darling Martha has bored us all so intensely with her talk of the importance of the classes that George teaches, we wouldn't mind her being guilty."

Grace rolled her eyes. "Mike Blake said that Gustav had a new plan to get Drew's picture. And no matter what you say, I think that the painting somehow figures into all of this. Gustav just looks guilty."

"My dear, Grace, you must forget about that picture. It means nothing."

"Right now I'm going to have to forget about everything except making beds. Yelling at the employment agency didn't seem to do me a lot of good and unless they have a change of heart and send someone over this morning, I'll be doing double duty. I'd better get myself in gear." Grace put the last dish in the top rack of the dishwasher, turned it on and then began wiping down the counter with a red and white checked dishrag. Theodora could think what she wanted. Grace knew the picture was important.

The doorbell rang at eleven fifteen. Grace paused from making Erwin Quick's bed and frowned. Did she dare hope it would be someone from the temporary agency? She ran down stairs and pulled open the front door. Her mouth opened in surprise.

"Sandy?" Grace looked at the young blonde she had pumped for information at Halcyon Nursing Home.

Sandy shot Grace a questioning look. "Hey, you're the same woman I talked to yesterday at Halcyon. Mrs. Applebee from the agency tried to call, but all she got was the answering machine. She told me to go ahead and drop by. She said you were raising hell." Sandy cleared her throat and looked hopeful. "Mrs. A said the job might become permanent."

"Please come in. I'm only the inn sitter. Mr. Wimberly owns the B&B and he's the person to decide who will be hired on a regular basis." The girl standing before her wouldn't have been her first choice, but she was desperate enough to use anyone.

"I just put in my application this morning. I had no idea you were at Halcyon scoping out help, I thought you were hunting for a job for yourself." Sandy stepped inside and glanced around the hallway.

"You can start right now." Grace led the young woman to the office, got her telephone number, stashed her purse, and then hustled her up to Erwin Quick's room.

"You may recognize some of our guests from elsewhere, but don't mention it to them." She hoped that would be enough to keep Sandy's mouth closed. "We change the towels every day and the sheets every three days if a guest is staying on." Grace handed Sandy a chart. "Bed making is a big deal at Wimberly Place. It's necessary to be as quick as possible in case the guests want to come back to their rooms."

"Maxie would have been a whiz at that." Sandy pulled back the comforter and smoothed the sheets. "She could make a bed quicker than anyone I ever saw. She'd whip off the dirty sheets, put on fresh ones, and even have the person in it cleaned up before you could say squat. If she could have kept her hands off of the patient's stuff, she'd still be at Halcyon."

And alive, Grace thought with a pang. It was a minute before she could speak.

"Yes. Maxie was great. Her singing must have cheered the patients. I know it brightened my day."

"You call that squawking singing? Maxie couldn't carry a tune to save her life. I kept telling her to put a sock in it, but she wouldn't shut up."

Grace felt an urgent need to distance herself from Sandy. I'll leave you with your work. When you've finished cleaning all the bedrooms come downstairs and dust. I'll be in the kitchen if you need me."

Grace met Erwin Quick and Sydney on the stairs and decided to delay their meeting Sandy for awhile.

"The new maid is cleaning your room, but she'll be through in a minute." She flashed a too-bright smile. "Could I make you a cup of tea while you wait?"

"Tea would be nice." Erwin leaned on Sydney's arm and the couple strolled toward the sitting room. "So, you found a new maid?"

"The agency finally sent one," Grace said. "Finding help isn't easy."

"Let's hope that the new maid will be luckier than Maxie," Erwin said.

Chapter 21

Grace couldn't believe it had been eleven days since she had fled from San Francisco and landed in what seemed to be the Land of Oz. She had given up expecting the phone to ring and hear Brand on the other end. This fact added an extra heaviness to her heart. Drew was right, she must find some way to pay for Brand's airfare and insist that young man come to California immediately. Yet she found herself hesitating before sending another, more direct email message. When she searched for a reason for the vacillation a new stab of guilt penetrated her heart. The shameful truth was that she didn't want to deal with a sullen and unhappy teenager on top of everything else. So I guess I'm as selfish as I've trained my son to be, she thought with a heavy heart.

She had settled into the life of an innkeeper with more ease than she had expected. The days were busy, but while working, she pondered who had killed the naked guy. It scared her to think that one of her new friends might be the murderer. But people had secrets. Theodora and Pansy were bound to have secrets, even though they seemed open and guileless. After all, they were in their sixties. But were any of these secrets connected to the murders? A gut feeling told her the answer was, "yes." Grace knew she needed to pry, and the thought of prying into friends secrets with suspicious intentions made her stomach cramp.

She also needed to schedule a meeting with Sergeant Harper and tell him about the mustard tie. It wasn't a meeting she looked forward to. She even wondered if it was a wise thing to do. He might doubt how she found the tie. Maybe she should just toss the wretched thing in the trash and forget about it. An obvious truth suddenly hit her. Having this evidence wasn't going to make her look like a clever sleuth. It was going to make her look guilty as sin! What had she been thinking? She threw a cup of walnuts into the large batch of brownies she was mixing for the afternoon tea and gave the stiff dough a few hard turns. She had to find the real killer. It was the only way to prove her innocence.

Another hard question assaulted her brain.

How could a couple of public schoolteachers afford to hang out in a bed and breakfast for such long periods of time? This question stumped Grace. Granted the place was more like a residential hotel than a bed and breakfast, but it was still much too expensive for the average income on an unlimited basis.

Grace scraped the batter into an oversized buttered Pyrex dish, slipped it into the heated oven, and set the timer.

She picked up a duster with fuchsia feathers and walked into the dining area where Sandy was polishing the massive Victorian silver tea service.

"When the oven timer buzzes I want you to take out the brownies and set them on the counter to cool. I'm going to be upstairs for awhile."

Sandy shot Grace a martyred look.

"I didn't know I was going to have to cook," she said. "Rubbing this grungy pot with this yucky gunk seems bad enough. Shouldn't I get more money for cooking?"

"I haven't asked you to cook," Grace said, feeling the burden of supervising the unwilling. "You're going to pick up a pot holder, pull a pan out of the oven, and set it to cool on a rack on the stove."

Grace ran upstairs to Theodora and Pansy's room, raised her hand and knocked before she could change her mind. How did she ever end up in the business of prying into her friends private affairs?

"Come on in!" Theodora shouted with a throaty warmth that made Grace feel ashamed. "Pansy left the door unlocked when she went downstairs earlier."

Grace pushed open the door.

"Aren't you afraid to leave your room open with a murderer lurking around?" Grace asked, stepping inside. Theodora, swathed in a flame silk peignoir sat at her dressing table surrounded by an artistic array of cosmetics. Grace felt suddenly dowdy in beige cotton capris and white shirt.

"I knew it was you." Theodora smiled up at Grace. "I hope you aren't in here to flick that duster about. I'd much rather that you sat down and kept me company while I finish touching up my face."

Grace lowered herself gingerly onto the edge of the bed, balancing the duster between her knees. She racked her brain to think of a polite way to pry into Theodora's private affairs.

"This is a lovely room," she hedged, looking at the lavender and white lace curtains. "Actually I think it's my favorite." Grace shifted her weight, squirming around and showing her nervousness. "You stay here almost every summer, don't you?"

"Oh yes," Theodora answered. "And often during winter holidays, too. Wimberly Place is more of a home than my apartment back in Marshall."

"Marshall? Is that the town where you and Pansy teach? I don't remember hearing of a Marshall, California?"

"It's in Oregon. And yes, we've both lived there for years. Pansy teaches art, you know. She's actually quite a good artist in her own right. She has an excellent eye, although she lacks originality." Theodora finished patting foundation under her eyes then smoothed it with a wedge-shaped sponge. "Our ex-husbands still live there so we don't like to hang around any more than necessary."

"I've always gathered that your divorces weren't friendly ones."

"That's putting it mildly. Pansy's possessed a mountain of money and a black temper and mine dumped me for a Barbie Doll trophy wife." Theodora looked serenely at Grace. "But don't waste any pity. Pansy and I are strong women, and too stubborn to allow ourselves to be run out of town. Both Scorpios, you know. You do know what Scorpios are like, don't you?"

It wasn't a question that needed answering, so Grace just nodded. She wanted to stop. Let it drop. Secrets should be left alone, especially when you liked both secret keepers. But she knew there would never be any real peace in her life until she learned the truth of what had happened in her room.

"No wonder you both prefer to hang out here when school's not in session." She waited for a response, but Theodora just picked up an over-sized powder brush and dusted her nose. Grace tried to read her friend's fixed look of indifference.

"I'm sorry, Theodora. It's awful of me to pry."

"But you intend to keep trying, don't you? Why not just ask what you want to know?" Theodora smiled.

The thought crossed Grace's mind that having smart friends could be a mixed blessing. She took a deep breath and plunged in.

"I was wondering about Drew and Pansy," Grace said.

"Then why don't you ask them?" Theodora held her mascara wand eye level and looked at Grace.

"That would be the decent thing to do. The truth is, I just plain don't have the guts. I thought it might be easier to pry it out of you."

Theodora threw back her head and laughed.

"My dear that's so bad of you, and so un-Grace-like that I think it might deserve an answer."

"Drew and Pansy are obviously in love. It seems odd that they haven't married."

"It's economics, my dear. As I said, Pansy was married for years to a cruel and wicked man. When she finally found the courage to divorce him, the judge awarded her a very healthy alimony. If she remarries, she will lose the comfort in which she now lives." She looked keenly at Grace. "You should try and live on a teacher's salary."

"You seem to manage quite nicely," Grace said. "Perhaps I need your secret."

Color drained from Theodora's face. She dropped her powder brush and gave Grace a stricken stare.

Chapter 22

Grace sipped hot French-roasted coffee and sighed. She loved coffee. Drinking coffee was one of life's purest pleasures. She felt sorry for people who didn't like the bitter brew, who didn't know how to enjoy its rich, almost sensual pleasure. She pulled two boxes of brown eggs from the refrigerator, set them on the counter then headed out to get the morning paper.

The smell of rain was in the air. The cool morning air hit her with an invigorating shock. Mornings are the best time of the day, she thought. Why did I waste so many years sleeping late? Even though she hated the first few sleep-fighting moments when the alarm sounded, it was worth the misery of pulling yourself out of bed. After she was up and her head cleared, she loved the quiet solitude of dawn. The beauty of morning was the one good thing she had gained from these enforced early morning risings.

She walked barefooted into the dew-covered grass enjoying the clean wetness, picked up the paper and slipped off the plastic sleeve, glancing at the headlines.

More about the Mexican sweat shop. How could anyone ever enjoy money they leeched from someone else's misery? Then she remembered the ton of money she and Charlie had made from their collection agency. She shrugged. She was paying in spades for that one. Her lawyer had called yesterday and mentioned that she might have to file bankruptcy.

She wished she had the moral strength to refuse such extreme measures, but she knew that when all of the chips were down she'd probably cave in and file. If she didn't, it would take her the rest of her life to pay off those bills that Charlie caused. If she could stay out of jail, that was. She flipped to the cartoon section, read Cathy then grinned. Cathy was a woman after her own heart.

A car pulled up to the curb. Grace looked toward the brown four-door Crown Victoria then glanced at her watch again. What was Sergeant Harper doing at Wimberly Place at five-thirty in the morning?

She watched him stride toward her. His top shirt button was unfastened and the navy tie hung loosely knotted an inch below where it should have been. Standard uniform for Harper, she thought. A lightweight brown jacket was thrown over his shoulder, and his expression was grim.

Uh oh, Grace thought. Looks like there's more trouble headed my way.

Harper's face brightened when he spotted her and his dour expression turned into a boyish grin.

"Hey, there," he said.

"Hey back." Grace smiled. What was he up to? A friendly Harper was scarier than an angry one.

He walked close, invading her space. What surprised her was that she liked it.

"You look good in the morning." His brown eyes were warmer than the coffee she had just drunk and turned her knees to liquid. Was she losing her mind? Another man was the last thing she needed.

"You're hardly a discerning connoisseur of women." She smiled. "I'm wearing thrift shop clothes and no makeup."

"Yeah, but that's what I like. You look like a woman who just rolled out of bed." Harper looked down at her, close but not touching. She could smell his after-shave, woodsy and cheap and suiting him. Unexpectedly she wanted to rest her head against his shoulders and breathe in the scent of him. Instead she stepped back. Madness added to murder—she must be losing it.

"This is a little early for a social call." Grace moved toward the front door, motioning him to come with her. "So I'm assuming that it's business." She stepped onto the sidewalk, her wet feet plastered with blades of grass.

"I need to speak to one of your guests," Harper said.

"At this hour?" Grace asked.

"Yes, at this hour."

"I can't say that I'm really surprised," Grace said. "Can I guess which one? I've been playing amateur sleuth."

"That's a damned stupid thing to do." Harper gave her a hard look. "This isn't a chapter from some English tea-cozy. You say the wrong thing to the wrong person and you could get dead." He put a hand to the small of her waist and guided her forward, reaching to open the door.

"I'm taking that as a no." She grinned up at him.

"Take it as a serious warning." Harper used his fingers to make gentle circles on her back that felt so good she wanted to close her eyes.

"Is that coffee I smell?" He cast a hopeful look toward the kitchen.

"Yeah, and I'll give you a cup if you tell me who you're after."

Grace walked through the kitchen door and over to the sink. She grabbed a paper towel and wiped her feet, then grinned at Harper.

"The going barefooted is genetic. I'm an Okie, you know."

"You never stop surprising me, Mrs. Cassidy." Harper grinned watching her rinse her hands. "Maybe that's why I find myself telling you things I never meant to say."

"So tell me who it is you're hounding this morning." Grace rinsed her hands, grabbed a white ceramic mug from a bleached-oak rack then reached for the coffee.

"I need to talk to Theodora Westmacott," Harper said.

Grace almost dropped the glass pot. Her hand jerked and hot black liquid splashed on the counter.

"Theodora? Are you kidding? At this time of day?" she asked. "Theodora's a night person. You bang on her door at this time of morning and she'll break your fingers."

Harper moved back into her space. So close she could feel the very essence of the man. Almost as if he was physically touching her.

"Don't burn yourself." He took the pot from her and poured his own coffee.

"Do you suspect Theodora of...?" Grace swallowed and struggled for the right word. Who knew what he was thinking, and she didn't want to put ideas in his head. "...of some wrong doing," she finally said.

"I have questions to ask." He wore his cop-face, and that part of Harper always scared Grace.

"You can't seriously think that Theodora had anything to do with the murder? She's a woman. And she's old to boot."

"With proper training, breaking a neck doesn't take that much strength. She studies Oriental forms of self-defense."

"She takes Tai chi classes!" Grace swung back to the sink, grabbed a bowl and began cracking eggs.

"You pretending those eggs are my head?" he teased.

"Every one of them," Grace opened the next box of eggs then grabbed a large copper skillet from the rack overhead and threw it on the burner. Next she switched on an electric grill for the Canadian bacon. "Suspecting Theodora is the dumbest thing I ever heard of."

"Theodora attacked her ex-husband with a fourteen-inch chopping knife." Harper sipped his coffee watching Grace over the rim of his cup. "Not that it's any of your business, and not that I should be telling you this."

"Really? She did that? Anyway, it doesn't matter if she did. Ex-husbands don't count. If Charlie were here I'd be chasing him through the house with a meat cleaver."

"Then lucky for him he's been spotted in Barbados." Harper kept his eyes on Grace.

"He has? You know that for sure?" Grace turned back to her eggs, grabbed one from the carton and cracked it so hard against the bowl that it smashed flat spilling egg and shells down the side of the bowl. "Damn," she breathed under her breath.

"I suspect he has moved somewhere else by now, but I'm using what contacts I have to try and find where he lands."

Grace knew he was attempting to do her a favor, but she couldn't bring herself to thank him. Instead she picked shells from the bowl of eggs and rinsed them down the sink.

"The jerk," she said. She pulled a container of bran muffin batter from the refrigerator where it had been stored overnight and began dropping spoonfuls into paper-lined tins.

"What's that stuff?" Harper asked peering over his coffee cup.

"Bran muffins," Grace said. "You stir them up and they keep in the refrigerator for up to two weeks. Handy for times like this morning when your breakfast plans have been screwed up by unexpected company." She glared at Harper. "This morning it's going to be scrambled eggs, grilled Canadian bacon and orange juice."

"Sounds good to me," Harper said. "I usually have a doughnut."

"Well, don't think you're invited to eat here." She scowled at him. "Not if you're seriously suspecting Theodora."

"Would you mind going upstairs and telling her I need to see her?" Harper asked.

"Oh sure, right after I bake muffins, cook the bacon, juice a dozen oranges, and whip up eggs for Blenkensop and Mendelsohn who will be down in about ten minutes." She shot him a furious look.

"Guess I'll do it then. Thanks for the coffee." Harper walked to the sink and rinsed out his cup.

"Wait!" Grace said. "It would be better if I gave her the bad news." She shot him an exasperated look. "Just sit down at the table, give me ten minutes to finish here and I'll get her."

"I'm on a tight schedule." Harper looked at his watch.

"I'll make extra everything," Grace said. "You can eat the best breakfast you've had in years." She pulled a string-bag of oranges from under the counter.

"You talked me into it." Harper walked to the end of the counter and poured himself another cup of coffee. "How can I help?"

"Slice oranges while you tell me why you suspect Theodora." Grace handed him a walnut-handled knife.

"Did she ever mention to you that she owns part interest in the Mexican sweat shop venture?" Harper asked.

Chapter 23

Grace left Harper sitting at the dining table with Mendelsohn and Blenkensop and ran upstairs to wake Theodora. It wasn't a job she coveted since Theodora's hatred of early-morning rising was legendary. If Pansy spent the night with Drew, as she often did, there would be no one standing between her and Theodora's wrath.

It took five minutes of brisk knocking and calling to bring Theodora to the door. The woman was sleepy headed, bleary-eyed, and highly indignant.

"What time is it?" Theodora asked, pulling open the door. She stood wearing a filmy rainbow nightie with arms akimbo.

"About six-fifteen," Grace said.

"Six-fifteen?" Theodora yelled. "What the hell is going on? Is the building on fire? *Everyone* knows that I never arise before eight."

"It's worse than a fire, it's the police." Grace pushed her way inside. "Harper is downstairs and he wants to talk to you."

"At this hour? Is he insane? Are you insane for telling him it's all right to wake a person in the middle of the night?"

"I don't have a choice, Theodora, and neither do you. He's here on official business. I braved your early-morning wrath for friendship's sake, so please don't shoot the messenger. You're going to need all the friends you have." Grace shut Theodora's door and switched on the overhead light. "Right now Harper's wolfing down breakfast, and I'm hoping that will mellow him out a little. You need to dress and come down as soon as possible."

"This is ridiculous. I'll report him to his superior. I'll have the bastard's badge for this insolence." Theodora walked to her bed and sat down. "I'm going back to bed. Tell him I'll be down at nine. That's early enough." She plopped down and pulled the covers back over her, even covering her head.

"Can't do that," Grace pulled the covers away, walked to the window, and opened the drapes. Dim sunlight spilled over the bed.

"Oh, hell!" Theodora yelled, sitting up straight. "What is wrong with you?"

"I think you'd better talk to him." Grace walked to the closet, pulled open the door, and began sorting through clothes. She found a comfortable looking beige cotton shift, pulled it off the hanger, and threw it at Theodora. "Pull that on and we'll run downstairs and get the ordeal over."

"This ugly thing? It looks like a damned shroud. The only place I'd wear that would be to a funeral, and then I'd have to be the corpse," Theodora yelled. "My cousin Gladys gave that to me and the only reason I even brought it was because she was watching me pack. You know how polite I always am."

"Except at six in the morning," Grace said with a grin. "None of this is my fault, Theodora. Now hop in the shower to wake up, pull on something, and come downstairs. I'm going to make you a cup of tea to help you get your eyes open. You're going to need all of your wits about you."

"What do you mean?" Theodora asked.

"Harper said he wants to question you about the Mexican sweat shop scandal." Grace watched the color drain from Theodora's face.

Ten minutes later Theodora was dressed in the beige shift and headed downstairs with Grace trailing alongside trying to speak encouraging words.

"I would never believe that you were knowingly involved in anything really immoral," Grace said.

"That's very trusting of you," Theodora said. "But would you please stop talking for a minute? I need to think."

"Maybe it would be better if you just told Harper the truth, whatever that is."

Theodora stopped mid-step, turned and gave Grace a horrified look.

"You must be joking," Theodora said.

Harper appeared at the foot of the stairs. He studied the two women with a resigned expression on his face.

"I was just getting ready to come up," he said.

"Cut the woman some slack, she had to dress. Now come along this way, we can use my office for privacy," Grace said.

"Where did you get this 'we' stuff?" Harper asked.

"Theodora will need me," Grace said. "If she decides she wants an attorney, I can call one for her."

"Would you like to have an attorney present, Mrs. Westmacott?" Harper asked.

"No," Theodora said in a beaten tone that terrified Grace. "No attorney."

Harper ushered Theodora into Grace's office and shut the door, closing Grace outside.

"Mrs. Cassidy?" Mendelsohn's voice called from the dining room. "Is anything wrong?"

Grace rushed in, forced a plastic smile, grabbed the coffeepot, and poured him a fresh cup. Blenkensop raised his cup for a refill without lifting his eyes from the Wall Street Journal.

"Anyone want sugar?" she asked, ignoring Mendelsohn's question.

Ten minutes later she was pounding on Drew's door. Pansy opened the door with a calm but surprised air.

"Grace?" Pansy raised her eyebrows in a question. "What a nice surprise. Come on in, Drew will be pleased to see you." Her delicate fingers checked the buttons of her crisp long sleeved blouse, making sure all were fastened. Grace was so worried she didn't even smile.

"Sorry, but this isn't a social call. Harper's upstairs quizzing Theodora about the Mexican sweatshop." Pansy lost her smile, but Grace refused to show mercy. "The poor thing looks absolutely terrified. You've got to tell me everything you know about this mess so I can figure out how to help her."

"Oh dear," Pansy pressed a small white hand over her heart. "Then it's all out in the open?"

"Yes, and smelling to high heaven." Grace's throat tightened at Pansy's contrite expression. The small woman swallowed and then began to talk.

"Theodora never did anything illegal. Not really. She was completely duped and acted in good faith and total ignorance. That couldn't be illegal, could it?" Pansy closed her eyes a minute then seemed to regain her serenity. "Of course that wouldn't keep the whole thing from being horribly embarrassing to her. She told me that exposure would completely ruin her life."

"How in the world did such a thing happen?"

"That's a long story." Pansy stepped outside and pulled the door to the apartment shut behind her. "We won't bother Drew. He tends to become annoyed and vocal over this subject." She walked toward the swing. "The whole problem began as a question of economics. It wasn't Theodora's fault, a woman has to live, you know. It's not easy to make ends meet when you're single."

"So Theodora started a sweatshop?" The two women stepped onto the swing's wooden slat foundation and then sat in the swing. Early morning mist and the sweet scent of flowers almost beguiled Grace into a sense of peace. Instead she gazed sternly at Pansy who shrugged as if she were a child scolded by her mother.

"Of course not, Mr. Blessing, the Spanish teacher at Marshall organized and started the sweatshop. He was the one with all of the contacts. Theodora just provided the capital."

"Just the capital? Pansy, none of this could have happened without Theodora's money to back the venture."

"Now, now," Pansy said. "It's not as bad as it sounds. When Theodora got a final settlement from her divorce she received a dreadfully unfair amount. Her husband had flaunted his young girlfriend in poor Theodora's face until she was livid with rage. Then the arrogant man asked our Theodora to stay as his 'official' wife while he kept his tart on the side." An uncharacteristic anger glinted in Pansy's eyes for a brief moment before she continued.

"Theodora, who is very proud and independent, told him to go eat grass and left with one small bag." Pansy thought about her words for a minute. "Of course she didn't actually say 'grass.' Her word had only four letters and was more graphic."

"Pansy! Get on with the story. We're running out of time."

"Yes, of course. Drew often says I tend to walk a winding path." She smiled. "Of course he also says it's charming and delightful."

"Pansy? Now isn't the time to be charming or delightful. Stick to the point."

"Very well, although I swore the man's name would never again cross my lips. But this awful 'person' was so selfish and vindictive over Theodora's spirited rebellion that he fought her over every spoon. He even had the audacity to claim she had deserted him."

"That's rotten, but didn't Theodora have a lawyer to protect her rights? Didn't the courts make the man share their assets?"

"Theodora's stubborn nature served her badly at that time. She was so hurt and traumatized she wouldn't listen to a word of advice and refused to hire a lawyer. She told her narcissistic husband to take whatever he wanted, that she could support herself without any help from him. You see, she'd never tried living on just a teacher's salary alone and had no idea what she was saying. Her husband was quite affluent and she had been accustomed to living with a great deal of comfort and style. I don't think it really occurred to her how much her life would change until much later. The presiding judge was a middle-aged man who had just survived an expensive divorce himself. He allotted Theodora a very small portion of the marital assets in cash and that money was all she had. So it was imperative she make a good investment."

Grace's heart hurt for the pain her friend must have suffered at the hands of a husband she had loved and trusted. But she still had to know the truth about Theodora's involvement or she would never be able to help her friend. She hardened her heart and spoke in a stern tone.

"So she started a sweatshop with her nest egg."

"Please quit saying that. Mr. Blessing knew she had this money and approached her for financial backing to a business venture, which he claimed would provide jobs for people who needed work. He made it sound as if Theodora was helping illegals earn a wage until they could obtain their green cards. He was a fellow teacher, so at first she thought it was some sort of humanitarian thing. By the time she learned differently it was too late. Mr. Blessing threatened that they would both go to jail if she told the authorities the truth." Pansy sighed. "You'd think a person could trust a kind-looking older man named Blessing, wouldn't you?" Pansy paused again and shrugged. "And I expect that she also had become accustomed to the luxury of the income. Money is addictive, and we all have feet of clay."

But Grace didn't want to believe that Theodora was addicted to money. "I can't believe this. Theodora's tougher and smarter than that."

"And smart people never make mistakes? But regardless of her errors in investment judgment, she had nothing to do with the murder. You have to believe that."

Murder? Who said anything about murder?

"Excuse me?"

"She swears that dreadful man was already dead when she went up to your room to have her conference, and I for one believe her."

A cold fear ran through Grace's body, followed by hot anger.

"Huxley invited Theodora to my bedroom for some kind of a conference?" The unfairness of being unwittingly snared into such a mess swept over Grace. She suddenly felt as if the whole world had conspired to make her life both dangerous and difficult. Her rage settled on the deceased Mr. Huxley. She sucked in a deep breath and raged on.

"How dare he? I paid good money for that room and my privacy was violated. And by a man who couldn't even keep on his clothes." Then she remembered that her rent check had bounced. "Or at least I tried to pay. How dare anyone come into my private room without an invitation from me?" Grace knew that she was ranting. Frustration ruled and the whole situation seemed to be madness. "Why on earth did he have to choose my room?"

"Because it was supposed to be vacant. It wasn't anything personal, dear. The room was being remodeled, for goodness sake. How were we supposed to know that Mr. Wimberly would rent the room before the renovations were finished? That awful Huxley's plans had been set up the day before you arrived and that's when he gave invitations to his victims."

"Invitations? Like it was a tea party?" Grace stared hard at Pansy.

Pansy paused and cocked her head to one side, thinking. "I always thought of it as an invitation, but it was actually more like an ultimatum."

Grace rolled her eyes. "Forget the etiquette, just tell me how did he got inside my room?"

"By picking the lock, of course. The man had absolutely no ethics," Pansy stated with prim disapproval. "Both Theodora and I were outraged at his audacity. He snooped until he somehow learned of Theodora's secret and demanded that she pay him money." Pansy lowered her voice to a confidential whisper. "The man was evil personified."

"And then suddenly he was dead."

"Please stop acting as if Theodora murdered that odious man. She didn't. She caught one glimpse of his murdered body and then came right back to my room."

"And the two of waited calmly for me to come back so you could stick me with finding his naked body? Talk about audacity—you both pretended to be surprised—making me think that I had lost my mind."

Pansy touched the base of her throat as if shocked by Grace's outrage. She blinked hard, her face innocent looking when she spoke. "But we were surprised. Theodora said he was fully clothed when she saw him." Pansy stretched her toes to the ground and pushed the swing.

"He was fully clothed? And already dead?" A terrible thought hit Grace. "So when had he been stripped naked? Did Theodora catch the killer in the middle of the crime? Maybe he stepped into the closet when he heard her coming."

The blood drained from Pansy's face. "It's a miracle that Theodora wasn't murdered, too."

"Unless the guy's clothes were taken later, but why would the killer come back? What was so important about his clothes?"

Pansy just shook her head, and Grace thought the little woman looked as if she were relieved that her misdeeds had now been forgotten. Grace frowned.

"But you and Theodora still set me up," Grace said.

"We meant you no harm," Pansy said in a timid voice.

"But you stuck me with finding the body."

"It wasn't like that. We knew you were innocent. It never occurred to us that the police might think you were in anyway involved."

Grace studied Pansy's guilty and miserable expression and her heart softened a tiny bit. She knew what it was to be in a bad spot. But she also wondered if Pansy had an appointment to meet the greedy Huxley. Did Pansy also have a secret sin?

"Okay, so Huxley was using my room to exhort money from people while I was out walking. Did you go to see him?"

"No, of course not, Drew forbade it."

"But you know who else visited him? Did Drew go?"

Pansy studied her shoes as if the solution to all of their problems was hidden somewhere on their surface. She ignored Grace's question.

"Poor Theodora was terrified that her students would find out she was connected with a sweatshop." Pansy gave the swing another little push. "Just imagine, after spending years teaching children that character is more important than possessions, this awful mess threatens to explode and make her look like a complete hypocrite to the young people she cares the most about. It's more than anyone should have to bear."

Grace sighed "The fact that Huxley was blackmailing Theodora gives her a strong motive for murder."

"Don't be silly. Theodora wouldn't hurt a fly." Pansy paused, frowned, and then reconsidered her words. "Well, she wouldn't kill anyone in a fit of anger, anyway. She would calmly think it through and then execute them in some painless and tidy sort of way."

Tidy? A tidy murder? Grace shivered. Huxley's death had indeed been tidy. Inconvenient but very neat.

"Pansy, don't say that when the police are around. A broken neck qualifies as tidy—who knows, it may also be painless—for sure it's quick."

"I intend to be discreet. You can depend on me not to blab to Sergeant Harper. Anyway, there were others in Mr. Huxley's room besides Theodora." Pansy closed her eyes, and assumed a guileless expression. "When I went back into that room with you I sensed that many souls had passed by the body after the poor man left this world."

Grace sighed and resisted rolling her eyes. "Can you remember what time Theodora went to Huxley's room?"

"It was exactly three o'clock. I'm sure because Huxley said the time had to be on-the-dot, so Theodora and I sat and watched the clock until it was time for her appointment. We weren't even able to enjoy our tea." Pansy gave a regretful sigh and Grace rolled her eyes. Keeping Pansy on track was harder than putting socks on an octopus.

"Then Huxley was murdered before three o'clock and stripped sometime afterwards. It was about one o'clock when I parked in front of Wimberly Place and walked inside to find a place to stay." Grace thought a minute. "By the time I had stashed my suitcases and walked downstairs it must have been about one-thirty or a quarter of two."

"That's right," Pansy said. "You chatted with Theodora and me for a few minutes then headed toward the beach. I remember glancing at my watch just as you left. It was exactly one forty-five."

"So Huxley came to my room some time after one-thirty and he was dead by three. That's an hour and a half for someone to murder him. He probably had other appointments before Theodora showed up, and I need to know who they were. Do you have any suggestions?"

"That evil man may have been blackmailing everyone in the building for all I know, except for our newlyweds, of course."

"That's too general, I want names and reasons." She waited for an answer, but Pansy just smiled innocently. "Did you see Huxley go up the stairs while you and Theodora were drinking tea?"

"No. Never." Pansy gasped. "Oh my, if we didn't see him, that means someone let him in the side door so he could sneak up the servant's stairs. That deadbolt would have been hard to open without showing obvious signs of being tampered with."

Grace frowned. Maxie had abandoned her cleaning supplies on that staircase and had never retrieved them. Perhaps someone tricked the innocent young woman into becoming involved in a crime? Grace bit her lip so hard she could taste blood.

Chapter 24

Grace quizzed Pansy another ten minutes and got nothing but nonsensical philosophy. She left the little woman and ran back upstairs. To her surprise Mike and Ashley Blake sat at the dining room table drinking coffee and eating muffins and orange marmalade. It was the first time since the couple had checked in that she had seen them wearing anything except Wimberly Place robes. Matching Hawaiian shirts and Gap cargo pants made for a nice change, she thought.

"We've come for some of your delicious eggs." Ashley flashed a dazzling smile. "Mr. Blenkensop just left and he said this morning's were the best ever." The young woman fingered the collar of her multicolored shirt. "But I'd like one of your omelets if you don't mind."

"Omelet?" Grace echoed. Oh, dang. She was expected to cook and there was no way to get out of doing her job. She didn't want the others to know that Theodora was being grilled in the next room, so she had to pretend everything was normal. "Uh, sure. Just give me a minute."

"We could use some more coffee, too," Mike said with a charming grin.

Grace shot a quick look at the closed office door. "Have you seen anyone come out of there?" she asked.

"Nope," Mike said. "It's been quiet as a tomb."

"A tomb, huh?" Grace frowned. That wasn't good. Not when Theodora was involved. She walked to the door, put her ear against the panel, and listened. A low murmur of voices sounded through the wood, but no one was yelling. Was that a good omen?

She went into the kitchen, cracked eggs into a clean bowl and whisked them, grabbed her other ingredients from the refrigerator, and started the omelet pan heating. She was getting faster. She carried orange juice to the Blakes and poured them more coffee then she sped back into the kitchen to finish the omelet. She slid the halved omelet onto two plates, added mango salsa, a touch of parsley and some cantaloupe slices then carried the hot plates to the Blakes hoping for the best. Could anyone call this a career, she wondered?

"Anyone come out of that office, yet?" she asked.

Mike was kissing Ashley, he grinned back at Grace. "Not a soul. Who were you expecting?"

Grace shrugged the question away. She grabbed two mugs from the Victorian sideboard, filled them with coffee, snagged the basket of muffins, and walked to the office door.

"Coffee time," she called out in a voice loud enough to reach Harper.

A chair scrapped the floor then the door swung open.

"Okay," Harper said. "You've stayed out longer than I had expected, and coffee would be good."

Grace looked over at Theodora who was pale but composed.

"How about some coffee and a muffin?" Grace asked.

"I'd rather have tea and a lawyer," Theodora said, looking wan but determined.

"Inn sitting sucks," Grace said to the empty kitchen. It was eleven o'clock and she had been double-timing it all morning. Pansy never showed for breakfast and Grace figured she was hiding out with Drew to avoid being quizzed by Harper.

Grace had called Theodora's lawyer in Marshall, Oregon and thought the man sounded out of his depth. He had mumbled something about locating a colleague to better assist Theodora then hung up. After this disappointment Grace served breakfast to the rest of the guests, cleaned up the kitchen and with the help of Sandy made all of the beds and put out fresh towels. She had just assigned Sandy to laundry duty when the phone rang with a call from Theodora's lawyer. Two minutes later Grace pounded on the office door where Harper was still questioning Theodora. She waited a minute then pushed her way inside.

"I can't believe you're still grilling this poor woman," Grace said to a frayed looking Harper.

"Grilling?" Harper broke into a grin, which gave him a boyish look. "It sounds like you've been reading Mickey Spillane."

"Why aren't you questioning Blenkensop or Mendelsohn? Both of them are better suspects than Theodora."

Grace glanced at Theodora and was shocked to see her friend's eyes had lost their usual sparkle. The woman looked exhausted and years older than yesterday.

"I have the name of your new lawyer in San Francisco." Grace walked to Theodora and gave her a slip of paper along with a hug. "He wants you in his office at three o'clock this afternoon." Grace turned and glared at Harper. "Which means I'm springing her right now."

"Springing her?" Harper laughed. The sound was warm and human and Grace liked him in spite of herself. "Mrs. Westmacott isn't under arrest. Her activities with the sweatshop haven't yet proved to be illegal. Immoral maybe, but not illegal."

"Don't say that, Sergeant." Theodora's voice quavered. "I never meant for anyone to be exploited.

"Then prove it by telling the truth. If you people would all just quit lying, I might get this mess sorted out."

"No one has lied to you Sergeant," Theodora said. "We may have forgotten to mention a few things, but lie? Never!" She flounced her beige tunic and looked toward the window with a stubborn set to her face.

"Theodora, wait and talk to your lawyer before saying another word." Grace realized she was giving this advice much too late.

"I've been telling her all morning that she can go just as soon as she explains to me her connection with Arnold Huxley and her movements on the day of his murder." Harper scowled at Theodora. "I want to know if that snake tried to blackmail you about the sweatshop."

"Don't answer that question," Grace snapped.

"When did you turn into Perry Mason?" Harper asked.

"You're trying to create a motive for Theodora to have murdered Huxley," Grace said. "I'm trying to protect her."

"No, Grace." Harper used her given name for the first time, and a shiver slid down Grace's spine. "You're being a pain in the butt."

"Come, Theodora." Grace took Theodora's hand and pulled her to her feet. "We're finished here." She put a firm hand to her friend's back and pushed her toward the door.

Theodora blinked, glanced at Harper then fled as if for her life.

"Hold on a minute, Mrs. Cassidy," Harper said. "I have something for you." He reached into his pocket and handed her a cameo earring. "One of my men picked up this little bauble in your room right after Huxley was murdered. I've been meaning to return it to you."

"Oh." Grace stared at the earring in surprise. She took a deep breath. Her life had been so complicated she couldn't even remember wearing earrings on the day of the murder. But she must have, there was Aunt Jewel's earring staring at her like a silent accusation.

"Thank you, Sergeant. I've been so busy I didn't even notice it was missing. I haven't bothered to put on jewelry. The earrings belonged to my great-great aunt. I would really hate to lose one." She smiled at him realizing he must have bent a few rules to get the cameo back to her before the case was closed. "I'm sorry if I've been a pain."

On sudden impulse she grinned impishly before fleeing to her room to put away the earring. She pulled a satin jewelry case from her dresser and poured the contents onto the bed.

Grace sucked in her breath.

In the jumble of gold metal and bright stones lay both of her cameo earrings.

Chapter 25

Grace pounded on Theodora's door with the cameo clutched in her hand. She knew that she should tell Harper that the earring found beside the body hadn't been hers, but for some reason she headed to Theodora instead. Maybe because she'd hid Huxley's tie in the refrigerator and it seemed two-faced to bring trouble to someone else. Especially if that someone was a friend, although Pansy seemed more the cameo type than Theodora. She pounded again. Theodora opened the door a crack.

"Oh, Grace. It's you. I'm so glad to see you. I thought..." Theodora was still wearing the beige shift and had not yet bothered with makeup. There were dark circles under her eyes and she had a haunted look about her.

"I think that Harper will let you alone for awhile." Grace walked into the room and held out the earring. "Does this belong to you?"

Theodora looked at the earring and raised an eyebrow.

"I'd never wear such an old fashioned thing, Grace dear. They simply aren't me. I once inherited some cameos, but I gave them to a niece that I like."

"Sergeant Harper found this one in my room after Mr. Huxley was murdered. He thought it belonged to me. I have very similar pair, but this one isn't mine, so I'm looking for the owner."

"It isn't mine, or Pansy's either. She never wears anything in her ears except pearls." Theodora raised her eyebrows and smiled. "Oh Grace. This earring is a real clue!"

"I agree, but who could it belong to?" Grace sat down on the bed. "Now, Theodora, I'm sharing information with you, and I need for you to tell me everything, and I mean *everything*. I already know that Huxley was blackmailing you about that Mexican sweatshop. So there's no need to embroider the truth."

Theodora's face changed into virtue itself.

"Don't look at me with those innocent eyes. If you don't fess up I'm not telling you another thing." She looked at Theodora and waited expectantly.

"Grace, I swear I didn't kill him. The man was dead when I went into your room. And he had on all of his clothes. I still can't imagine who might have stripped him naked or why. Pansy and I were shocked when you told us the body was naked. That's why we insisted on looking for ourselves." She frowned. "Anyway, how did you know I had already seen the body? Did Pansy blab?"

"Only after I twisted her arm. Why didn't you just call the police? Why did you let me become involved? Suspected?"

"My dear, isn't the answer obvious?" Theodora walked resignedly to her dressing table and sat down. Her reflection in the mirror watched Grace.

"Not to me. You pretended to be my friend, but you pulled me into this murder when it had nothing to do with me."

"The man was killed in your room. I know that's unfair, but it wasn't my fault. We were both victims. Besides, I didn't even know you then, and you were the only safe person to involve. You were the only person I knew for certain had not killed Huxley."

"You set me up because you knew I was innocent?" Grace knew she was being unreasonable, but she felt justified.

Theodora picked up a bottle of moisturizer, unscrewed the top, and began patting lotion on her face. "How could we know that Sergeant Harper would put you on his suspect list? The fact that you had no place to go certainly wasn't our fault, but we did help as much as we could."

"I feel like such a patsy." Grace smacked her fist into a velvet pillow. "Everything in my life turned to garbage at the same time. I hate my rotten luck!"

"I know darling, and I don't blame you one tiny bit for being angry. But please believe me. I didn't kill that poor man, although I was angry enough to do so."

Grace felt more frustrated than angry. After all, she had just met Theodora and Pansy. They owed her no loyalty on that first day.

"Okay, okay. But you owe me the truth about what happened," she said. "And I mean the complete and unvarnished truth. Make sure no inconvenient little details slip your mind."

Theodora took a deep breath and then blew it out slowly. "All right, if you insist. But I warn you, it's going to make you mad all over again, and I hate it when you yell at me. It's so un-Grace-like."

Grace grinned in spite of herself. "I'll try and hold on to my temper," she said. "Just don't skip any vital facts."

Theodora sighed, and then thought for a minute. "The whole mess was set into motion because of that wretched seascape of Drew's. I told Pansy that she should never have painted it." Theodora glanced at Grace then began patting concealer under her eyes. "She's a genius with copy work, you know."

"Pansy painted that beautiful seascape? But it looks so old." Grace thought about that for a minute. "Are you sure it isn't a Winslow Homer?"

"Of course, I saw the work while it was in process. I've always thought it such a shame that Pansy can't create original works. She's only gifted at making copies."

"This doesn't make any sense. Why lie and say the painting is real?" Grace sucked in her breath. "Was he only pretending that he wasn't going to sell it? Was there a scam going on?"

"With Drew involved? Never. The thing was, about a year ago Drew got behind on his rent because of all the medical bills, and Wimberly threatened to evict him. You know Wimberly, he wanted more than just Drew's word for collateral. So Pansy painted the picture, aged it, and in Wimberly's presence we all oohed and ahhed about how wonderful it was that Drew had been able to keep one treasure from his past." She picked up a magnifying mirror and studied her face.

"Don't you just hate your pores?" Theodora asked. "Mine are like craters and they look just ghastly! I think that maybe I have post menopausal acne." She touched one finger to a red spot on her chin.

"Theodora!" Grace yelled. "Quit worrying about your complexion and tell me about the picture."

"Of course darling," Theodora used a foam sponge to smooth foundation over her face, carefully covering the incipient pimple. "Wimberly almost wet his pants when he thought Drew had a real Winslow Homer. He was well ac-

quainted with Mendelsohn's greed for art and he thought
he'd cheat Drew out of a treasure and make a fortune selling
it." Theodora picked up a brush, dipped it into powder, and
began dusting her face.

"The bastard!" Grace said, and then bit her lip. Mama
would have been shocked. A lady never curses, Mama always
said.

"That's Wimberly. True to character he made Drew sign a
promissory note using the picture as collateral. Not that
Drew did anything illegal. He was very careful never to claim
on paper the picture had been painted by Winslow Homer.
He was equally careful to make enough payments to
Wimberly to prevent him collecting the painting. One look at
the seascape by an expert and the whole scheme would have
been exposed."

"Let me guess," Grace interrupted. "Gustav Mendelsohn
got impatient and went after the painting on his own."

"Bingo. Drew found himself in a really bad spot. He
couldn't sell the painting, because it was pretty much
worthless. He needed the illusion of authenticity to stay in
the inn. So he just refused to sell, and Pansy and I told everyone that it was one of those prideful, manly things, and
they bought it. Mendelsohn was eaten up with lust for the
painting so he hired Huxley to scrape up all of the dirt he
could on Drew with the intention of forcing him to sell. In the
process Huxley found out about me."

"Your connection with the Mexican sweatshop?" Grace
said.

"Oh, Grace. I'm so ashamed that I ever got messed up in
that dreadful scheme. I deluded myself into believing it was a
perfectly decent thing to do. It just shows you what terrible
things can be caused by greed." Her eyes began to tear and
she dropped her mascara wand.

"Hey, don't be so hard on yourself." Grace walked to the
vanity and handed her friend a tissue. "You didn't know what
that unscrupulous teacher had planned."

"But I should have. I have enough sense to know you
don't make large amounts of money doing good deeds for the
underprivileged. I just went into some sort of denial. I
wanted so badly for it to be all right." She dabbed at her eyes
with the already damp Kleenex.

"Welcome to the human race," Grace said.

"Indeed. Anyway, we all thought that room, your room, was going to be empty." She cast an accusing glance at Grace who smiled back. "It was hardly our fault that you showed up out of the blue and persuaded Mr. Wimberly to rent you an unfinished room. By that time there was no way to get word to Huxley." She threw an eyebrow pencil back into the jumbled heap of cosmetics. "That man is so greedy. If dear Beth hadn't been busy packing for Hawaii, you would never have convinced *her* to rent you such a room."

"I just wanted a place to sleep." Grace recalled how she had insisted to Wimberly that any room would be fine, finished or not.

"Well, Huxley asked me to meet him up in what we thought was a vacant room." She lowered her voice. "He had one of those gismos that opened locked doors, you know. I was supposed to bring money, and I did. But when I showed up, that awful man was already dead."

"And he was wearing his clothes. The murderer could have just finished killing Huxley, and slipped into the closet, waiting for you to leave."

"I thought of that, and still grow cold with fear over the thought."

"Yet you haven't told this to Sergeant Harper?"

"How could I? It gives both Pansy and Drew a motive to have murdered him. And it would let the cat out of the bag to Wimberly that the painting is worthless. That means Drew would no longer have the security of knowing he won't be asked to leave."

"I see your point." Grace thought a minute. "We must learn how Maxie fits into all of this. Obviously she knew who the murderer was and waited too long to tell anyone." The memory of the young woman and her delightful chanting made her heart ache. "There's much more to learn. Do you have any idea who this earring might belong to?"

"It could be Sydney Davenport's," Theodora said. "I saw her wearing such a pair once."

Chapter 26

Finding Sydney alone without Erwin was a problem. Grace couldn't remember seeing the couple apart. She pounded on Sydney's bedroom door suspecting that Erwin would also be there. When Sydney answered and flashed her endearing homely smile Grace's heart twisted.

"Hi, I wonder if I could speak to you in private?" Grace forced a smile feeling much like Benedict Arnold.

"Of course," Sydney wore a red and white-stripped tunic, red latex pants and white Nike's. She reminded Grace of a mammoth barber pole. Sydney turned and called over her shoulder to Erwin. "I'll be back in just a minute, darling."

"The guest's sitting room happens to be empty just now, perhaps we could talk there?" Grace led the way down to the landing. She glanced around to make certain no one was listening. "I wanted to ask you if this was your earring." She held out the cameo.

A bright smile spread over Sydney's face.

"I've been looking everywhere for that," Sydney said with a smile, and then she frowned. "Why didn't you just give it to me? Why bring me down to the sitting room?"

"Because Sergeant Harper found this earring in my room beside Arnold Huxley's body. He gave it to me thinking it was mine."

Color drained from Sydney's face.

"Oh, my God," She said. "Oh, my God." Tears sprang into her pale blue eyes. "I didn't kill that man, Grace. I swear I didn't."

"What time were you in my room?"

All color left Sydney's face. "I wasn't there—why would I be in your room?"

The lie was so obvious and the woman so panicked that pity touched Grace's heart, but she couldn't afford to soften."

"Then Erwin must have dropped it when he visited Huxley, who was a blackmailer."

"No, no. Erwin is a total straight shooter, and the kindest man I've ever met. When Mrs. Quick insisted on Maxie being fired at Halcyon, Erwin found the poor girl a job here."

"Come on, Sydney. Huxley was blackmailing you, wasn't he?"

The tears stopped and Sydney glared at Grace. "He was already dead when I went upstairs to meet him. The room was supposed to be empty. I'd never have gone if I had known you had moved in." She shot Grace an accusatory look as if the murder could have been avoided if only she had stayed somewhere else.

"Why was he blackmailing you?" Grace asked refusing to be sidetracked by defending her choice of inns.

"Oh that dreadful man, he said early Californians mined for gold, but he mined for dirt—human dirt—and he bragged that he always found it. Can you imagine anyone being so evil? He threatened to tell Erwin unless I paid him money for his silence."

"Sydney, if you didn't kill him, you're a victim here. I don't want to hurt you. But you must tell me what Huxley was blackmailing you about."

Sydney clapped a hand over her mouth while tears leaked down her cheeks.

"I'm not asking so I can spread the information around. If your secret has nothing to do with these murders I won't even tell Harper. I promise."

"Why not just give the earring back to me?" Sydney pleaded.

"Because Harper thinks that I might be the murderer."

Sydney's expression clouded and she stuck out her bottom lip, much like an oversized child determined to have her own way.

"What I should do is give this piece of evidence back to Harper." Grace watched Sydney swallow and seem to shrink in size.

"Very well. Since you put it that way I suppose I have no choice." Her eyes accused Grace of cruelty to elderly people. "It was almost ten years ago," Sydney dropped her gaze. "An indiscretion of my early fifties, Mother had just died and I was feeling so terribly lonely," she heaved a sigh.

"I'm sorry. I know what it's like to lose your mother." Grace fished a clean tissue from her pocket and handed it to Sydney who dabbed her eyes and took a deep breath.

"Huxley somehow learned that I had an affair with Wilbur Wimberly during that sad time all those years ago."

"What?" Grace said then immediately regretted the word when Sydney's face flushed a deep red.

"It was a terrible mistake and Huxley made it sound so ugly, as if I slept with every man I came across while nursing a patient. Such an accusation could even harm my career. Most of my clients were elderly and very conservative." Sydney swallowed and Grace's heart went out to her.

"So, Mrs. Wimberly was sick back then?" Grace asked.

"Not our dear Beth. It was Wimberly's mother. She was an evil old thing and was ill with congestive heart failure. A tyrant of a woman, she was." Sydney shuddered. "But Wimberly seemed such a devoted son that his concern touched my heart. Later I realized that like many bullies, he was just scared of his mama. But as I said, it was a bad time for me. I was lonely. Wimberly came on so smoothly, and I wasn't accustomed to attention from men. I just sort of folded under his charm."

Charm? Grace bit her lip to keep from speaking the word aloud. She stretched up to put her arm around the tall woman and patted her shoulder. If Huxley was gouging money out of Sydney, what would prevent him from extracting it from Wimberly? Wimberly was the only person who knew she was renting the unfinished room. Had he agreed to the rental in order to deliberately set her up? She put the thought on a back-burner to ponder later.

"Then I met Erwin during his wife's final illness. She was a very difficult patient, but he was a real gentleman." Sydney's face relaxed into pure happiness. "We were just perfect together. At long last I have found my dream-man." She sighed and looked down at Grace. "But I never told Erwin about Wilbur Wimberly and myself. My Erwin is a bit old fashioned and would never understand about my having an affair with a married man."

"Then why did you agree to vacation here at the inn?" Grace asked.

"Because this is where Erwin likes to stay," Sydney said, as if that explained everything. She cast a worried glance upward toward her bedroom door. "I want to keep my man happy. I would have paid all the money I have to keep Erwin from knowing about Wimberly." She dropped her voice to a whisper. "And for sure Erwin wouldn't understand about giving into a blackmailer. Now remember that you promised not to tell anyone, Grace."

Grace looked at the plain face alight with trust. Her heart sank. If only she would be able to keep that promise.

"What time was your appointment?" Grace asked.

"At 3:30. That horrible man was already dead. I almost had a heart attack. Then I fled back to my room and prayed no one would think I was involved. I swear it."

"Was he naked when you saw him?" Grace asked.

"No, he was fully clothed—even wore a tie—if you can believe that. I was astonished to learn that he was found naked later." Sydney's voice dropped to a conspiratorial and sympathetic tone. "No one blames you for murdering that evil man, but none of us can understand why you took his clothes." Her smile turned condescending. "Perhaps you don't know about dental records, dear. They identify a body every time."

"Thanks for the tip," Grace said dryly, as her thoughts sped to other questions. This jibed with what Theodora had told her the truth, at least about Huxley's clothes. But why in the world did the killer come back and strip the body? It made no sense. What could be so important about some second-hand clothing? Or had people come in and out of the room so quickly the murderer didn't have time to leave the closet and finish the job? Or even worse, was Theodora the one hiding in the closet?

Sydney patted her chest and blew out a relieved breath. "Oh, my. I think I feel better for having unburdened myself. And it's so comforting to know that you've promised never to tell the police."

Grace opened her mouth to protest when the doorbell rang.

"Well I know you have to get on with your duties," Sydney said. "I'll just run back upstairs."

"I didn't exactly promise," Grace called after her. The doorbell rang several times in succession and she sighed at the visitor's impatience.

"But you did," Sydney's words trailed after her, reminding Grace of a little girl's plea.

"I said I'd try." Then Grace realized she was talking to herself. She ran to the bottom of the stairs, threw open the door and cried out in delight.

Her six-foot-two son stood on the porch with his duffel bag in one hand and his laptop in the other. A big grin lighted his face. "Oh, Brand!" Grace threw her arms around the young man and held him close. He laid his cheek against the top of her head and hugged back without dropping his luggage.

Was he really there or was she hallucinating? Either way was bliss, so she stood silently feeling the strength of his young muscles and breathing in the smell of him. Rejoicing.

"You didn't call, so I thought you didn't care."

"Your email surprised the shit out of me," Brand said. "I knew you were in big trouble or you would never have braved the internet. I know how much you hate it. I didn't call again on purpose because I didn't want to spend the money." He kissed her on top of her head and drew back to grin down at her.

Grace's heart swelled with pure joy and she grinned back. Brand! Her baby had come to be with her.

"How on earth did you manage to buy a ticket? How did you find me here?" Grace drunk in the sight of her son: his long blond hair tumbled across his eyes, his scruffy jeans and faded University of Oklahoma sweatshirt with arms and neck cut away, were just as she remembered. The unkempt child of her heart had never looked better to his mother. She hugged him again and felt the warmth of his body. Only now did she realize how desperately she missed and needed him.

"I'm glad to have you home," she said. And strangely enough, even in a bartered inn hundreds of miles from Oklahoma, she knew that they were a family once again and wherever they were would indeed be home.

"How did you know where to find me? And where did you get the money to travel?" Grace stood on tiptoe to kiss his cheek.

"I had an open return ticket to Tulsa, so when I got there I called Mabel. You know, Dad's office manager? She told me some of the shit that was going on and where you were staying. I sold my high school ring so I could buy a ticket on out to San Francisco. Then I thumbed a ride here." He put his bag on the floor and carefully laid the laptop beside it.

"But Brand, that ring was fourteen caret gold and had a real ruby in it. You loved that ring."

"It doesn't matter now. What's bothering me is that Dad ran off with some bimbo and left you without any money. My own father is nothing but a crook—and after all of the lectures he gave me." Brand shook his head, his young eyes bright with hurt and indignation.

"It sounds like Mabel told you a lot." Grace pulled her boy into the hallway and cast a glance down the dark foyer. Now wasn't the time run into Wimberly. Brand dragged his stuff through the door.

"Yeah, and it looks like I've got a shitload of trouble to straighten out." Brand looked around the hallway with a determined expression.

"Yes. And it's wonderful to have you here to help me." Grace gave her son another quick hug, her heart swelling with pride. The two of us will manage just fine. You'll see. Other things have happened, too, here at the inn. I'd better fill you in on the details." She glanced toward Wimberly's quarters at the back of the house.

"You mean that murder shit? Mabel said something about that too, but that couldn't have anything to do with us."

"Could you please use another word? Preferably one that contains more than four letters?" She reached up and tousled his hair.

"Oh yeah," Brand said. "Sorry about that. I forgot you don't like the word shit."

"Actually, I have nothing against it when used in moderation. I've heard that the word started as an acronym for 'ship high in transit,' and was once used to mark crates of manure being transported aboard ships. But that could just be another urban legend."

"Really?" Brand frowned. "Where do you hear this sh..., 'er, stuff? On the history channel?"

"Never mind, you must be starving. Come back to the kitchen and I'll fix you something to eat." She grinned at him. "Breakfast has become my specialty for these folks at the inn, and it's what you're going to get right now."

"You're working as a cook?"

Grace smiled at her son's expression. He couldn't have looked more shocked if she had told him she was keeping a bordello.

"And as a housekeeper and office manager and whatever else might be needed at the moment."

"No shit?" Brand gazed at his mother in admiration. "That's awesome."

Grace opened her mouth to correct his language when footsteps pounded down the staircase. Her heart lurched. *Please don't let it be Wimberly.* She looked up to see Sandy racing down the staircase dressed in black cutoffs and chartreuse tube-top and sighed with relief. Even Sandy was better than Wimberly.

"Well, hi there." Sandy's voice played the flirt and her gaze fused to Brand's body. "Who are you and where did you come from?"

"Sandy, I'd like you to meet my son, Brand. He'll be staying with me for a few days, but I haven't cleared his visit with Mr. Wimberly and his presence needs to be our little secret. At least for right now."

"Your son? No shit?" Sandy said with a broad smile, her eyes never leaving Brand's face.

At least these two young people speak the same language, Grace thought.

Chapter 27

Grace woke up in the middle of the night during a weird dream. In it she had struggled to hang Drew's painting over a table when her mother appeared and insisted she exchange the beautiful seascape for a framed road map. Very strange.

The distant hall clock chimed twice. Only three more hours and it would be time to roll out of bed and begin breakfast, again. She rolled over and tried to settle back into sleep.

Brand's rhythmic breathing from a pallet on the floor brought a smile to her lips. It was good to have her son back in her life, even if she hadn't yet broken the news to Wimberly that he was there.

She had worried about Brand's reaction when he learned they would have to sleep in the room where Huxley was murdered.

"Murdered? Right here in this room?" he had said. "Cool. Wait until I tell all of my friends."

Then she remembered her half-million-dollar debt back in Tulsa and frowned. There was no way she could pay back that kind of money, at least not working as a substitute inn sitter. She had laughed about her huge debt to Brand, making light of the whole mess in an effort to dispel his panic. And somehow the laughing had eased her worries, then. But now her precarious situation came back with the force of night-terrors. She would spend the rest of her life in poverty and debt. To escape the burden she thought again of the dream.

She hated roadmaps. The wretched things seemed difficult to read and almost impossible to refold correctly, at least for her. Grace's first attempt at map reading had been in the fourth grade when her class assignment had been to plot a trip from Tulsa to Chicago without parental help. Most of the kids had taken to the task like ducks to water, but Grace thought it was an assignment from hell. She spent the evening pouring over the map. She cried until her sinuses clogged, then went to bed in a state of hopeless desperation. When she awoke in the morning, she knew exactly how the map worked. Mama had said it was her subconscious mind answering a question asked right before falling asleep. In the fourth grade, Grace had considered it a miracle.

"Okay, subconscious," Grace breathed softly. "What happened to the dead guy's clothes?" She rolled over and fell into a sound sleep. When the alarm went off at five, Grace knew exactly what had happened to Arnold Huxley's clothes. What ticked her off was that it had taken her so long to figure it out.

She had looked at the problem the wrong way around.

"Is it time to get up?" Brand groaned and started to rise.

"Go back to sleep," she whispered. "And remember to stay in this room, at least for now. I'll bring you some breakfast when I can."

She jumped out of bed and headed for the shower, treading carefully through Brand's trail of clothes leading from the bathroom. Her mind raced ahead and her movements were on autopilot.

Huxley's body had been too clean. The room and the bed were too clean. The air she breathed while looking at the body was too clean. That damned potpourri smell. She had noticed it immediately, but had given the fragrance no serious thought at the time, and she should have. It now seemed obvious that her room must have been cleaned and then hosed down with deodorizing spray after the murder had taken place.

She remembered now that Maxie's dead body stunk to high heaven. She had walked into the room and spotted Maxie lying on the bed, her neck at a right degree angle, her skin the color of gray wax. But the most vivid memory was the stench. Maxie had soiled herself when she died. Arnold Huxley had been immaculate. He had been too clean.

Had Sergeant Harper made this connection, Grace wondered? She lathered apple-scented shampoo into her hair. Maybe. The man had a mind like a stainless steel food processor and he missed very little. She remembered the mustard colored tie hidden in Wimberly's crisper and frowned. Harper would have a cow when he found out.

Grace turned off the steaming water and grabbed a thick white towel. There was only one person who could have managed the cleanup without being noticed and that was Maxie.

Grace figured that the young woman just did what she had been trained to do at her former job, she cleaned up after the dead. Maxie would have thought it normal to strip the bed, replace the linen, and bundle up the soiled laundry. Only later would she have realized she made a mistake. The poor thing must have panicked and decided to carry the dirty clothes back to her own apartment and hide them in the Dumpster. It would have been very like Maxie to separate the filthy items from the unsoiled ones. His wallet and papers were probably under a mound of garbage at the city dump.

Harper's machine-gun questions about the murdered man's clothes probably terrified Maxie, and she was too scared to confess her mistake. Later the young woman had tried to confess to Grace.

I've done something bad, Missus. Grace remembered Maxie's words and guilt swept through her. She should have paid attention. How she wished she had listened when she had had the chance.

If Maxie let Huxley inside Wimberly Place he must have tricked her someway. Or perhaps she unexpectedly saw him on the stairs? That would have been when she dropped the supplies. Yet that didn't make sense. She would have told someone immediately. Of course Mendelsohn, greedy for the seascape, might have let him in. She should already have considered that.

Grace broke free from her reverie, finger combed her hair, and decided to let the curls dry naturally. Clothes were becoming a problem, too. Everything suitable for work needed to be washed. After looking in her almost bare closet, she pulled on navy linen pants and a yellow silk shirt, leaving her thrift-store shorts and a red T-shirt soaking in the lavatory. She'd find a minute to rinse them out later, and hang them in the shower to dry for tomorrow. But now breakfast needed cooking.

It was a darned shame that her subconscious mind seemed able to handle only one question at a time.

All of her guests seemed to have plans, so breakfast was over earlier than usual. Even Theodora was up and about. Grace glanced at her watch. Ten o'clock. Sandy had just volunteered to carry a tray up to Brand, acting so obviously secretive that Grace feared everyone in the inn would catch on to her son's presence.

After Theodora and Pansy left for their Tai chi class, Grace stacked the plates in the sink and ran hot water over them. At that exact moment it occurred to her that the ideal place to house Brand would be with Drew. Just the thought made her feel better.

Drew would be perfect to keep Brand while the two of them were stranded in California. His was a private apartment and therefore could have guests. And better still, Drew was the kind of person Brand would respect. He was the ideal grandfather figure and would be a positive influence on her son. Grace felt sure that Drew wouldn't mind having a young man sleeping on his floor.

She ran back upstairs and found Brand sitting before his laptop with Sandy standing behind him watching the screen like some sort of techno groupie.

"Sandy, I need you downstairs cleaning up the kitchen," Grace said in her best no-nonsense voice.

"I'll do that just as soon as Brand finishes getting this information about the Cayman Islands," Sandy said. "The two of us may fly there and try to find his dad."

"What?" Grace almost yelled.

"I may fly there," Brand said with a quick grin at his mother.

"Really?" Grace's voice was edged with skepticism, but she put off asking what he planned to use for money. "Well, right now Sandy is flying downstairs to earn her living. First she has to clean up the kitchen then she's doing the marketing." Grace opened the door and pointed.

"I'll see you later, Brand," Sandy said with a shrug and strolled out.

"Brand, we have enough problems right now without adding Sandy to the list," Grace said.

"Hey Mom, she's the one hanging around me. I'm just looking for a cheap ticket so I can track down Dad and get this mess straightened out."

"Right now you need to pack your clothes and come downstairs with me. I want you to stay with a permanent lodger in the basement." She lowered her voice. "I think I'm close to knowing who's the murderer."

"You do? Who?"

"Later," his mother answered. "When I'm sure."

Ten minutes later the two of them were standing in front of the entrance to the basement apartments with Brand's gear stacked beside them. Grace pounded on the outside door hoping to raise one of the tenants.

"I can let you in this door, but there ain't no use knocking at Drew's," a quavering voice spoke from behind. They turned to see a grizzled old woman who looked to be pushing a hundred, coming around the corner. She pulled a faded red wagon filled with a colorful mixture of odds and ends. A variety of aluminum cans, a pair of used yellow Keds with their laces neatly knotted together, a child's blue T-shirt trimmed in lace, and two badly thumbed Sue Grafton paperbacks were tumbled together in a cheerful looking heap.

"You must be Mrs. Murphy," Grace said, noticing an intelligent glint in the faded blue eyes.

"That would be me. Mrs. Aloysius Alpin Murphy." The old woman pulled a key from her pocket and jabbed it into the lock. "Drew ain't here. He's down to the beach taking a walk with his woman, but he always keeps an extra key under the mat right in front of his door. You could wait inside his place if you wanted. The key's for his woman, you know, but he won't care if you use it."

"Been Dumpster diving?" Brand grinned and pointed at the wagon. "That's the way I managed to move out of the dorm and into an apartment last semester at school."

"You what?" Grace said. Something Mrs. Murphy had said needed thinking about, but Brand's speech disrupted her concentration and she couldn't remember what it was.

"I got into Dumpster diving. Lots of the kids do that to get by. There's some great stuff that people throw away." Brand grinned at his mother. "Guess things have changed a lot since you were a kid, huh Mama?"

"This young man's right about the Dumpster," Mrs. Murphy said. "It's just crammed full of fine things. What I can't sell someone around here can always use." She shot Grace a hard look. "You wouldn't believe what folks throw away, and most of it is good stuff."

Grace sucked in a hard breath.

"Did you recently find a mustard colored tie in a Dumpster?" Grace asked.

"As a matter of fact I did." Mrs. Murphy jerked the door open and pulled at her wagon. "I pick up lots of ties. People don't wear them much anymore and they're always chucking them into the trash. It was an ugly thing so I gave it away." The back wheels locked on the door jam and Brand squatted to lift the wagon clear for her.

Ugly, perhaps, Grace thought. But mustard was a shade of yellow and Maxie might have loved it.

"Did you give it to the pet thrift shop at Five Oaks?" Grace grasped Mrs. Murphy's arm to keep her from escaping into her own apartment.

"Sure did. I do anything I can to help out those sweet little dogs and cats. I like animals better than I like most people." She tried to move away but Grace held fast.

"Me too," Brand said. "I had a cat when I was a little kid. She died when I was in high school, but I'm going to get another one when I graduate."

"Where did you find the tie?" Grace asked, ignoring Brand and trying to keep Mrs. Murphy on the subject.

"Well, let's see." Mrs. Murphy stroked her chin and frowned. "That would be the apartment building at fifth and Madison. Not one of those big complexes, but a nice little cinder-block affair. I learned about the place from that retarded girl who used to work here, she lived there until someone killed her the other day. But I guess you already knew that." The old woman pulled her arm loose from Grace with a surprising show of strength.

"You get yourself busy now, missy. You and me both got our chores to take care of." Mrs. Murphy paused a minute and beamed at Brand. "And if this good looking young fella intends to bunk in with Drew, I'm sure he'll be more than welcome. Drew's always taking in one stray or the other." She walked away rattling her wagon behind her.

"Come on, Brand." Grace reached under the mat and fished out the key. "You heard the woman." She unlocked the door and pushed her way into Drew's apartment feeling uncomfortably like a housebreaker. "I'll just write him a note explaining everything."

"Are you sure my moving in without permission is okay?" Brand asked. "Who is this old guy, anyway?"

"He's a good friend, and you're going to like him. You can leave your stuff here and we'll walk down to the beach and see if we can find him."

"If you say so." He opened a closet door and stashed his gear.

"I'll lock up and put the key back where it was." Grace sat down to write the note and Brand stepped outside. When she joined him, Sandy was also there. Gage sighed.

"Brand and I have to go now, Sandy."

"Can I come along?" Sandy said.

"It's just an errand," Grace answered.

"Well, I'm glad it isn't anything important," Sandy said. "I thought I'd talk Brand into coming to the market with me so he could carry the heavy stuff back."

"Sure, if you really need me. Mom can probably handle this errand better by herself." He grinned at his mother. "I'd just soon not be present when you beg a bed for me."

"Okay. I guess I can understand your embarrassment. Go along with Sandy and enjoy yourself." Grace glanced at gray clouds gathering overhead. "But it looks like rain, so be careful not to get soaked."

"Mom! I just got back from a trip to Europe. All by myself." His ears turned a bright pink.

Sandy rolled her eyes and Grace laughed.

"So take off," she said. "And have a good time." She turned in the opposite direction and headed toward the beach.

The storm clouds thickened. Grace walked briskly toward the beach, and Mrs. Murphy's words echoed in her mind. She stopped. Her breath caught in her throat.

"Dear God," she breathed aloud. "Now I remember what Mrs. Murphy said that seemed wrong."

Chapter 28

A monstrous idea popped into Grace's mind and her first reaction was denial. She walked three blocks arguing with herself then realized that concrete evidence was what she needed. She abandoned the search for Drew, and sprinted after a city bus pulling up at the corner. She managed to leap aboard just before the bus belched carbon monoxide and moved on.

Grace braced herself, feet apart, against the motion of the vehicle and dug change from her purse. She quizzed the fortyish male driver about directions then dropped coins into the meter. She accepted a transfer needed for another bus and lurched her way to a seat in the back. She needed thinking time.

Mrs. Murphy had called Pansy, "Drew's woman." Grace remembered her own grandmother using that phrase and to Grandma it had always translated into "wife," never the modern "girl friend." Since Mrs. Murphy was from Grandma's era, it was possible that Drew and Pansy were married. If they were, then not only the picture, but also their marriage was also motive for murder.

Theodora said that Pansy collected megabucks in alimony from her evil-tempered ex-husband who had loved abusing the little blonde. He had fought Pansy leaving him and the alimony payments should have stopped if and when Pansy and Drew married. The stories Theodora told about Pansy's ex described a man who wouldn't hesitate to file criminal charges against a former wife who had crossed him. And Grace felt sure that the calm and sensible Drew would kill to prevent Pansy from going to prison or coming to any harm. The man worshiped her.

The thought of Drew as a murderer, made Grace heart-sick. But, the truth was, she barely knew the man and as a SEAL, he would have been trained to kill. Grace shivered, and hugged herself for warmth. Of all the people at Wimberly Place, she had trusted Drew the most. Not because of anything he said, but because of the very essence of the man, himself. She closed her eyes for a minute and admitted the truth to herself. She loved him because he reminded her so much of her father. *But Daddy would never have killed Maxie.* Huxley maybe but not Maxie, yet and her instinct could be wrong. After all, she'd married Charlie. And what if Drew and Pansy weren't married? Maybe she was making a mountain out of a molehill, as Mama used to say. She searched her mind for another solution.

Pansy said that many people passed by Huxley's body, and Grace suspected that was the truth. Theodora and Sydney for certain and there could have been others. Mendelsohn certainly had a motive. It was no stretch to visualize the suave German committing murder, either to save himself or for gain. Huxley could easily have turned on him and blackmailed his own client. Blenkensop seemed unlikely, but unlikely people probably did commit murder. If he had stolen software from a hapless teen, and wanted to hide that knowledge, he was definitely in the running. She needed to consider every possibility.

Wimberly's smirking face leapt into her mind, and this was a suspect she enjoyed pondering. She should have given him more thought earlier. He was the person who had rented her the unfinished room, although he pretended reluctance. He could have watched her leave, and then killed Huxley. Then Grace frowned. Much as she would have liked Wimberly to be the culprit, she couldn't imagine him doing anything so physical. It seemed more likely he would have bored the man to death.

Grace sighed. How did Maxie's murder fit in with Huxley's? Maxie must have seen the murderer on that fateful day. For some reason she wasn't killed at the time, perhaps because the killer thought the maid wasn't clever enough to understand the truth, or else that she would keep her mouth shut. But that would mean the killer was someone she knew and cared about. Drew fit that profile perfectly. Grace shut her eyes tight. She hated such thoughts, but they wouldn't stop coming.

The bus rumbled on and the jolting rhythm of the movement seemed somehow to comfort Grace and help her organize her thoughts. She frowned, concentrating on Maxie.

Drew would have hated killing Maxie, and first tried to reason with her. But no one had planned on Grace unex-

pectedly winning Maxie's trust. The maid's sudden attachment to her had surprised even Grace. Such an unexpected
event might have panicked Drew into desperate action.

Regret swept through her heart and settled into her soul.
Maxie, sweet and innocent and trusting. Once again strains
of the young woman's singing sounded in her memory. Grace
pressed her hands against her ears, but the music wouldn't
stop. Grace steeled herself for the task at hand, and the fact
that a dear friend might be the murderer.

She glanced outside at the darkening clouds and shivered. If Drew or Theodora proved to be the villain, then she
could no longer trust her own judgment. Brand's appearance
was wonderful, but had she put him in danger? She frowned.
Maybe she should send him away. But where could he go?
She had no money and no close relatives. You couldn't dump
a nineteen-year-old man with casual friends when he
couldn't even be trusted to pick up after himself. Besides,
something about the new Brand told her he wouldn't leave if
he thought his mother was in danger.

The library looked as if it had been built in the 1970's, old
enough to be dirty but too new to have any character. She
hated the place until she walked inside and smelled the
books. Then she sighed and relaxed. It was a library. One of
the places she loved most in the whole world, ugly or not. It
was like coming home.

Grace engaged the help of a middle-aged librarian
wearing a brown shirtwaist dress and sensible shoes. The
woman set her up to scan the local paper for marriage list-
ings. She began a year ago and then worked backwards.
When she reached five years past she gave up and walked
over to the librarian.

"If a couple wanted to get married, didn't want to travel
far, and yet needed to avoid a listing in the local paper, how
could they accomplish that feat?"

The woman brushed back a wisp of gray hair from her
face, and thought a minute without even looking surprised.
Grace figured that librarians got all sorts of weird questions.

"The happy couple could drive to Oakland. Their marriage would be listed in that city's paper instead of ours."

"Do you have any copies of Oakland's paper?" Grace asked.

Forty-five minutes later Grace had the information she needed. She thanked the librarian and stepped out of the building into a heavy downpour.

"Perfect, now the weather matches my life!" She had no choice but to step into the storm and head toward the bus stop. Water streamed down, and it was like walking through a car wash. Hair plastered against her face and she pushed the soaked strands away. It was just as well she hadn't wasted any time on blow-drying that morning. "Half my kingdom for an umbrella," she said and then grinned. Who would want half of the world's largest debt, she wondered? Suddenly something moved under her foot and an indignant meow caused her to stumble on the last library step.

"Oh, shit!" she reverted to Brand's language and then gave a wry smile at her own hypocrisy. A soaked orange-striped tiger kitten yowled at her feet. He looked wet, angry and hungry. Worst of all he looked pitiful and forlorn and more than a little loveable.

"Sorry sugar," Grace said to the cat. "I didn't see you. Are you hurt?" It meowed again and she tried to step around the animal but the kitty moved with her, twining itself around her feet as she walked, almost tripping her.

"Mew?" The sound was no longer angry, and seemed almost a question.

"Look kitty, who do you belong to?" Grace asked, glancing around for another bystander who might be persuaded to take responsibility for the stray. All she saw was rain and cars. She looked back at the thin cat. "The answer to that question seems obvious," she said listening to the fast moving traffic. "Someone dumped you here, didn't they?" Anger washed through her. "Odious person!" she said trying to redeem her vocabulary. "How can anyone be so cruel?"

The cat mewed his agreement and continued to move with her as she tried to walk. Grace edged toward the bus stop and the animal followed underfoot.

"Hey sweet guy," Grace said. "You can't come with me. I'm practically homeless myself." She looked up and saw the city bus moving toward her. "Besides, that bus driver would never let me take you aboard."

"Meow?" the cat answered, and Grace could hear him purring through the noise of the engines.

"Maybe someone else will come along. I haven't asked, but I'm pretty sure that Wimberly has a "no cats" rule."

But instead of a kind stranger rescuing the kitten, a picture of the soft bundle of fur crushed under a bus wheel flashed vividly into Grace's mind. At that exact moment the cat began licking her leg with his rough tongue, purring louder.

"You're such a sweetie, but I can't rescue you."

The bus was almost upon them. The cat looked up at Grace, eyes large and round and helpless.

"Oh, what the heck!" Grace said. She picked up the cat, dropped him inside her oversized purse, and stepped aboard the bus.

Chapter 29

"He's adorable." Theodora sat in a kitchen chair, looking at the cat. "But you'll have to hide him from Wimberly."

Theodora wore black pants and a puce and teal flowing top, complete with her favorite jet beads. Grace supposed this costume was what Theodora considered her business attire since she had donned it to drive to San Francisco later in the afternoon to once again visit her newest attorney. The woman looked drained and frightened and Grace's heart ached for her friend.

"I'll figure a way around Wimberly," Grace said. "It will be nice to have the little guy around. He'll be a distraction."

The kitten stood before a Maritime Rose Haviland saucer lapping milk that Grace had warmed in the microwave.

"It was raining. Someone was going to run over the poor thing."

"It's stopped raining now," Theodora said with a teasing smile.

"Too late." Grace laughed. "I'm in love."

Grace wondered where her much larger stray was just now. She hadn't seen hide or hair of Brand since he and Sandy had left the inn hours ago. "Anyway, what else could I do? He was homeless."

"Like you," Theodora said in a soft, indulgent voice.

"Yes," Grace said. "Like me."

"What about..." Theodora cleared her throat. "Kitty facilities?"

"Potting soil for now," Grace reached under the sink and pulled out a plastic bag. "Wimberly will never know, and this will be fine until I can buy some real litter." She grabbed an empty raisin-bran box from the counter. "I have a tray all prepared."

"See?" she said. "I removed a side panel and taped the ends together. It's going to work just great." She poured dirt into the box and carried it to a small opening between the refrigerator and the stove. "I'll just slip my handy-dandy little kitty-pot into this nook until I can find the right minute to sneak everything upstairs."

"What are you going to name him?" Theodora asked.

"An apt name would be Trouble," Grace said with a wry smile. "But I'll talk it over with Brand, and he can help me decide. He's a special cat and needs a special name."

Later, back in her room, Grace found herself talking to the cat, a sure sign of how lonely she was.

"I'm going to smack your roomie Brand until his teeth rattle," Grace said to Trouble/Whatever, dropping the purring kitten onto the floor of her bedroom and setting his litter tray in a corner. The cat meowed and rubbed against Grace's ankles.

"I'm not kidding. It's two o'clock and I haven't seen him or his friend Sandy. "And where are my groceries? Just when I'd had a moment's hope that Brand might be maturing he pulls a trick like this."

The orange cat meowed again, jumped up on Grace's bed and began kneading the chenille bedspread with his claws.

"That's right, you settle yourself down for a nap, I've got to call Sergeant Harper and eat a large piece of humble-pie." The kitten looked at Grace and blinked. "Nasty tasting stuff, humble-pie." Grace sat on the bed and dialed the portable phone she had carried from the kitchen. "This particular pie you wouldn't like. Cats hate it even more than humans, and God knows that we hate the taste with a passion." It took almost ten minutes of dangling on the phone to find out that Harper was unavailable. She left him a message to call her as soon as possible.

Grace watched the kitten close his eyes and nod off to sleep. She smiled, thinking how pleased Brand would be when he saw the animal then frowned when she remembered her new theory on the murders. She desperately needed to bounce her ideas off of someone, but every person she knew seemed to be connected with the murder, either directly or indirectly. That thought left Grace feeling the sharp edge of loneliness. She reached over to touch the cat for comfort and felt his motor start.

She glanced at her watch. Running an inn was something that wouldn't turn loose of her. She had managed to get the place tidied up, but it looked as if those kids weren't going to turn up with the pastry she had ordered, and that meant she needed to stir up something for afternoon tea. Sandy might just find her little butt fired if she wasn't careful. But first Grace needed to retrieve Brand's gear from Drew's apartment. With her new fears about Drew she wanted to distance those two as quickly as possible.

Grace ran downstairs then outside to the basement apartments and pounded on the door. If Drew didn't answer, she'd just get the key from under the mat, and pick up Brand's stuff. No one needed to be the wiser.

Drew opened the outside door with a scowl on his face. He had notes pinned to his shirt as if he had been working on his book. When he saw Grace he grinned.

"Hey there little girl. I've been missing your company. Where have you been keeping yourself?"

"With my nose right against the grindstone," Grace said trying to keep things light. "I guess you've figured out that the gear stowed in your closet belongs to Brand? I've come to drag his junk back up to my room and out of your way."

"Come in, come in. No need to apologize for anything. Mrs. Murphy gave me a glowing report of your son and said he was to bunk in with me. It'll be nice to have a young man around for awhile. I don't mind in the least. But what things are you talking about?"

"We dumped his duffel bag and laptop in your closet this morning. Maybe you haven't happened across them yet." She managed a stiff smile, trying to keep the charm going. "But I've decided that Brand and I need to spend more time together so we can get reacquainted. I've come to retrieve his things and take them back to my room."

"Are you sure you don't want him to stay down here? You could still see him as much as you wanted, and Wimberly wouldn't be able to give you a hard time about keeping the boy."

The garden gate creaked and Grace turned to see Walter, the gardener, walking toward them frowning. He pulled off his ball cap and wiped sweat from his forehead. He was carrying his softball bat so Grace figured he was on his way either to or from practice with the Golden Oldies Team.

"Hi, Grace. I didn't expect to see you out here. That cop fella just stepped inside the front door. Did you know he was here?"

"No thanks for telling me. I'll run up and see what he wants," Grace said, ignoring Walter's question. Grace's heart raced. The station must have forwarded her message, but she didn't want Drew to know she was suspicious. I'll take a raincheck on that coffee."

"Sure thing," Drew said.

Grace decided to worry about Brand's luggage later. She might even get Harper to come back with her, she mused as she ran back to the kitchen.

It was the first time she could remember being glad to see Harper. He slouched at the kitchen table leaning back in his chair with one foot extended, the other tucked beneath his chair. He had helped himself to a cup of the coffee left warming on the counter. His dark eyes locked with hers and she caught her breath. She thought about flashing her version of a dazzling smile, but was afraid of making a fool of herself.

"You called me at the station? Wanted to talk?" Harper's voice seemed surprised.

"Yes, serious talk." She stepped toward the stove to distance herself from his appeal. "You hungry? I have breakfast stuff I could fix."

"Coffee's fine." He sipped from the cup, raised one eyebrow. "Damn fine."

"You look hungry to me." She walked to the refrigerator, took out three brown eggs, butter, some leftover grated Monterey Jack, and a bottle of Tabasco. She switched on the gas jet and pulled an omelet pan from the overhead rack. Harper watched her beat the eggs. His eyes were hungry.

"I've been doing some serious thinking." She poured the eggs into sizzling butter. "I put a few things together that I'm willing to share." She lifted the edges of the omelet to let it cook, watching Harper out of the corner of her eye to see if he bought her story.

"Sharing's good." Harper said.

"I'll tell you what I know and also what I surmise." She folded the omelet and gave him a dazzling smile, the one she had been afraid to risk earlier. She mentally crossed her fingers.

"And what am I supposed to do in return?" Harper asked.

"Take me on as partner in solving this murder." Grace swallowed but didn't drop her gaze. "I'm not going to be able to go on with my life until this mess has been straightened out. Let's work together."

"You're too young to be Jessica Fletcher and I'm too smart to be her fall-guy." Harper's jaw twitched, as if he suppressed a smile. "But I think that's the sort of thing you're suggesting?"

"Exactly that," Grace grabbed a delicate flower sprigged luncheon plate from the cabinet, filled it with eggs and set it in front of Harper along with a sterling silver fork.

His gaze bored into her eyes. Silence filled the room for a long minute. He glanced down at the eggs then picked up his fork.

"Deal." Harper shoved a forkful of eggs into his mouth, closed his eyes. His groan sent another shiver down Grace's spine

"You're one hell of a cook," he said, then took another bite. "I'll eat. You talk."

"There's a bunch of stuff I need to tell you." Grace pulled out a chair and sat down, leaning forward.

"You've been playing sleuth?" Harper said with his mouth full.

"Yes. I've learned things." She paused a minute. "Oh, yes. There's another thing. My son has returned from Germany."

"He's here at the inn?" Harper stopped eating and raised an eyebrow.

"Well, right now he's supposedly buying groceries with Sandy, my new maid." Grace grinned. "But I suspect that they're actually at the beach playing kissy-face, because I haven't seen either of them since they left hours ago."

"Sounds like a fun game." Harper grinned then finished the omelet. "I expect you're glad to have your kid out here."

"I can't even tell you how happy I was to see him. And he seems to have changed, matured. I was going to let him bunk in with Drew, but I've changed my mind." She looked up at Harper. "I think Drew might have murdered Huxley and Maxie."

Harper quit drinking coffee and stared at her.

"I was downstairs retrieving Brand's gear when Walter dropped by and said you were here."

"I don't see the kid's stuff," Harper said.

"No, I'll have to go back."

"You think the man's a murderer and you're going back to his apartment? Are you out of your mind?" In his agitation he bumped the table and his plate rattled precariously on the edge.

"Look out for the dish," Grace said in a cold voice. "That's a piece of Apple Blossom Haviland. You break it, you pay for it."

"What the hell do I care about a plate? You're driving me nuts, Grace. Anyway, what makes you think that Maynard is the killer? I find that hard to believe."

"It was something Mrs. Murphy said then I spent a couple of hours at the library doing research. Pansy and Drew were married about four years ago. Did you know that?"

"Yes." Harper grinned. "I think you need to leave the sleuthing to me. This is no big news flash. Maynard told me about the marriage the first day I talked to him. He knew I'd find out anyway and thought it would be better coming from him." Harper picked up his coffee cup. "He was right."

"And you don't think that might be a motive for murder? Pansy receives alimony from her first husband, and has been doing so for the entire four years of their marriage. Their divorce decree calls for the money to stop if she remarries. She'd have to pay back every penny if her ex-husband knew about her new marriage."

"I talked to her about it. Pansy doesn't see taking the money as fraud. To her it was money earned. After calling and talking to that ex-husband I'm inclined to agree with her." He raised an eyebrow and gave her a teasing smile. "The only thing I care about is the murder." Harper drained the last drop of his coffee then set the cup on its saucer with exaggerated care, grinning up at Grace. "See? Even I can be house broken by the right woman."

"I don't know why I'm wasting my time telling you any-thing." Grace felt herself blush, and it did nothing to improve her mood. "Drew telling you about their marriage means nothing. It's true that you'd have found out anyway."

"Damn straight. I'm good at what I do," Harper said without cracking a smile.

"Then I don't know why I'm bothering with this conversation," Grace said.

"Because I'm a fun guy to talk to?" Harper wiggled his eyebrows.

"Why does every man in the world think that eyebrow wiggling is funny?"

Harper exploded in laughter and Grace could have bitten off her tongue.

"Since you're so smart I guess you also know what happened to Huxley's clothes?" she said.

"What?" Harper sat up straight. "Are you saying that you know?"

"I think so. Inept little me found his tie at a thrift shop."

"His tie? I don't believe it. How do you know it's his tie?"

"I don't know for sure, but Walter Slovak, the gardener, saw a stranger who was wearing a mustard-colored tie go through the back door of Wimberly Place on the afternoon of the murder." Grace walked to the refrigerator, pulled open the door and hauled out a small brown paper sack. She reached inside, stripped away the layer of aluminum foil she had added for safety, walked over to Harper and held up the tie.

"I don't know about this." Harper said.

"I'm certain that it's Arnold Huxley's tie," Grace said with no small amount of self-satisfaction.

"Then where's his other stuff?" Harper took the tie between two fingers and studied it. "I'd love to go through his pockets."

"Probably in a heap of garbage somewhere in the city dump."

"Sit down and tell me the whole story." He rubbed the palm of his hand over the first hint of stubble on his cheek.

Grace studied his fingers, not slender and tapered as Charlie's had been, but strong and more dependable looking. She took a deep breath and began to talk.

Harper sat grim and unsmiling while Grace related her trip to the nursing home, the information about Erwin Quick's deceased wife, and how she had happened onto the tie at the small shopping center. Then she recounted everything she had learned.

"Do you know anything else?" Harper had his notebook out taking notes. "Don't skip anything. Most of this I already knew, but tell me everything you can think of."

Grace paused, thinking of Sydney' secret about Wimberly. She bit her lip. In spite of Harper's doubt, she was almost certain that Drew was the murderer. Why ruin poor Sydney's life?

"That's pretty much it," she said.

"You're a hell of a bad liar." Harper snapped his notebook shut and stuck it back into his shirt pocket. "And I think you're wrong about Drew Maynard. I got some first-class testimonials from top-level navy brass. Said they would trust Maynard with their lives." Harper stood and looked at Grace. "Would you leave the police work to me? You don't know what you could get yourself into."

"Maybe you'd like to give me back the tie?" Grace snapped. "And you could forget about how the dead guy's clothes disappeared in the first place. I was the one who figured that out and told you, remember? I saw you taking notes. I thought we had a deal, but you're not sharing what you know. You lied to me!"

"Temper, temper." Harper dropped the tie back in the brown paper bag and held it in salute, walking toward the door. "Thanks for not storing this in plastic. You're smart, but you're way out of your depth. I need you to back off of my territory. You got a pen and paper? I'll give you my cell number. Call me if you get worried about anything. You just stick to inn keeping, you were born to cook, not to catch killers. That's my job."

"You arrogant...." Words failed Grace. She grabbed the first thing her hand touched and hurled it toward him. The Havilland luncheon plate smashed into the facing of the kitchen door, right next to Harper's head, and shattered.

"Get out of my kitchen. I don't need your damned telephone number. I can take care of myself."

"That dish go on your tab or mine?" Harper asked then fled as if for his life.

Grace stood for a minute trembling with anger. Then she found the whiskbroom and dustpan and swept up the shards of china and hid them in the bottom of the trashcan. Only then did she remember that tea was less than two hours away. She grabbed a cookbook off the shelf and was scanning recipes when Sandy strolled in carrying two bags of groceries.

"There'd better be pastry in one of those," Grace said.

"Sand tarts and ladyfingers," Sandy answered fishing out a smaller sack. "I thought that was just the sort of crap old folks like to eat in the afternoon."

"Did you now?" Grace drew a deep breath. "Where's Brand? Did he go back upstairs to our room?"

"Brand? Shit, no. We ran into that old guy that lives in the basement and Brand took off with him. That was right after we left you this morning."

Chapter 30

"What do you mean Brand went off with some old guy? I thought he was with you," Grace screamed at Sandy.

"I didn't know I was supposed to be watching him! This old geezer found us at Starbucks where we were having a double latte and he said you needed Brand back at the inn." Sandy popped her gum and glared at Grace. "I didn't go along because I don't want to spend my time hanging around old folks. When I worked at the nursing home I had to talk to those people, but no one's paying me for that now. Anyway, I had to buy that stuff you wanted, didn't I?"

"Okay, okay. Just tell me exactly what time it was when Brand took off with this guy." Grace dug her nails into the palms of her hands.

"Like I told you, it was about ten or so. Brand and I had just gotten our coffee." Sandy ran her fingers through her spiked hair. "I had to finish drinking mine all by myself, but I didn't mind too much because the waiter was pretty cute." Sandy yawned and looked at the groceries. "You don't expect me to unload this stuff do you? I thought I'd just go on home, since I've been here eight hours already. Besides, I've got a date tonight and I think that I may want to break up with this guy I've been seeing."

"Yes. Go home. I'll manage." Fear rose in Grace's heart but she managed to keep her voice steady. The idea of spending one more minute with Sandy was unbearable.

"See you in the morning." Sandy started out the door then looked back. "It's okay to tell Brand that I'm breaking up with my boyfriend if you want to." She fluttered a finger wave then walked out the door.

Grace pulled Harper's business card from her pocket, cursing herself for not taking his cell number. Her hand shook so hard she could hardly dial. The voice that answered was female and decidedly unfriendly.

"Harper isn't available," the woman said.

"My name is Grace Cassidy and I need him to call me. Could you get that message to him? It's urgent."

"Sure." The voice sounded both bored and annoyed. Grace's heart sank.

"This is police business," Grace said. "It's critical."

"I'll leave him a note," the woman said.

"But I need him now...." But the phone was dead in Grace's ear. *There was no one but her to save Brand.*

She scanned the kitchen for some sort of weapon. There was no way she could overpower Drew in a struggle. She would have to outsmart him and needed something small and easy to hide, like mace. She pulled open a drawer and saw some tools and a tiny can of WD-40. Whatever chemicals comprised the spray, a squirt in the eyes should hurt. She stuck the WD-40 into her pocket, tucked a screwdriver into her waistband, and pulled her shirt out to cover both items before racing downstairs.

Grace pounded on the door. When there was no answer she let herself in with the key from under the mat and ran to the closet. Her stomach twisted. Brand's stuff was gone.

The sound of a key in the outside latch gave her time to shut the closet. Drew pushed open the door and jumped when he saw her.

"Sorry to startle you. I came back after that coffee you promised me." She forced a smile but her knees felt liquid.

"Sure thing, I already have hot water plugged in. He walked to a shelf and grabbed a jar of instant coffee along with two chipped cups. "You see Walter in the garden? I've been looking for him," he said.

"I think he was working in the flower beds," Grace said. If Drew thought someone was nearby so much the better.

"Cream or sugar?" He asked and she shook her head. If there was ever a time for black coffee, this was it.

Drew's apartment had seemed warm and cozy when she was there before. Now it seemed like a death chamber. She accepted a cup from Drew, walked to the seascape, and studied the picture. *Did you kill someone for the woman who painted this?* The question seemed so loud inside her head it was a minute before she realized with relief that she hadn't asked it. She took a deep breath to calm herself. Small talk was a better plan. Stall, find out where Brand was.

"It's a great copy." She pointed to the picture. "Pansy has a unique gift."

Drew walked up to stand beside her. He viewed the painting with pride, smiled, and then began unpinning notes from the front of his shirt.

"So you've found out the truth about the picture? Did Theodora tell you?" He walked to the south wall and skewered his notes onto a cork bulletin board. He kept smiling. "It fooled Mendelsohn, which was no small feat. Wimberly, of course knows nothing about art, so fooling him took no effort at all."

"Ah yes. And I doubt if Huxley knew art either."

"What?" Drew stopped smiling. He stared at Grace.

"I know everything, and none of it matters to me. All I want is to know where Brand is. Nothing else is any of my business. I only care about my son." It was true. Even her debt to Maxie paled in comparison to her love for her son. "Tell me where he is and I promise you that Brand and I will be on the next plane out of here. You'll never hear from us again." Grace felt the can of WD-40 pressing against her bare skin.

What was she doing? She'd just given everything away. This was never going to work. Anyone cruel enough to murder Maxie wasn't going to care about her, much less about a college kid he'd never seen before. She had to do better.

"I don't believe that Pansy knows about anything. I'll tell you what. Release Brand to me and I give you my word of honor never to mention anything to Pansy or to the police."

Grace knew her promise was weak at best. She was saying the first thing that came into her mind, speaking words that scarcely made any sense even to her.

"My God." Drew watched her, white-faced. "You think I murdered Huxley? And Maxie? You think I'd kill Maxie?"

"I don't think you meant to. But you're trained in combat. Huxley ticked you off. Threatened your *wife*. Breaking an enemy's neck would be second nature to you. It probably happened before you even knew what you'd done. Reflex action."

"You can't be serious?"

"I know that Huxley threatened to expose Pansy, threatened to tell her ex-husband that the two of you were married. There's no way she could pay back all of the alimony she had received. Not after four years. Her ex wouldn't have a second thought about throwing her in jail for fraud. No one could blame you for killing someone who threatened to hurt Pansy."

It was a minute before Drew answered. His face had lost color and he seemed to instantly age ten years. "Okay, so I might kill a man like Huxley given the right circumstances. But Maxie?"

"I think she saw you the day you went upstairs to murder Huxley. She was going to confess the whole thing to me and the secret would be out. You were only blowing smoke when you suggested someone meant to murder me instead of Maxie. She had to be silenced."

"I'd already had my little talk with Huxley the day he tried to set up a meeting with me. We had us a little straight-talk, and believe me, when he left he wanted no part of bothering either Pansy or me."

"But I don't care! All I want is my son back." Grace's hand shook and she pressed it hard against her stomach. "Please tell me where he is. I know that his things are gone from your closet. You saw me open the door."

"Your boy's things have disappeared from my closet?" Drew's gaze fell to the bulletin board and seemed to freeze. "Oh my God." His shoulders slumped and he seemed to age instantly.

Grace stepped closer to the collage of notes and memorabilia pinned to the board to see what Drew was studying with such intensity. An old photo, black and white and shiny, was pinned beside the notes. It was the snapshot she had observed earlier, the one that had quickened some sort of memory. Two handsome young sailors were wearing snappy uniforms and wide grins. They stood with the self-assured ease of the very young.

"That's you." She tapped the picture with its edges curling and starting to crack. "The other guy looks familiar too."

"You may not believe this," Drew said, "But sentimentality and kindness can sometimes cause more grief than cruelty."

Grace wondered what that remark had to do with the price of corn in Iowa, but decided to play along. "That's a strange philosophy. I'd have to know more before I could give an opinion."

"Pansy has always predicted that my strong points, not my weaknesses, would be my downfall. Perhaps she was correct." He sighed.

"That's your excuse for snapping Maxie's neck as if it were a twig?" The words were out before she thought. Her hand flew to her mouth, but it was too late. The words couldn't be recalled.

"You think that you've put it all together?" A muscle worked in Drew's jaw, but his face never changed expression. "And I do think you have gotten very close. Pansy always said you were an intuitive thinker. A rare combination, she told me. You would think that after all of these years I would listen to Pansy. People think she's an airhead, but actually she's very perceptive."

Grace's mouth went dry. She'd done an extremely stupid thing for an intuitive thinker. With great effort she controlled the sudden urge to glance toward the door in order to judge the distance.

"A man's nature is to protect the things he loves, the things that are his. I can understand killing for a woman like Pansy."

"You don't understand." Drew's strong fingers laced together and twisted. His knuckles cracked. Grace balled her fists to keep her hands from shaking.

"Perhaps you'd like to hear what I know and how I surmised it?" she said, surprised at the calmness of her voice. And like Scheherazade she spun her story, taking more time than was needed in order to prolong her life.

Drew sat silently musing after she had finished. Grace's heart pounded and she rested her hand on her shirt where it covered the screwdriver.

"You have all the pieces but one," he said. "I'm the wrong man."

Chapter 31

The sound of knuckles pounding on the door of Drew's apartment was a welcome interruption for Grace who hoped it might be Harper. But instead Walter stood on the steps looking worried. He still held his bat.

Good, Grace thought, that trusty old bat might come in handy as a weapon if things turn nasty. Drew hesitated, and Grace knew he didn't want the man anywhere near her.

"Hey Walter, come on in." Grace swept a hand toward Drew's sitting area and closed the door after Walter stepped inside.

"Could we talk a minute, buddy?" Walter asked Drew. "There's something I need to run past you." Walter shot Grace a worried look, and she wondered if he knew she was in danger.

"I'm trying to find my son, Brand," she said. "He flew in yesterday and now he seems to have disappeared." Surely Walter would help her in spite of the two men's friendship. The smell of whiskey on his breath caused a twinge of worry, but the man was always drinking. Walter cocked his head to a jaunty angle and something clicked in Grace's memory. She glanced at the photo on the bulletin board and realized the other guy was Walter when he was a young man.

"It was you!" she said. The booze-worn old gardener was so changed from the carefree sailor in the photograph, that she hadn't made the connection before. "I just this minute realized that."

Walter's smile vanished and was replaced with a hard dangerous looking glare. "You damned snooping woman!"

Grace stepped backwards and sucked in a breath. Shock momentarily paralyzed her. Walter's hands tightened around the bat handle and she stared in horror as the man morphed from Dr. Jekyll to Mr. Hyde.

"Why couldn't you just mind your own business? I knew you were going to be trouble, and tried to get you to leave. But no, you had to hang around and stick your nose into other people's business."

Time stood still. Drew had said that he was the wrong man, but she hadn't believed him. Sandy said Brand had left with the 'old guy,' and she had jumped to the conclusion that was Drew. It had never occurred to her that Walter fit the same description. The old drunk had always seemed so harmless. Like some sort of stereotypical joke. This couldn't be happening. Why didn't her alarm ring and awake her from this nightmare?

"Walter!" Drew yelled. "She's talking about recognizing you in that old picture. She didn't mean any thing. Give me that damned bat."

Walter didn't seem to hear him and stepped closer to Grace. The dangerous light of insanity blazed in his eyes. A sudden understanding iced her heart. *Walter was the killer.* It took all of her will power just to keep breathing. Stay calm and think, she told herself. You've got to answer him, but stay calm. She drew a deep breath.

"Of course I was talking about the picture. Whatever did you think?" Grace was so terrified and her knees so weak that she could hardly stand. To her own surprise her voice sounded normal. This small miracle encouraged her enough that she was able to force a phony smile. "You were down-right hunky back in those days."

She could see that Walter wasn't buying her flattery, and she steeled herself for action. She had to save herself so she could rescue her son. Almost as if reading her mind, Walter threatened Brand.

"You'd better do what I tell you, or that boy of yours is dead."

"You hurt Brand and I'll kill you." The words were out of Grace's mouth before she could stop herself. Not even biting her tongue until she tasted blood could snatch back the ill-spoken words.

Walter opened his mouth and emitted a primitive battle yell, then lifted the bat and swung at Grace. Drew stepped between them with surprising speed, taking the force of the blow. His left arm dangled uselessly at his side. Surprise swept across Walter's face.

"Hey buddy, I didn't mean to hit you. Why'd you step into the line of fire? You know better than that."

Grace inched toward Walter. If only she could grab the bat, but he saw her and tightened his grip, shooting her a menacing glare.

"I did you a favor," Drew said. "Can't you see that I'm trying to help? We're going to get you into the hospital where trained people can take care of you. I need to go too, so they can look at my arm. We can go together."

Determination never left Drew's face, but Grace could tell that the man was barely able to stand. His voice was pain-filled and not much more than a low croak. Age and injury had taken its toll and Grace knew she couldn't depend on this courageous man for much assistance. The spirit might be willing, but the flesh was too injured. Her hand moved toward the WD-40 in her pocket while Walter raged at his friend.

"Hospital? Why would I need to go to the hospital? I'm not sick." Walter's eyes shifted back and forth between Grace and Drew. "I'm not going to any nut house," he yelled.

"Give me the bat, Walter. And tell me where you've got that boy. Why on earth did you kidnap him, anyway?"

"I overheard him tell the new maid that his mom may have solved the murder. I saw them leave together and followed. Then I tricked him into coming back with me."

"Where you hide the boy?" Drew's face was white and his lips were pinched with pain, but his voice resonated leadership. The wounded old man narrowed his eyes and somehow managed to straighten his shoulders. "I still outrank you, sailor, and I order you to tell me where the young fellow is."

Walter scowled his rebellion, but as Drew continued to glare, the gardener seemed to shrink in size. Finally he shrugged in resignation.

"He's stashed in my apartment. Fed him Everclear until he passed out, he took to drinking like a duck to water." He chucked briefly, sounding something like the old Walter. "Now don't you worry, buddy. I've got everything under control."

Brand was alive! Relief swept through Grace. Then she remembered the cases of alcohol poisoning at the OU frat houses, and her heart sank again. Could Brand tolerate that much liquor?

"This isn't the way to handle the situation, Walter. You've gone too far. Why did you kill Maxie? She was a helpless little thing and wouldn't have hurt anyone."

"Didn't have any choice now, did I? A SEAL's got to do whatever is necessary. Remember? You were the one who trained me. Just break their necks if you have to. Don't let yourself think about it. That's what you said, remember?"

"My God, Walter. That was during the Viet Nam War. Years ago. You were never trained to hurt innocent civilians."

"Innocent?" Walter looked confused. "Huxley wasn't innocent. That bastard was going to get Pansy into terrible trouble. He told me so." Walter licked dry lips and his eyes flickered. "He tried to talk me into helping him get your painting." He nodded toward the fake Winslow Homer. "But I wouldn't do that, not ever. I know how much it means to you."

"Are you telling me that all of this carnage was over that damn painting? The picture's a fake. It's practically worthless. Huxley was no threat to Pansy, not after I got through talking to him."

"A fake? You never told me it was a fake. And you never said you talked to Huxley neither." Walter swallowed hard. "Anyway, he knew about my almost getting a dishonorable discharge, and he was going to tell Wimberly. He found old Schwartz and pried the information out of him. You remember old Schwartz, don't you? Never could keep his damn mouth shut."

"Huxley was bluffing," Drew said. "You shouldn't have let him scare you about that old stuff."

"I didn't care so much about him getting me into trouble. I killed him to protect Pansy." Walter's eyes shifted back and forth between Drew and Grace, the bat held ready to strike. "I wasn't going to let my buddy's wife go to prison. I didn't want to kill Maxie. I tried to talk some sense into her, but I couldn't. She was going to tell Grace that she took me up the back stairs to meet Huxley on the day of the murder. We argued for awhile and she called me a 'dark man.' Talk about crazy!"

The dark man! Grace shivered, remembering Maxie had spoken these same words to her, but she had thought the maid was talking about Harper.

"I had to shut her up now, didn't I? There was no other choice." Walter gripped the bat and gave it a little test swing. "Now just step back and let me do my job."

"Give me that damned bat you maniac." Drew reached for the weapon with his good hand. Walter blinked in surprise, raised the bat, and swung it against Drew's head.

"Drew!" Grace screamed as he crumpled and fell to the floor. "My God Walter, you've killed him." She knelt beside the body and searched for a pulse. Relief swept through her when she discovered a faint beat.

"Didn't want to," Walter said. "Old Drew turned against me. Never thought my buddy would turn against me."

Grace looked at Drew's unconscious body and knew the only way the two of them would stay alive was if she kept her head. She took a deep breath and then slowly stood. Drawing courage from somewhere deep inside herself she spoke, forcing herself to use a kind and reassuring tone.

"It was just another accident, Walter. I can make the police understand. We're all friends. Let's don't kill Drew, we'd miss him." She spoke to Walter in the same voice she had used on Brand when he was small and in trouble. "Drew will come around."

"Drew has changed. He's been full of hisself ever since he started writing that book. Damn fool idea, writing a book."

Grace decided to change tactics and appeal to Walter's military background.

"Look. I'll take full responsibility for this entire mess. I'm the innkeeper, and that makes me the person in charge here, sort of like the captain. We can't go around killing our crew now, can we?"

Walter's eyes glazed over with panic. He looked at Grace as if trying to figure out if she was telling him the truth. Then he frowned.

"You're shittin' me, ain't you?"

"Of course not, Walter," Grace said. "I want to help you. I'll prove it by tying Drew up. After he awakens he'll be calmer, then we can help him understand that we're all in this together. We're friends, remember?" She watched his antagonism weaken, and then pressed on with her arguments.

"Theodora wouldn't like it if you hurt either Drew or me. She would be so disappointed. You wouldn't want to upset Theodora, now would you?

"I love Theodora. And I hated killing that little retarded girl. Theodora has to believe that I never meant to do that. But Maxie was going to tell. I couldn't let her tell our secrets, could I?"

"It's going to be all right, Walter." Grace said. "Let's just take care of Drew and then you can show me where you've hidden Brand. Everyone will be pleased to see him alive and well."

"He should be okay. At least the last time I saw him he was breathing," Walter said.

The wild look in Walter's eyes seemed to have calmed. Grace took a deep breath and slowly reached for the bat. Immediately Walter jerked back, and a new anger, hot as fire, shot from his eyes. "Stay away from me, you tricky bitch!" he yelled.

It was now or never. Grace grabbed the WD-40 from her pocket aimed the spray at his eyes, and fired. He screamed and clutched his face. The bat fell to the floor and Grace grabbed it.

"Stand back, Walter," she said. "Don't make me hit you."

Walter charged toward her, tears streaming down his face. Grace gripped the bat, braced her feet, and swung. She heard wood crack against the side of Walter's head and he fell motionless at her feet.

By the time Sergeant Harper and the ambulance arrived, Grace had Walter's hands bound tightly with a thread-bare red striped dishtowel, and had helped both men to regain consciousness. Walter sat slumped against the wall, whimpering while Drew and Grace tried to comfort the distraught man.

Harper walked in with the ambulance attendants and his gaze immediately shot to Grace. Relief washed over his face and he managed a smile.

"I guess you were right. You were able to care of yourself." He stepped to her side and lifted her to her feet.

Grace threw herself into his arms, buried her face against his shoulder, and sobbed. When she could take a breath she looked at him.

"Give me your damned cell phone number," she said.

Chapter 32

Grace perched on the edge of a plastic and chrome chair in Drew's apartment and looked around at of her friends. She was glad for Harper's presence. For the first time she could remember the detective didn't make her feel uncomfortable, but safe. There seemed to be something reassuring in his presence. She glanced at Brand stretched out on the floor on a blanket just underneath the fake Winslow Homer painting. The young man lay half-dozing, half-listening to the conversation, and she breathed a silent prayer of thanks for her son's safety. Harper had found him bound and sleeping in Walter's room and brought him to her.

Drew sat on the sofa between Pansy and Theodora. His face looked drawn and years older than yesterday, Grace thought. He had refused an ambulance and now wore a make-shift sling.

"I hate hospitals," Drew said. "I've already spent too much time in those antiseptic hell-holes. I've had enough injuries in my life to know that my arm isn't broken but just badly bruised. As you can see, Pansy put a long forgotten luncheon cloth to good use."

"If your arm doesn't feel better by morning, I'll drive you to the emergency room." The tone of Pansy's voice and the look she swept toward Drew convinced Grace this little woman could charm her husband into submission any time she chose.

Drew smiled tenderly at his wife then shifted his gaze to Harper.

"I knew that Walter had problems, but I never dreamed he was dangerous," Drew said. "How could he have hurt poor Maxie? The little thing must have been terrified."

"It's too horrible to imagine, even now. None of us suspected Walter." Pansy leaned upward and kissed Drew's cheek. "The aura of darkness often hovered over him, but I just assumed it was his alcoholism and sent healing thoughts in his direction. It's very hard to be critical about people we love."

Drew studied Pansy's face and his expression softened. He seemed to almost recover some of his former youthful appearance. "Thank you my cherished one," he said gently, and then turned his focus to the group. "Walter got into some trouble years ago in the service, but I thought that was all behind him. I thought he was taking his medication and was doing fine."

"I can't believe that I didn't find out about any prior trouble," Harper said. "I ran a thorough check."

"We were able to keep the incident out of his Navy records." Drew shook his head and sighed. "Walter was a real hero when he served his country and had the medals to prove it. No one wanted to cause him any grief. I thought he was going to be all right. And for years he was."

"I adored the man," Theodora said. "He was charming and kind. He even caused the thought of marriage to cross my mind. Briefly." She fanned herself by fluffing the edge of her billowing scarlet shirt then used the hem of a sleeve to dab at her eyes. "I can't envision the same person who picked peppermint leaves for my indigestion breaking someone's neck." She sighed. "The men who are attracted to me! It gives one pause."

Grace nodded to show she understood and identified with her friend's words. "What will the authorities do with him after he gets out of the hospital?" Grace asked.

"I got a phone call from St. Matthew's about half an hour ago," Harper said. "Right now he's in the psychiatric ward for evaluation. He seems to have gone entirely over the edge, and thinks he's back in the war. He'll probably remain institutionalized."

"We must all go and visit him just as soon as the authorities will allow us." Pansy released Drew's hand long enough to straighten her Peter Pan collar. "We can take him daisies and babies' breath from Wimberly Place's garden. That should make him feel better."

"I think anyone could kill if the motivation was strong enough," Grace said. "I know that I would have done anything to save my son. When I swung that bat I never gave a thought to whether or not I might kill Walter." She looked at Brand and smiled. "Are you feeling any better, son?" she asked, raising her voice a bit.

"Please Mom. Quit yelling. Speak softly. I think that maybe I'm going to die," Brand moaned.

"Serves you right," Grace snapped. "Whatever could you have been thinking of, drinking Everclear? That stuff will destroy your brains cells."

"I didn't want to be rude to the old guy by turning down his hospitality. Besides, he seemed so harmless. How could I have known that he was going to tie me up when I closed my eyes long enough to make the room stop spinning?"

"I just hope you learned something from all of this," Grace said.

"Here's you a cushion for your head, son." Drew chuckled and threw Brand a small green pillow with tattered fringe. "I think you're going to need it."

"Thanks." Brand reached for the cushion and used it to cover his face.

"Don't be too hard on the boy," Drew said. "And we also have to forgive Walter and realize he went over the edge. The poor guy thought that he was protecting Pansy and me. Let's remember that Arnold Huxley was the real villain in this tragedy."

"That bastard made his fatal mistake when he told Walter that little Miss Pansy here was guilty of fraud and could go to prison." Harper smiled at Pansy with such affection that Grace once again marveled at the older woman's influence on men of all ages. "His intention was to stampede Walter into persuading Drew to give him the painting. Said that he'd forget everything he knew if Walter could manage it. The problem was that poor old Walter didn't know that the damned thing was a fake."

"We never told him for fear he'd let the cat out of the bag with Wimberly," Theodora said. "Walter believed our story that Drew would never part with the painting because it was some sort of family heirloom." Theodora rearranged the brilliant folds of her shirt and smiled at Grace. "When dear Walter was drinking he talked too much. He'd have told for sure."

"He wouldn't have meant to, of course," Pansy hurried to explain. "He'd just have kept hinting and winking until even someone as dense as Wimberly would have caught on."

"That's pretty much the same story I got from Walter," Harper said. "It seems that Walter told Huxley to go to hell, and Huxley got real nasty. Said not only was he going to ruin Pansy and Drew but that he also had some business with the little fat lady on the second floor who wasn't as high and mighty as she pretended to be. Huxley just kept going on and on. He threatened that both women would go to jail if Walter didn't persuade Drew to give up the picture. Walter said something inside him just snapped."

"So he broke Huxley's neck." A shiver slid down Grace's spine. "With his military training it must have been almost like a reflex action."

"Yes." Harper shifted in his chair and shot an admiring glance at Grace. "The old guy was in fine physical shape. Not only did he garden but he lifted weights at the Y, and played softball. He's as strong as a horse." The muscle in his jaw tightened. "Good thing you had the foresight to grab that can of WD-40."

"You'll never know how much I wished I'd taken your cell phone number," she said with a wry smile. "I'm so sorry that I had to hurt him."

"He's going to be fine," Harper said. "His head must be as hard as a rock. He has only a minor concussion."

"What else did he tell you?" Theodora asked Harper.

"Maxie let him inside the inn so he could talk to Huxley on the day of the first murder. When the second murder occurred he sneaked in while Pansy was visiting the basement, and slipped up to Grace's room to caution Maxie to keep quiet. But Maxie turned stubborn and said that she wouldn't. Said that she had to tell her Missus the truth. The pressure was too great and Walter killed her, too."

"She had tried to tell me earlier." A familiar guilt crept through Grace. "Only I was in a hurry to get down and see Mrs. Wimberly and start my new job, so I wouldn't let her finish. I thought she was just talking about trying on my clothes without permission."

"A most understandable mistake," Theodora said. "Maxie had a problem staying out of the guests' things, bless her heart. Pansy and I used to look out for her and warn her when someone was coming. Perhaps that was why she had such a loyalty to us and didn't tell anyone that I was in your room after Huxley was murdered."

"If you ladies had been open about everything, it would have helped," Harper said.

Both Theodora and Pansy smiled sweetly at Harper and he rolled his eyes.

"Never mind," He said. "I'm helpless against that damned charm. It kicks my butt every time."

Grace rescued him by asking a question.

"Was Huxley trying to blackmail the Blenkensops or Erwin Quick?" Grace asked Harper.

"It's my guess that he was, but there's no proof and no one is talking. But it no longer matters. My main concern was the murder and we have a confession for that from Walter. This was a hard case for me because the victim was such pond scum and all of the suspects were likeable." He grinned at Grace. "I hope that dilemma never happens to me again."

"What a morning! I thought the other guests would never leave the table so we could have some real conversation." Theodora popped another bite of Dutch apple pancake into her mouth, chewed, and then smiled at Grace. "These are much too delicious, dear. It makes people want to linger and stuff themselves. I thought that Martha was going to burst her seams before she finally left."

"She's right, Mom. Back when I was little, you were a great cook and nothing has changed." Brand picked up a gilt-edged platter holding the last piece of country ham and passed it to Pansy who waved it away. He extended the dish to Theodora who shook her head with an indulgent smile toward the boy. Relief swept across his face and he forked the thick slice of meat onto his own plate and attacked it with gusto.

"Have you heard my wonderful news?" Pansy put her delicate eggshell china cup back into its saucer and looked around. "Erwin Quick wants to buy the Winslow Homer, even though he knows it's a copy. Of course he doesn't want to pay a million dollars for it, but he's willing to pay a goodly amount. The money will be so convenient. I can't tell you how relieved I am."

"Pansy, that's great." Grace refilled the little blonde's cup then moved to Theodora's side and poured another. "What made him decide to buy a fake?"

"A copy dear," Theodora smiled. "A copy and an excellent one at that. The picture is lovely and he and Sydney just want to enjoy it."

"That's great," Grace said. "Perhaps you can sell more pictures."

"She already has," Theodora said. Mendelsohn wants to commission Pansy to make copies of all his art. This little fiasco has terrified him so much that he's suddenly afraid a thief will decide to murder him in his sleep in order to steal his pictures. People do tend to judge the rest of the world by their own actions, you know." She swept her ringed fingers through the air in a graceful movement and then continued.

"He'll keep the reproductions at his estate in Germany and loan the originals to museums where they will be safe. His name will be on brass plaques in some of the best museums in the world." Theodora took her last bite, murmured in ecstasy, chewed then swallowed. "Heavenly," she said.

"I'll have enough money to make payments to my ex-husband for the alimony that I received after my marriage to Drew. If I can manage to do that he won't prosecute me for fraud." She flashed a brilliant smile at Harper. "The Sergeant was most kind in persuading him to cooperate. I should still have enough cash left to help Drew with his medical needs. Dear Gustav even has friends who are interested in my work. I intend to start a new career."

"Terrific." Grace sat on an ornate Victorian chair and glanced at Theodora. "How about you Theodora? Any more news about your legal problems?"

"My lawyer tells me that since I had no knowledge of criminal intent that I shouldn't be charged." Theodora took another sip of tea. "And he thinks that my volunteering for community service should help my case. Since I've always volunteered at the public library, teaching adults to read, life should continue as usual."

"Isn't it lovely when your punishment turns out to be your pleasure?" Pansy said. "The Universe is looking out for all of us. Isn't that a comforting thought?"

"I think the Universe is going to have her hands full with this bunch," Brand quipped. His mother shot him a dark look and he grinned back at her, unrepentant.

A door slammed in the direction of Wimberly's private quarters and Grace cast a worried glance in Brand's direction. How long would Wimberly allow her son to eat with the guests? She held her breath, dreading a possible conniption fit. For sure they would both have to leave when Mrs. Wimberly returned, but Grace had hoped for a few more days at Wimberly Place.

Wimberly rushed into the room wearing a Pepto-Bismol colored golf shirt and canary yellow pants. He didn't even glance at Brand, but looked only at Grace.

"Something horrible has happened." Wimberly's face was as pale as a ghost.

"Another murder?" Grace stood, her stomach tightening.

"Murder? Of course not. Why would there be a murder? It's much worse." Wimberly sank onto the chair Grace had vacated. "I was all ready to go out and play golf when my wife called me from Hawaii. She's met some young native fellow, and is going to divorce me and marry him. Can you believe that? She's staying in the islands. They're buying a Bed and Breakfast there." Wimberly hid his head in his hands and his shoulders began to shake.

"You're kidding?" Grace bit her lip to keep her lips from curving upward. The long suffering Beth had finally rebelled.

"If only I were," Wimberly looked up at Grace through his fingers with a hopeful expression. "My dear Mrs. Cassidy. Tell me that I can count on your help in my time of great need."

"You want me to stay on as innkeeper?" Grace asked, pretending indifference.

"Indeed I do. You are such a wonderful addition to our little inn. I've said so from the beginning. You're a woman with a great deal of class."

"That's what you said, huh?" Grace said with a droll smile. But her mind rushed to her problems. Why not? There was no place else to go. Things weren't any better in Tulsa, and she had no desire to face a horde of angry bill collectors. She had already commissioned an agent in Oklahoma to auction her furniture and personal belongings, and her house was up for sale. Creditors would get what little her husband had left behind. Not even Harper had been able to locate Charlie.

Any port in a storm, she thought, so why not Port Ortega? But still it was fun to let Wimberly dangle helplessly in the wind for a minute or two.

"It's critical that you continue on," Wimberly urged.

"Then of course you won't mind my son staying here with me?" She'd better press for the best deal she could manage.

The room went dead quiet. Wimberly frowned, thought a minute then forced his face into a fake smile.

"Not one little bit." Wimberly turned his plastic smile toward Brand who stared back, his open mouth filled with ham. "This charming young man could take over the yard work. Why he could even attend our community college right here in Port Ortega."

Brand took a minute to think over the offer. "That would be cool, I like California."

"What about my cat?" Grace asked. "He'll have to stay, too."

"Cat? What cat? You don't have a cat." Wimberly's bad excuse for a smile disappeared.

"You're wrong. I have a cat and I intend to keep him. It's a package deal. My son, our cat, and I. We three make a family." Grace glanced at Brand and saw a flush of pleasure sweep over his face. She smiled back at her grown son while hope warmed her heart.

Wimberly's face fused purple. He started to speak then swallowed.

"Of course." He seemed to choke then struggled onward. "A cat would be fine—as long as you keep the beast away from the guests."

"No problem." Grace crossed her fingers. Wimberly would learn soon enough that cats did as they pleased. "But there's the matter of my salary."

"Salary?" A look of pain crossed his face. "But both you and your son will be receiving room and board." I don't think I could manage a pay raise, too."

"That's too bad." She untied the apron she was wearing and tossed it on the buffet. "Come on upstairs, Brand. We have to pack." From the corner of her eye she watched her son nod without blinking an eye.

"I'll be right up, Mama." He chugged down the last of his coffee.

"Let me check my books," Wimberly said, in a vain attempt to save face. "Maybe I could manage twenty-five cents more an hour."

"How about a dollar?" Grace countered. Little enough since she now worked for minimum wage. She looked fondly at her son. If all else failed, maybe the two of them could take up playing poker.

"Fifty cents is my last offer." Wimberly's voice cracked.

"I don't think so." Grace turned to leave the room.

"Seventy-five cents and it's done," Wimberly said, swallowing hard.

Grace pretended to consider the offer that she was happy to get.

"Starting immediately," Wimberly said, breaking into a sweat.

The anxiety on Wimberly's face seemed like a down payment on better things to come. Finally she relented and smiled.

"Okay, we'll stay," Grace said.

CPSIA information can be obtained at www.ICGtesting.com
Printed in the USA
LVOW060947251011

251992LV00002B/2/P